PERFECTION IS MURDER

Bill, thank you for taking time out in your busy schedule to edit parts of my book —

Your friend
Rebecca Long
"Becky"

REBECCA LONG

© 2006 Rebecca Long
All Rights Reserved.

No part of this publication may be reproduced, stored in a retrieval system, or transmitted, in any form or by any means, electronic, mechanical, photocopying, recording, or otherwise, without the written permission of the author.

First published by Dog Ear Publishing
4010 W. 86th Street, Ste H
Indianapolis, IN 46268
www.dogearpublishing.net

ISBN: 1-59858-108-2
Library of Congress Control Number: 2005938656

This book is printed on acid-free paper.
This book is a work of Fiction. Places, events, and situations in this book are purely Fictional and any resemblance to actual persons, living or dead, is coincidental.

Printed in the United States of America

Writing my novel has been a creative and educational experience for me. It has given my imagination avenues that I never dreamed possible. Along the way, I have realized that I had a wealth of friends who supported and encouraged me toward the completion of my story. To these friends I owe a great deal of gratitude and appreciation. I thank you from the bottom of my heart.

There is one person that I want to express my love and appreciation to and that is my husband, Marshall Long. All the time I worked on my novel, he never discouraged me or complained about the time I spent away from him on the computer.

To you, Marshall, I dedicate PERFECTION IS MURDER.

With all my love,
"Becky"

PROLOGUE

Lauren Fulghum worked hard to get to her seventh year of medical school at Harvard University. She had many opportunities to date and to have a good time, but her studies were the center of her life. Lauren was attractive, charming, and taller than the average woman. She could have made a career of modeling, but she chose to be a pediatrician because of her love for children.

One early September day as she was coming out of the classroom, Lauren bumped into a student named David Williams accidentally. One of her books fell on his foot. He bent down to retrieve it, and when he looked up, their eyes met. David broke the silence when he asked if he could carry some of her books. Lauren thought this is my lucky day. He's nice looking and a sharp dresser in his blue jeans and madras shirt. From that time on Lauren Fulghum and David Williams were inseparable. One sunny day and good weather for sailing, David called Lauren to meet him at the marina. He told her he had borrowed a friend's boat to go sailing and he wanted her to go with him.

When Lauren got to the marina, she saw the boat with the name, "Gotcha," painted on the side of it. She asked David how his friend came up with that strange name? He explained that his friend had saved money for a long time and when he finally had enough, he bought the boat and called it, "Gotcha."

David maneuvered the boat out of the harbor, and they sailed for several hours out into the open sound. They were getting hungry, so David dropped anchor. They went down into the galley and had a picnic Lauren had prepared. After a satisfying lunch and casual conversation, they crawled into one of the bunk beds and made love.

Exhausted, David rolled over on his side. After a few minutes, he climbed out of the bed, knelt down on his knees, and asked Lauren to marry him. Her mind became blurred as she searched for the right answer. She definitely knew that she wanted to marry him but not before they finish school. From the tone of his voice and the look in his eyes, she knew that he wanted to get married right then. Tenderly Lauren leaned over and kissed David. She whispered softly that they live together in her apartment on campus until they finished school. After that, they could get a job, and then start married life on solid ground. David was disappointed, but he realized that she was right.

They couldn't have been any happier if they had been married until the day David received a call from his mother. She called to tell him that he would have to come home because his father was very ill. She needed him to run the family business.

Lauren begged David to take her home with him. He tried to reason by telling her that his time would be spent learning the business; however, the real reason David didn't take her was that he knew there were very few research facilities in Montana where he lived. She would be devastated not to be able to work on her project about childhood diseases.

After a year, their letters became less frequent and soon stopped all together. Lauren regretted that she didn't marry David, as he was the only man she ever loved.

CHAPTER 1

My God, she thought, her first year at Harvard University had been a real challenge. If it had not been for her parents' constant encouragement for her to excel in her studies, she might not have succeeded in graduating at the top of her class in pediatrics. As soon as graduation was over in June, she immediately sent applications to many hospitals. She continued to live in her apartment and to work in the library rather than go home while she waited for a job opening.

Lauren waited anxiously to hear from some of her resumes. It was a steamy and sultry afternoon in August when she left work and walked dejectedly to her apartment. When she opened the door, mail lay scattered on the floor where the mailman had shoved it through the slot. She scrambled through it, and the last letter was from Massachusetts General Hospital, in Boston. She tore into the envelope and read the good news that she had been accepted. Now that her job was settled, she had to find a place to live before the first of September. Soon it became apparent that finding an apartment was harder than getting a job. A place near the hospital would be nice so she could walk to work. At last, her real estate agent called with news that he had found just the place. She nearly fainted when he told her how much rent she would have to pay. After the real estate agent told Lauren that it looked like a typical colonial house with a stoop, two columns, and a raised panel front door, she felt better. It would remind her of home in Williamsburg, Virginia.

During the last week in August, she went to the apartment to clean it and to wait for the delivery of her furniture. She put on her coolest clothes: a pair of cut off jeans, and a short-sleeved white t-shirt with red Harvard letters sprawled across the front of it. With her hair tied up in a ponytail, she leaned against the kitchen counter and wondered how she was going to make her new home attractive with eclectic second-hand furniture. The sound of grinding gears from a truck broke her concentration. She opened the door and yelled, "Are you looking for Apartment 10?"

"Yes, ma'am! We're looking for a Dr. Lauren Fulghum."

"I'm Dr. Fulghum. I'm mighty glad to see you." Lauren called to them over the roar of the truck engine, "I wondered what I'd sleep on tonight. Bring in the furniture, and I'll show you where to put it."

The first thing they brought in was the chipped Wedgwood blue breakfast table and four chairs. She remembered her mom, at a yard sale, haggling over the price. She could hear her mom saying, "Honey, you might need it someday to set up housekeeping."

The movers steadily brought in the furniture and Lauren directed their every move. She continued to give orders as they noisily brought in a bedroom suite, a faded rose brocade sofa, and boxes of dishes, linens, and clothing. Now she was thankful her mom had saved the early-attic furniture. When the men finished, they walked to the door and waited in anticipation. Lauren went to the bedroom and came back with a generous tip.

It was late in the afternoon when she finished unpacking. Tired and hot, Lauren decided it was time to stop, take a bath, eat supper, and go to bed.

* * * * *

The alarm clock, on her bedside table, jangled her to consciousness. Lauren sprang out of bed ready to start her first day of work. Much too excited to eat, she gulped down some orange juice, showered, and put on her make-up. She slipped into a black skirt and a white short-sleeved blouse, and dashed out the door. The top was down on her Plymouth convertible as she drove along the street. The dampness of the early morning air rushed over her, awakening her body to the fresh air. Lauren was eager to meet and to get acquainted with the staff. Moments later the hospital came into view, and she pulled into the nearly empty parking lot. She grabbed her bag and found her way to the Chief of Staff's Office. The Chief Officer was a tall, rugged looking man with broad shoulders and olive complexion. His gray hair and mustache gave him an air of dignity. He greeted Lauren with enthusiasm as he waved his arm toward the circle of doctors. After introductions, he escorted her to a suite of offices. The Chief smiled and said, "We have a custom here of presenting a new doctor his or her first white jacket or better known as the "'Battle Jacket'. Here's your jacket."

Lauren answered with a chuckle, "I'm ready for the battle."

He smiled and said, "Welcome to Mass General. This will be your home away from home. It isn't plush, but soon you'll find it doesn't matter at the end of the day. Call me if you have any questions." The Chief Officer gave her a quick salute and returned to his office.

Lauren's eyes roamed around the meager furnishings: a dark oak desk, a brown leather swivel desk chair, a filing cabinet, and a worn red leather couch. It was drab, but she didn't complain—she had a job.

* * * * *

Three years passed since coming to work at Mass General, and she decided it was time to start a new life. Since her devastating break-up with David Williams, all she wanted to do was to work and to try to forget him. During that time, her practice had tripled. What free time she had was spent either on her computer or studying medical journals. The winter months slowly melted into spring and a rebirth of life surged into her body to get her back into reality. She felt like a butterfly coming out of its cocoon.

Every Wednesday afternoon, Lauren took her half-day off from work. She got into her dark green convertible, drove down Cambridge Street, and crossed over Longfellow Bridge to Massachusetts Avenue. She decided to go to Widner Library to check on some updated treatment for a rare childhood disease. Afterwards, she'd find a place to get a snack and a cup of coffee.

The wind tossed her hair as she cruised along the highway, but she didn't care. It was wonderful to breathe in the fresh cool air of April. Spring was dressing itself with a flourish of color: azaleas and rose gardens were in profusion; yellow forsythia formed borders as it sprawled along the driveways of homes; and, pink and red geraniums adorned window boxes. The scenery was extra exhilarating to Lauren after being closed up in a building day after day.

Lauren parked her car and went into the library. After several hours of intensive reading, her eyes felt tired so she decided to take a break. She drove around several blocks, parked her car, and walked along the brick-paved sidewalk. Her stride matched those of students as they strolled along the way. She felt as young as they did in her white peasant blouse, a flowing navy blue skirt, and white sandals. A quaint coffee shop that was squeezed between rows of colonial buildings caught her eye. It had a green and white striped awning that hung over a heavy-leaded glass door and posters in the windows claiming to have the best coffee on campus. A tinkling bell sounded when she stepped inside. The aroma of freshly ground coffee filled the room. Small round tables covered in green and white-checkered cloths cluttered the coffee shop. The only available table was pushed against a window overlooking the sidewalk. She rushed over to it and sat down.

A young and attractive waitress came to her table and

asked, "May I get you something?"

Taken by surprise with such quick service, Lauren stammered, "O-h-h- a- I would like a cappuccino." Like magic, the waitress reappeared with her coffee. Lauren thanked her and then leisurely sipped it while she reviewed her notes. Deep in thought, someone clearing his throat startled her. She looked up to see a man in jeans and a white T-shirt with Harvard U. emblazoned across the front of it. Her pulse quickened as she took in his smile, his black wavy hair, and his dark sensuous eyes.

He smiled and stared down at her lovely face and said, "Mind if I join you? This is the only available chair," he said politely as his muscular physique towered over her, his cup of coffee and sweet roll in his hand.

Flustered, she responded, "Oh...ah...sure. Have a seat."

"Are you sure? I can wait for another chair if I'm disturbing you."

"Oh, no, I was just looking over some notes. It's quite all right." Lauren went back to her notes and pretended not to notice him.

The man maneuvered his chair around to face Lauren. He interrupted her again, "I really appreciate your letting me sit here. I've been studying for hours, and I needed a break."

She glanced up from her notes, smiled, and asked, "What are you studying?"

Now that he had her attention, he cupped his hands around the coffee mug, leaned forward, looked into her beautiful blue eyes and said, "Law. I thought it was hard when I was in the service, but this is murder." Never letting his eyes leave Lauren's face, he slowly put the mug down, thrust his hand forward, and said, "I'm sorry I haven't introduced myself, I'm Jack Harper."

Lauren gracefully extended her hand. She stared into his dark brown eyes shrouded by the longest eyelashes she had ever seen on a man. Timidly she said, "Oh...ah...My name's

Lauren Fulghum. Glad to meet you. How long have you been at Harvard?"

He pursed his lips and said, "Oh-h-h, about a year and a half. It seems like a century. What about you?" Lauren still awed by his looks; his chiseled jaw, his slight cleft in his chin, and his dazzling smile, didn't hear his question. Jack chuckled and repeated his question, "What kind of history do you have?"

Embarrassed, Lauren tugged at a strand of her hair. She flipped it behind her ear and regained her composure. "I'm a pediatrician at Mass General." At that moment, a coo-coo clock that hung behind the counter chirped five times and interrupted Lauren's response. "Oh, darn, it's late!" she stammered. "I have to drive back to Boston. If I don't go now, the traffic will be horrendous." She jumped up and headed for the door.

Jack followed as best he could, but she was already a half a block away. Standing in the middle of the sidewalk, he called out, "When will I see you again?"

Lauren stopped the car, looked back over her shoulder and yelled, "I don't know! Maybe another time!"

Jack threw up his hand again and yelled, "Wait! When will that be?"

Quick as a rabbit, Lauren found a way to make a U-Turn and headed toward Jack and as she drove by him, she called out, "How about tomorrow. Same time?"

With a wide awesome smile, he gave her an okay sign as she drove away.

The image of Jack flashed repeatedly in her mind as she drove home: his handsome face, his physique, and his enthralling smile sent a thrill through every nerve ending in her body.

"Wow!" She muttered. "I haven't felt this kind of excitement in a long time." She turned up the radio and listened to the music as it floated through the air. Suddenly, reality set in.

Lauren clutched the steering wheel and cried out "Oh, my God! How am I going to get off work tomorrow?"

The next day, when the last patient walked out the door, Lauren dashed out of the hospital and risked getting a speeding ticket. When she neared the cafe, she said under her breath, "Oh, damn! Not a single parking space. He'll think I'm not coming." Lucky for her, a car backed out of a parking place just as she approached the coffee shop. Like a spider ready to pounce on a fly, she swerved into the space, bounded out of the car, and checked her hair as she passed the store windows. Satisfied, she took a deep breath and stepped casually into the coffee house.

Jack sat at a table facing the door. When he saw her, he rose and met her half way. Their gazes locked until Jack smiled and said, "I was afraid you might not show up." He took her hand and led her to his table. As soon as they were seated, he threw his head back, sniffed the air, and said, "There's nothing like the smell of freshly baked bagels and brewed coffee? It's wonderful. By the way, I've already ordered...is that's all right with you?"

A smile spread across Lauren's face as she responded cheerfully, "Sounds good to me." She made no attempt to withdraw her hand as the waitress approached them with their coffee.

For a week, they met every afternoon at five o'clock. Lauren looked forward to their conversations that covered many topics from old movies, current news, to his campus activities. It was a nice break to talk about something other than things that go on at the hospital. Jack asked if she would show him around the hospital so he could relate to the places she worked with staff and patients. It pleased her that Jack seemed so interested in her work.

At the end of the week as she got in her car to leave, Jack asked, "May I call you?" With a shy smile and a twinkle in her eyes Lauren said, "W-e-l-l...I suppose it would be okay," as she handed him one of her business cards. So with a carefree flick of her hand, she waved good-bye and sped off.

* * * * *

Jack called Lauren every day for several weeks reminding her of how much he missed her. When he wasn't calling, he was constantly asking her out either to a movie or to dinner. One Friday afternoon, he waited in front of her apartment with a big bouquet of roses. As Lauren drove up and saw him standing there with the flowers, she sprang from the car and threw her arms around his neck. She sang out, "Oh Jack, the roses are beautiful. They are my favorite flowers."

Jack smiled and said, "Lauren, they pale to your beauty." He bent down and kissed her.

"Oh-h-h, thank you for that lovely compliment." Lauren caressed his face with her hand and said, "You might as well move in with me, you're here as much as I am."

Shocked, Jack stepped back, threw his hands up, and said, "Wait a minute. Now if you really want me to, I will! I didn't know that you felt that way about me. You'd better be sure."

Lauren tilted her head to one side and with an impish smile, pointed her finger at Jack and said, "Maybe I spoke to quickly. You really don't know me. I'm not a very good housekeeper or cook. I don't have time for it. Since I've been with you, I've discovered you like things to be perfect." Lauren snickered, "Living with me could be hazardous to your health."

He grabbed her up in his arms. "I can't think of anything I had rather do."

"Jack! I never thought in a thousand years you'd move in. I…"

He kissed her before she could say anything else, put her down, and said, "We can share household expenses. I'll even help with the chores."

Lauren laughed almost hysterically as she stammered out, "I can't believe this is happening. You've made me very happy.

Let's celebrate."

The sun disappeared below the horizon as they walked hand-in-hand into the apartment. She got a bottle of wine and glasses from the cabinets. Jack walked over to her from the living room area, raised her face up to his, and kissed her tenderly. Holding up his glass he said, "Here's to a beautiful lady and a new life we'll share." After the toast, he put down his glass. "Oh, damn. I forgot. I can't move in until the end of June. My lease doesn't run out until then. But, as soon as July gets here, I'll pack all my stuff and bring it over."

Lauren sighed and said, "Oh- h-h, that's too bad, honey. But I suppose I can wait."

"We'll have to wait but in the meantime let's continue to have some fun. Come on let's sit on the couch and watch a movie." Jack flipped on the television to an X-rated movie. As the scenes became torrid, they became aroused. Their willpower gave way. They never knew when the TV station went off the air. When the clock on the mantle chimed 1:00 a.m., Jack's head jerked up and as he exclaimed, "Damn, when you're having good sex, time flies. I've got to go. I have an early class in the morning." He jumped up from the couch, flipped on the light, and said, "Don't get up. I'll let myself out. You'd better get some rest if you plan to work tomorrow." Before she knew it, the door slammed and he was gone. Once outside the apartment, Jack stopped on the top step and mused, "I believe I've hit 'pay-dirt'; a beautiful woman, an apartment, and the possibility of making lots of money."

After the shock of Jack's leaving so abruptly, Lauren got up, went to her bedroom, and as she dressed for bed murmured, "It's been a long time since I've made love. At long last I've found someone that can take David's place. Perhaps now I won't be alone anymore."

A few days passed with no word from Jack. Lauren convinced herself that he had been working hard on his studies. But when Saturday came, she fully expected him to come over that night. She prepared his favorite meal: steaks, tossed salad, and baked potatoes. She wanted everything to be perfect. The mantle clock chimed six times. Oh my, she thought, I've got to get dressed. Lauren flipped through the hangers in her closet. There in the back of her closet was a light blue silky dress she had bought on sale. Quickly she pulled it over her head, and it fell over her well-proportioned body, exposing a deep cleavage. Every fifteen minutes she checked her watch. Nine thirty. What had happened to him? Why was he late? Back and forth she paced and at each turn got angrier. Lauren stared at the phone. Why hadn't he called? Eleven o'clock. Where was he? Tears streamed down her face. She snatched off her dress, put on her gown, and crawled into bed. Fifteen minutes later, the phone rang. "Hello!" She shouted, "Who is this?"

"We-l-l-l," came a familiar voice. "You sound angry."

Like a smoldering fire drenched with water, her anger fizzled; she dried her eyes, cleared her throat, and purred like a cat, "Jack, why didn't you come over tonight? Where are you?"

"I'm at my apartment. I've been studying and I still haven't finished. I couldn't go to bed until I heard your voice." There was a pause and then he said, "I want to tell you something, I…"

Lauren broke in, "What is it?"

"Oh-h-h, I think you know."

"No—I don't. Tell me! You're driving me crazy."

"Okay, okay. If you really want to know, I'm in love with you." Lauren caught her breath and pressed the receiver closer to her ear to savor every word. "I wanted to be with you when I said it, but I couldn't wait until morning. I'll call you tomorrow. Sorry about tonight. Right now, I've got to finish a paper."

Lauren's closed her eyes and whispered, "That's okay. I understand. Goodnight, sweetheart." She hung up the phone, turned out the light, slipped into bed, and dreamed about Jack.

CHAPTER 2

July—moving time. There were many boxes full of books, sports equipment, and clothes. When he unpacked his belongings, he grumbled because there wasn't enough room to hang his clothes without them being crowded. To keep him satisfied, Lauren moved some of her clothes into the guest bedroom closet.

It had taken several weeks of adjustments for them to get used to each other. Now that their lives had settled down, Lauren wanted to get married. If they wanted to have children, they should start planning. She was thirty-one and it might take a couple of years to make a baby. Maybe if she used some psychology, it would make him take action. She was well aware that her scheme might backfire, but she had to try it. The next day she stopped at a gourmet restaurant near the hospital and picked up something for supper. She wanted to make a good impression. Out came her best china and crystal, candles were put in every conceivable place, and romantic music was set to play at the touch of a button. Lauren took a shower, splashed on her best perfume, and put on a sexy chemise.

When Jack walked into the apartment and didn't see Lauren, he called out, "What's so special tonight? What's with the fancy table and romantic music?"

Lauren sashayed into the room, puckered up her lips, and in her sexiest voice said, "Sir, our special tonight was prepared just for you: Chicken Kiev, Gourmet Rice, Broccoli topped with Hollandaise, Caesar Salad, Savory Bread, Lemon Mousse, and your favorite wine—a carafe of Chardonnay. She pressed her breasts against his chest, and with wet lips she kissed him fervently. She stroked his hips, slid her hands to the inside of his thighs, and then ran her hands up and down his back. Jack was mesmerized by her actions. It was unlike Lauren to be so seductive. She tried to hide her nervousness as she continued to move seductively around the room. Desperately, she wanted her scheme to work. When she stopped in front of him, looked deep into his eyes, and she said in an apologetic way, "Darling, I don't think this arrangement is working. I need to get on with my life. You've been wonderful, and I would hate to see you go. I really think it best that you get your own apartment."

Jack was stunned. He wondered if she was on drugs as he stammered, "Sweetheart! Are you saying you want me to leave?"

She walked to the kitchen and put the finishing touches on the meal. Lauren took a deep breath to bolster her courage. "Yes, darling, that's what I mean."

Jack dashed over to her, crushed her in his arms, and cried, "What can I do to make you change your mind?" He kissed her hard and with shortness of breath said, "I know—let's get married!" While they embraced, she looked over his shoulder, smiled as she batted her eyelashes in a victorious way, and whispered in his ear, "Well...darling, if that's what you want to do."

Jack held her at arm's length and laughed, "I don't know why I didn't think of it sooner. Let's decide on a date right away."

Now that her strategy had worked, she wanted to set a date immediately. As subtle as possible, she said, "Honey, let's eat. The food will get cold. Afterwards, we'll talk about setting a date." Everywhere Lauren turned, Jack reached out to her. She pretended to be annoyed so in a joking way said, "Jack would you mind sitting in the living room? You're in the way."

"Lauren! You've got me so horny, I can't think about eating."

"That's too bad. You'll just have to wait."

When they finished dinner, Jack took out his pocket calendar and said, "Okay, Lauren, how does a wedding on Saturday, August 28th, suit you? The fall semester begins in the middle of September; we would have a week for a honeymoon."

"Yes! Yes! That's wonderful," she cried. Without another word, she jumped up from the table and ran to the telephone. "Oh, Jack! I've got to call my parents and tell them the good news!" She crossed over to a small desk by the fireplace. Lauren called back to Jack and said, "While I'm on the phone, please start cleaning up the kitchen." The rattling of dishes distracted her. When she turned to see what was going on, she saw that Jack had a scowl on his face. It was obvious he was angry about something. It was too late to ask what was wrong because her mom answered the phone. "Oh- ah-ah-, Hello, Mom." The words tumbled out. "I'd like to come to see you this weekend. I've got some wonderful news. I've been dating a great guy for several months and we plan to be married August 28th. I'd like to be married in my hometown." There was a long period of silence. She wasn't sure if they had been disconnected? "Mom! Are you still there?"

"Yes, Dear. I'm still here. I was shocked by your news. You didn't mentioned anything about dating the last time we talked."

"I wasn't sure at that time how I felt about him but I know now. I'm really in love."

"Of course, Honey, it'll be so good to see you this weekend."

"I'm sorry it's such short notice. We'll talk about Jack and the wedding when I get there. I'll be at your house Friday evening at seven o'clock. I love you. Tell dad I love him too. Bye." Lauren looked over at Jack, and her forehead creased into a frown as she asked, "Jack, why did you get so angry while I was talking to Mom?"

In a disgruntled voice, "I don't do dishes. I never have and never intend to do them again."

"What!" She snapped back, "Does that mean you don't intend to help me with the chores?" Ignoring her question, he finished the last dish, folded the towel neatly, hung it on a rack, walked over to the sofa, picked up a book and started reading. Bewildered, Lauren followed him to the sofa, put her hands on her hips, glared at him, and asked, "What's wrong with you?"

Disgusted, Jack slammed the book down and said sarcastically, "Well, if you must know, that conversation with your parents really put a chill on my romantic mood."

"I'm sorry. I was so excited. I just had to tell Mom so we could start making plans for the wedding. Lauren bent over him and gave him a quick kiss on his cheek. After a few minutes, she called out from the bedroom, "H-o-n-e-y, dessert is ready."

CHAPTER 3

Thursday night, Lauren packed before she went to bed for her trip home. She wanted to be ready to leave Friday evening as soon as she got off work.

It had been a hectic day. There had been more sick children than usual. She was anxious to leave as she had three hours to catch her flight to Williamsburg, Virginia. As she was checking on her last patient, the electronic doors to the emergency entrance hurled open. A gurney with an unconscious child was rushed into the hospital. The parents ran beside it screaming, "Get a doctor! Where's the doctor?"

Lauren's head jerked up when she heard her name being paged, "Doctor Lauren Fulghum, ER! Doctor Lauren Fulghum, ER! STAT!" Adrenaline pumped into her tired body as she raced down the hall of the hospital. Her white jacket and long blonde hair flew in all directions as she dashed through the open ward doors, hurried past a black man clutching his abdomen, and past a battered woman whose face was bulging beyond recognition. The smell of blood hung heavy in the air.

A nurse called, "Doctor! Doctor! Over here!"

The minute Lauren saw the little girl she realized it was her patient, Christy. Lauren's eyes filled with compassion as she remembered her skipping into her office with a bright smile and a head full of red, bouncy ringlets. Now her mangled body lay matted with blood, and she was hardly recognizable.

Lauren stood by the nurse and in a low voice asked, "What happened?"

The nurse said, "She was hit by a car. Her parents insisted that you come."

"Call a neurosurgeon! I'll do what I can for her until he arrives." Lauren turned and saw Christy's parents tearfully huddled together in a corner of the emergency room. She forced a smile of hope. Then she turned to a near-by counter and picked up some sterile bandages and cleaned the blood from Christy's swollen face just as the neurosurgeon came in. While the doctor examined her, Lauren said to her parents, "Christy's in good hands. I think it would be a good idea for both of you to stay in the waiting room until we know more. I'm going back to my office. The neurosurgeon will let you know how she's doing." The parents choked back tears as they thanked Lauren, glanced back at their daughter, and left the emergency room.

Lauren returned to her office, but before she left the hospital, she called the neurosurgeon. Relieved that his prognosis was encouraging, Lauren hurried to the parking lot. She only had two hours to shower, dress, and call a taxi. She was ready to go. Lauren glanced at her watch and thought, "Damn! What's holding up that taxi?" Her patience had worn thin.

The sound of screeching brakes made her jump. The taxi swerved into the parking lot and the driver jumped out and apologized, "Sorry lady, heavy traffic." Lauren climbed in and slumped down in the back seat. The driver looked at her in his mirror. Lauren glared angrily back at him for being late. Expertly he drove through the congested traffic, reassuring her that he would be there in time for her flight. When he arrived at the terminal, he sprang out of the cab, helped her out, and handed her the suitcase. Lauren slapped a tip in his hand and ran toward the check-in line. With a few minutes to spare, she followed the other passengers who moved like a herd of cattle. Lauren wiggled her way over a passenger until she got to her seat next to the window.

Disappointed that Jack didn't make a concerted effort to go with her, she imagined his face in the reflection of the glass. His reason was that he needed to stay home and study. Sleep overtook her thoughts. Exhausted, she drifted off to sleep while visions of a white wedding dress swirled in her head.

CHAPTER 4

A few hours later she was awakened by the Captain's voice when he announced the plane would be landing in ten minutes. As soon as the seatbelt sign turned off, she squirmed out of her seat, dug her bag out from the overhead compartment, and shoved her way out of the plane. Afraid of a delay that would keep her father waiting, she hailed a cab to take her to her parents' home. The driver took her bag and asked, "Ever been to Williamsburg, Miss?"

"Yes!" She replied in a curt voice. "I used to live here. Please take me to 521 Columbus Avenue." The taxi shot forward, skidded around corners, and sped toward the address. When Lauren saw the familiar two-story house with white clapboard siding and dark green shutters, it gave her a comforting feeling.

The tall, stately pines cast shadows against the house and across the well-manicured lawn. Her parents, Ben and Polly Fulghum, sat on the porch waiting for her. Her dad, sixty-four years old, was handsome as ever in his blue jeans and red plaid shirt. He still had a head full of beautiful white, wavy hair that framed his tanned face. His six-foot tall athletic body suffered only a slight protruding stomach that hung over his belt.

Her mom was wearing a simple, short-sleeved dress, with a small flower design, complete with an apron tied around her waist. Her hair hung straight below her ears with bangs that barely brushed her eyebrows. Polly's strawberry colored hair was sprinkled with gray, and she was still a lovely woman who had aged gracefully. As soon as the taxi stopped, her parents ran down the walk with outstretched arms. Ben reached through the open window, paid the driver, and sent him on his way. Then he turned to speak to Lauren, but Polly was already bombarding her with questions.

Lauren laughed, "Mom! Please, one question at a time. I'll be here for two days."

Polly squeezed her hand and exclaimed, "Honey, I'm so excited to see you. I want to know everything at one time. When you called and told me your news, I wanted to ask a dozen questions but you seemed to be in a hurry. C'mon baby, let's go inside and talk. You and your dad can sit in the kitchen while I finish cooking supper."

Ben put his arm round Lauren's shoulder and said, "Ok Polly, we'll be there in a few minutes." Then he turned and pointed with his other hand and said proudly, "I just finished mowing and trimming the lawn. I want it to look perfect on your wedding day. I've planted flowers that will be at their peak then."

"It's beautiful, Dad. You've manicured the lawn to perfection."

As they walked into the kitchen, the aroma of spaghetti sauce permeated the room. Lauren stopped and took a deep breath. "Y-u-m-m, it smells delicious. I've really missed your cooking, Mom."

Ben pulled back one of the ladder-back chairs that surrounded the pine trestle table. "C'mon honey, let's sit down." He looked across the table at her. "I believe you get prettier every time I see you but you do look a little tired. Are you working hard?"

Lauren, looked him straight in his eye's and said, "Dad, don't worry about me. I love taking care of children. The only problem is that it takes most of my time. Wait a minute, Dad," as Lauren called out, "Mom! I'm starving. When can we eat?"

"It's ready." She served them plates of spaghetti, ice tea, piping hot Italian bread, and tossed salad. Polly gave a short blessing and before she was through, Lauren had already twisted the noodles around her fork and shoved a large portion into her mouth. Polly laughed at her and said, "There's plenty more. You don't have to eat so fast."

"I can't help it."

Polly waited for Lauren to slow down eating before she asked her questions. "Honey, we'd like to know something about Jack. Is he working while he goes to school? Will he help you financially?"

"He tells me that he will get a job just as soon as he finishes this semester. He needs to spend all the extra time studying so that he can finish school in good standing." Lauren continued to eat but she thought about the promise Jack had made to her about getting a part-time job. He hadn't even tried to get one. She'd been paying all the bills and giving him extra money. Lauren put her fork down and said, "Don't worry, Mom. He'll get a job."

Polly put her hands in her lap and tore a paper napkin into shreds. Her curiosity got the better of her. "Didn't he want to come with you? What are his parents like? It would be nice to meet him before the wedding."

"Mom! Let's not discuss Jack or his family tonight. I'll tell you all I know about them after we get the wedding plans completed." Polly backed off the questions as she realized it was upsetting Lauren.

Ben, puzzled at Lauren's vague response, said in a condescending voice, "Lauren, you're our only daughter. We've always wanted you to have the best of everything, including the best possible husband. It's only natural that we want to know all about him."

Lauren's nerves gave way. She slammed her hand on the table and yelled, "Damn it! Don't you think I know what I'm doing? Give me a break. Better yet, when Jack comes, you can ask him about his financial situation and his family. I'm going to my room."

Ben and Polly looked at each other and were stunned at Lauren's sudden outburst. Polly jumped up from the table and started washing dishes.

Ben tried to console Polly and whispered, "She'll be all right. I could tell she's been working hard and now with a wedding to plan for—it's overwhelming."

When Lauren got to her room, she sat down at her dressing table and looked in the mirror and thought, Mom and Dad don't understand. They haven't met Jack and can't imagine how wonderful he is. They're treating me like a child. What do they know about the way young couples live in today's world? Why can't they accept Jack without any reservations? They should be glad that I'm getting married. Lauren got up from the dressing table, took a shower, put on her gown, turned off the light, and climbed into bed. She pulled the sheet up around her shoulders and watched the streetlights flicker through the fluttering lace curtains.

* * * * *

The next morning, she peeked at the clock by her bed. Shocked at how long she had slept she exclaimed, "Seven o'clock! I've got to go to work!" She stopped in the middle of the room and muttered, "What am I doing? I'm home. I don't have to go to work." She slipped on a light blue seersucker robe and a pair of blue scuffs, and tiptoed downstairs to make coffee. She was surprised to see her parents already up and busy doing their chores.

Polly chirped, "Good morning, sleepy head."

Ben asked, "Did you have a good night's sleep?"

"I think I must have died when I hit the bed. It feels good to be home again. I apologize for cutting you short last night. I was just plain exhausted."

Polly kissed Lauren on the cheek and said, "We understand. Sit down and have some breakfast."

Lauren raised her coffee cup and quipped, "Madame, I'll drink to that."

After breakfast, Polly cautiously asked Lauren, "Why do you want to get married so soon? It takes longer than four months to get to know someone that you will spend the rest of your life with. You don't seem to know anything about his family or what he did before he met you. Maybe Ben and I could fly up there one weekend and meet him?"

Before Polly could finish her questions, Lauren blurted out, "Mom, I'm thirty-one! I really don't have time to be choosy! I'm going on my gut feeling that we'll be happy. I want a family before I get too old to have children. If I've made a mistake, I'll have to live with it. If you don't mind, let's go on with the wedding plans."

"Lauren, after I talked to you the other night, I thought you might need me to help find a place to have the wedding and reception. I don't mean to take charge and if there is anything you don't like, you can change it."

"Thanks, Mom. I was hoping that you would start organizing the wedding. I just don't have time."

Polly pulled out a list of things that she had already accomplished. "I've got the church, the preacher, place for the reception, videographer, and photographer. The videographer told me he would like to have photographs of you and Jack."

Ben exclaimed, "That isn't a problem. We have hundreds of you. Lauren and I can pick those out while you take care of other chores!" Polly forced a smile to cover up her feelings for the way Lauren had raised her voice about the questions she had asked. To keep Lauren happy, she would go along with the wedding and keep her thoughts to herself. Ben pulled a large box full of photographs from one of the cabinets. He grinned as he picked up a picture and said, "I'm mighty proud of this one," as he held it up. "Here you are in your robe when you graduated from Harvard with honors. Lauren, you've been everything we could ever want in a daughter. You've never disappointed us."

"Thanks, Dad, I'm the lucky one." Lauren put down a handful of pictures and said, "I've got some things I really need to do. If it's okay, pick out what you like. Whatever you choose will be all right with me." Lauren turned back to her notes and marked off wedding bouquet, church, flowers, shoes, and wedding dress. Since it was going to be a small wedding, she would have only one attendant, Camille Bloomfield. Lauren looked up from her notes and said, "Mom, I need to go upstairs." As she started up the stairs, about halfway up, she stopped and looked over the banister rail into the living room. She wished, one day, her apartment would be as beautiful as her parents' home, which was decorated with antiques in the Williamsburg period. She adored the tall, antique grandfather clock in the foyer and loved to hear it chime. A portrait of her dressed in her black graduating robe holding a diploma from Harvard University, which hung over the mantel, caught her attention. Thoughts of the past triggered painful memories of her college years. She gripped the handrail of the stairs until her knuckles turned white. A decision about a man that she loved, while working on her degree, turned into a disaster. She blamed part of it on her parents for the pressure they put on her to excel in everything. It was true they had sacrificed, but she had, too. It took all her time to maintain high grades to please them. They constantly reminded her not to get serious with anyone until she had finished college. It would have been impossible for any man to live up to her parents' expectations.

Her resentment toward her parents for being so strict during college disappeared like a puff of smoke when she walked into her bedroom. High school memories rushed over her. The night before she had been too tired and sleepy to look carefully at her old room. Her mom had always loved pink and never changed anything, especially those pepto bismol walls. Lauren strolled around the room and touched the posters of rock stars that had long ago lost popularity.

There was one of Elvis Presley—dead but not forgotten. Banners from various high schools hung randomly about the walls camouflaging some of the pink. All the pictures had made her feel nostalgic and sleepy. Lauren lay down on the bed and looked up at the canopy with string tassels hanging from every crocheted point. Her hands rubbed the coverlet that was made in the wedding ring design. Her mom had promised it to her on her wedding day. The grandfather clock's deep resonant gong shook Lauren out of her nostalgia. Get up, she thought, I've got things to do.

At that same moment, her mother called, "Lauren! Jack's on the phone."

She scrambled to get the telephone. "Hello, honey. It's good to hear your voice. I've missed you."

"Lauren! You sound a little sleepy."

"I went to bed late last night and I overslept. What are you doing up so early this morning?"

"Now don't get upset! I'm packing."

Lauren cried out, "Packing! Where're you going?" She felt weak in her knees. Oh, my God she thought, he's leaving me!

"I've decided to fly back home for a few days. I need to talk to my parents about some financial matters. My bank account has dwindled down to nothing. I'm hoping they will sign a loan to help me with my education and our wedding expenses."

"Do they know you're coming?"

"I called Mother to let her know. I don't care whether my father knows or not."

"Does she know we're getting married?"

Jack snapped back, "Damn it, Lauren. That's why I'm going, remember?"

Lauren forged ahead, "Well...Jack, it would be nice to know if they're coming before the wedding. I'd like to meet my future in-laws before we're married."

"Not a chance. You'll be lucky to see them the day of the wedding. I'll fill you in on all the details when I get back. I can't talk anymore. I've got to go."

"O-k-a-y. I suppose I'm getting a little nervous. Call me when you get back home."

"I will—bye"

Before he hung up, Lauren cried out, "Wait! I nearly forgot. Ask your mother to send pictures of you from early childhood on up through college. Anything will do. I'm having our photos put on the beginning of our wedding video."

Jack sounded sarcastic in his reply, "Do you think that's necessary?"

Lauren was getting annoyed with Jack's sarcastic replies and said, "Since I don't know much about you, I would like to see what you looked like as a child. Get some pictures of your parents, too."

"My parents didn't believe in taking pictures. I doubt there'll be any. I can't talk anymore. I've got to catch a plane. Good-bye, Doc."

Lauren quickly said, "I love you. Have a safe trip." A click sounded at the other end of the line. She wondered why he always got angry every time she mentioned his family? Maybe one day she'd find out. Before going downstairs, she slipped into a pair of khaki shorts, a T-shirt, and tennis shoes.

The pungent odor of spicy tea filled the kitchen. While her mom talked on the phone, she poured a cup of tea and looked around the kitchen at the familiar pictures and antiques her parents had collected over the years. Her mother asking a barrage of questions to someone on the telephone interrupted Lauren's memories of the past. Polly's voice seemed to rise with each question, "Which room will you use for the reception?" Before they could answer, she said hastily again, "Will you send me a menu to select from? " Her mom finally stopped talking and listened to the manager's response. Polly's face had a look of concern when she turned around and saw Lauren. "Oh, Lauren," she said, "I do hope the manager of the Williamsburg Inn will make this reception an especially memorable event for you." Polly walked over to the stove, poured herself a cup of tea and took a sip. "It takes a lot of planning to put on a wedding, and I want this to be extra special for my baby. Now that all those decisions have been made, you and I can talk. How was Jack when he called?"

Lauren shrugged and said, "Fine. He's flying to White Plains, New York, to visit his parents for a couple of days."

Polly took the towel she had in her hand, and unconsciously rubbed a spot on the table. "I really wish you had known Jack a little longer."

Lauren tilted her head to one side and said firmly, "Mom—I understand your concern. I know what I'm doing. Jack has stirred feelings I haven't felt for a long time. You never knew how close I came to getting married before I graduated from Harvard. I was crushed when things didn't work out. I swore I would never let that happen again. After that, I poured myself into my career. Jack came along and filled that void." Lauren reached over the table and held her mom's hand, giggled a little, and said, "My biological clock is ticking, and if I intend to have a family, I had better start working on it."

With a solemn expression on her face, Polly said, "Lauren, I'm trying to understand. I suppose I'm just a worrier."

Disappointed that her mom didn't understand her feelings, Lauren walked around the table and put her hand on her mom's shoulder, and said, "I know you'll like him once you get to know him."

CHAPTER 5

After Jack's conversation with Lauren Saturday morning, he dressed and left for the airport. An hour later, when he stepped into the doorway of the plane, he wished he wasn't going home. If it hadn't been for his mother, Sarah, and asking for a loan—he'd never go back. His father, Vernon Harper, whom he abhorred, was the last person in the world he wanted to see.

The flight from Boston to White Plains took only an hour. Here he was twenty-nine years old, and it had been eleven years since his last visit—except for a couple of hours at his graduation from North Bridge Military Academy. He gazed out the window of the cab at a town that hadn't changed very much in eleven years. The four-block downtown area had the same old painted storefronts with canvas awnings covering a third of them. Cars were parked horizontally along the street with no worry about meters to feed. Time stood still as he reflected on how fast the years had gone by: four years at North Bridge, five years in the regular Army, and two years as an instructor at North Bridge Academy.

Not a leaf stirred in the late afternoon. The humidity was stifling in August. His parents' house was the same: a plain two-story, white clapboard house with a porch that stretched across the front. He remembered that his father refused to plant shrubbery around the house because it would cost too much. The lawn looked like a mixture of weeds and volunteer grass, but was neat and appeared to be mowed regularly. He glanced up in time to see his mother standing on the porch. She dabbed at the perspiration on her forehead. She hadn't changed the way she always dressed. It seemed to be her basic uniform: a short-sleeved blue and white-striped blouse and a navy blue skirt. That was the way his father wanted her to dress.

Jack bounded out of the cab and dashed up the steps. He'd forgotten how small and fragile his mother was until he embraced her. Holding her at arms length, the image of her all these years remained the same except the passing of time had left its mark. Her blonde hair, now totally gray, was neatly pulled back and twisted in a knot at the nape of her neck. Her gray-green eyes, that once seemed so alert, drooped with age and her beautiful face was crosshatched with lines. A sudden rush of anger came over him as he remembered what she had endured living with his father.

Sarah's expression lit up like a sunbeam at the sight of Jack, and she cried excitedly, "Jack, you look wonderful! You haven't changed a bit. I knew you would be as handsome as ever. You've taken good care of yourself." She took him by the arm and led him across the porch to two rocking chairs. The warped boards creaked as they walked on them. Sarah sat down in one of them and motioned for Jack to sit in the other one. As she rocked, the monotonous thump of the rockers irritated Jack.

He grabbed the armrest of her chair and said, "Mother, the sound of your chair reminds me of the times father hit me with a wooden paddle."

Sarah looked pitifully into Jack's eyes and said, "Oh, Jack, I'm sorry. It never dawned on me that was the way it sounded."

Finally, Jack smiled, "Tell me what's been going on in the neighborhood for the past 11 years."

"There's not a lot to tell." Sarah entwined her fingers nervously as she glanced toward the front door. Satisfied to see that no one was around, she continued talking. "All your friends have grown up, joined the army, or gotten married. I go to church and volunteer at the Red Cross Center, but that's about the extent of my activities." Sarah lifted her head up, looked into Jack's eyes, and said, "My life's been very dull until you told me that you were coming home and getting married. There're a lot of questions I want to ask; first, how's school, how did you meet Lauren, and what are your wedding plans?"

Jack laughed, "Slow down, Mother. I'll fill you in on everything." Jack reached over and gently held his mother's hand, "Before I answer your questions, I want you to answer a question for me that has been on my mind for a long time. Why didn't you leave father?" He watched his mother blink nervously. She tried to pull her hand away, but Jack held it until she gave him an answer.

Again Sarah's eyes darted around to see as if Vernon might be lurking behind a window or a door. She leaned toward Jack and whispered, "I was afraid to tell you before, but since you know how he treated me over the years, you're entitled to an explanation. In the beginning, I thought I loved him. It was only after several years of marriage that his true personality emerged. For many years I thought seriously about leaving him. Once I got as far as the bus station, but he was there waiting for me and made me come back. He said he would kill me if I ever left again. To make sure I understood what he said, he slapped me so hard I fell to the floor. Before I could get up, he raped me. The only good thing to come out of that experience was that I became pregnant with you. You were my salvation. Had you not been born, I believe I would have killed myself. Now…I'm old. I have no place to go." Sarah took a deep breath and continued. "As long as he controlled my life…he left me alone. He runs this house like a military camp. At times I've felt like a prisoner of war. Your father gets angry if his meals aren't on schedule. He acts like a raging bull if I'm a minute late. Everything I do around here has to be done on a military schedule." Suddenly Sarah jumped up and said, "We'll talk later." His mother glanced back at Jack as she reached the front door, and said, "Son, take your bag upstairs, and I'll call you when supper's ready."

Jack lingered on the porch. He looked down the street and recognized a house where he used to play ball with four brothers. A frown creased his face when he remembered the beatings he got if his clothes got dirty while playing. He shrugged his shoulders as memories surfaced. As a child he was terrified of his father. The pressure was always on him to be the best scholastically and in sports. Vernon Harper expected perfection. Jack's thoughts faded away when the dark clouds of night followed the sun as it disappeared below the horizon.

Jack stepped inside the door, flipped on the hall light, and saw his father coming down the steps. Vernon halted midway when he saw Jack. Their eyes met. Jack didn't retreat from his piercing stare but stood as tall and ramrod straight as his father. He noticed how he had not aged as his mother had. The creases in his face and the traces of gray in his black wavy hair only intensified his good looks.

A glint of light flashed off the belt buckle his father wore. Jack would never forget that belt. It made his hatred rise like a wall of raging fire. To help restrain an angry outburst, he clinched his fist and flexed his jaw and said in a terse voice, "Hello, Father." Then lied, "It's good to see you again."

Vernon continued down the steps, and coolly replied "Hello, Jack. I hear you're getting married."

"Yes…you heard right." Jack was proud of himself for not saying, yes sir and not saluting. "We'll be getting married the last weekend in August. Lauren and I hope you and Mother will come to the wedding."

Vernon replied indifferently, "We'll see," and without another word continued down the stairs and disappeared into his office.

Jack went up to his room and tossed his bag on the bed. He looked around. Nothing had changed. His mother had kept it just like the day he left home. He always wanted to hang posters of sports heroes and banners, but in the eyes of his father, it wasn't military enough. His room had the appearance of a hospital clinic: white walls, drapes, tile floor, and even stark white bed linens. The only things that weren't white were the black wrought iron bed, the brown desk, chair, and dresser. As hard as it was to admit, his father was right about keeping things perfect and organized: clothes put away neatly, toys in their proper place, and books stacked orderly on the shelves. His discipline had helped him get through the service. Upon opening his suitcase, he picked up his jacket and shook it to get out the wrinkles. A metal object hit the floor. It was a medal he had been awarded for excellent marksmanship at North Bridge. He wanted to show it to his mother. It reminded him of another medal a long time ago.

* * * * *

His father sent him to a school where everyone had to wear the standard dress code of dark blue dresses for the girls, dark blue pants and shirts for the boys. His father transferred him to this school because it reminded him of a military academy.

At thirteen, Jack Harper was just beginning the eighth grade. One day his teacher asked each student to bring something interesting to show the class. He chose to take his father's treasured medal for sharp shooting. The big problem was to get the medal back on the wall before his father returned home from a veteran's meeting.

When the last bell rang, he dashed to his bicycle and rode at break neck speed to get home. He leapt off his bike and ran up the front porch steps two at a time. When he entered the house, to his dismay, his father waited for him at the foot of the stairs. Jack knew he was in trouble. Anger creased his father's face.

Vernon yelled, "Jack, do you remember what I told you about my medals? Well! You have gone too far this time! The sharp shooting medal is missing! Where is it?"

Jack stammered, "I took it to school and…"

"You what? Took my medal! Go to your room!" Jack shrank past him on the stairs concealing the medal in his hand. He was angry, too, because his father didn't give him a chance to explain. It didn't matter what he said. A beating was inevitable. In a few minutes his irate father stood in the doorway of his bedroom, hands on his hips, eyes glaring. He growled, "Where's my medal?"

Jack was determined not to tell his father how he wanted to brag on him, and especially now since he was about to get a beating. He stood by his bed, braced his shoulders, and answered defiantly, "I lost it."

Vernon roared, "I'll teach you a lesson you won't forget; undress, bend over the bed!"

He whipped the leather belt out of his pants and began to lash Jack's back. Again and again, his father struck him until welts covered it. Jack squeezed his eyes closed and clutched the bedspread to keep from crying. When the whipping stopped, he felt the blood run down the sides of his back as it reddened the white bedspread. Dead silence for a few minutes and then Jack heard the door slam and his father stomp downstairs. He buried his head in the covers as the dreadful pain throbbed through his body. The blanket absorbed muffled screams, "I hate your old medal! I hate you! I hate you!"

Exhausted, Jack fell asleep. Later, the aroma of fried chicken awakened him. Sarah tiptoed into his room and placed a tray of food on the desk. He stumbled over to it, sat down, and tried to eat. To keep from disappointing his mother, Jack struggled to eat a piece of chicken.

Sarah stepped behind Jack's chair and saw the bloody streaks on his back, which evoked pitiful sobs, "O-h-h-h, my Son. I want to help you, but you know I can't. You know what your father would do if he caught me up here." Sarah's sobs quieted down as she whispered, "Son, before you go to bed, take a warm shower, that'll help. When you've finished eating, hide the dishes under the bed. I'll get them later." Jack knew the consequences if his father found out she had fed him; she'd get a beating, too. He loved her even more for the risk she was taking. Jack hugged her. She kissed him on his cheek, and slipped out of the room.

The next morning, Jack carefully eased out of bed to keep the swollen welts from bleeding again. He took another warm shower and put on a white, cotton T-shirt to keep blood from showing through his blue school shirt.

On his way down the stairs to the kitchen, Jack considered telling his father a story that maybe the medal fell out of his pocket at school. But, when his father tromped out of his office cursing about the missing medal, Jack changed his mind. They both went into the kitchen and sat down at the breakfast table. His father never acknowledged Jack's presence. A cold silence hung over the stark white room.

His mother turned from the stove, forced a smile and said, "Good morning, Son. How do you want your eggs? Do you want toast or biscuits?" Jack stared at the red dishcloth in her hand, the same color of his blood. Right then he vowed he would never give his father a reason to beat him again as long as he lived in his house, and one day he would avenge himself.

"Son! Did you hear me?"

"Oh! I'm sorry...I-I-I'd like scrambled eggs and toast, please."

Sarah served their plates and sat down. The clicking of utensils against the white plastic plates offered little solace. Jack found it hard to eat being around his father. He yearned to hear a sympathetic word from him. If only he would say, "Son, I'm sorry. Will you forgive me?" But he knew that wasn't going to happen.

Jack saw his mother glance at the kitchen clock over the

cupboard, "Better hurry! You'll be late for school." Although it was painful to walk, he clenched his teeth and walked boldly out of the house to keep his father from seeing the pain on his face.

While in school, the day was a blur. His thoughts focused on what he could do with the medal. Even his pain was forgotten. When the last class bell rang, Jack dashed for his bike to peddle his way home. Dark clouds had gathered and a misty rain fell as he approached the highest bridge that spanned the Hudson. An idea came to him. He stopped, got off his bike, and looked over the rail. He pulled the medal out of his pocket, held it over the side, dangled it between his fingers, and let it fall. The medal flipped over and over until it was out of sight.

Uncontrollable, pent-up emotions poured out of his body as he cried, "Revenge…at last revenge!"

As he approached his house, he was surprised to see his mother waiting for him on the porch. She said excitedly, "Your father has gone out of town for the day. Better put the medal back before he gets home tomorrow."

Jack's eyes opened wide with dread and he yelled, "I can't! I threw it over the bridge into the river."

Sarah slapped her hands against her hips and exclaimed, "You what! You mean to say the medal is gone? Oh, my God! Go get in the car. We'll go to the Army Surplus Store and try to find one."

Without a minute to spare, she sped down town and looked frantically for a parking place. After they parked, they hurriedly walked into the store. They saw a man standing behind a counter. He was about as tall and thin as a six-foot fence post, haircut like a bristle brush, and complexion as ruddy as a steel wool pad. He chewed on a short stub of a cigar and spoke gruffly, "What 'cha want?"

Sarah glared at him, "We want to look at your war medals."

The tone in Sarah's voice jolted him to respond politely, "Yes, ma'am! What kind of medal?"

"A sharp shooters medal."

"Okay," he mumbled. He pulled out a large tray and placed it on the counter. Sarah and Jack fingered through the hodgepodge of army medals.

Soon Jack cried out, "Look! Here it is!"

"Thank goodness," Sarah sighed. "You can tell your father you found it." She turned to the disheveled man, with the medal in her hand and asked, "How much?"

He grunted, "Five bucks." Sarah tossed the money on the counter, thanked him, and dashed out of the store.

Jack nearly vaulted out of the car even before his mother stopped. He ran to his father's office, hung the medal back in its proper place, and then he swore out loud, "Father, you'll never see your original medal again—you'll never beat me again even if I have to lie, cheat, or run away." Jack slammed the office door and went to his room.

* * * * *

Before going down for dinner, Jack sat on his bed, picked up his own sharp shooter medal and rubbed it until it glistened. He wanted to show it to his mother but decided it might bring back too many bitter memories.

Later, at the dinner table, he asked, "Father, have you made up your mind about coming to our wedding?"

Vernon took his time before answering, "Well, I'm not sure. Sarah and I have talked about going to Kiawah Island for a vacation about that time. Maybe we could work our plans to coincide with your wedding."

Jack leaned back in his chair, crossed his arms, and tried to control his anger. His face was flushed as he said sarcastically, "In other words, you'll come if it meets your time schedule! I don't really give a damn whether you come or not as long as Mother's there."

Vernon frowned and looked at his son, and said vindictively, "You should be thankful we'd come at all. I don't approve of your getting married. I don't believe you're financially able, and I'm sure as hell not going to loan you any money." Vernon paused for a few seconds and then said, "Since you've been gone, I've published some articles on military discipline. I thought you might like to know that."

Jack jumped up, causing his chair to fall over, and said with indignation, "That's great! You certainly are an authority on punishment! All you're interested in is how great you think you are! If you were so great, why didn't you make General?" Jack picked up the chair and sat down. There was a long period of silence.

Vernon glared at Jack with eyes that could have killed. In a few minutes, when he had cooled off, he dropped his gaze, picked up his fork, and continued to eat. When he had recovered from Jack's outburst, he asked him as though nothing had happened, "Did you resign from the Academy?"

It took Jack by surprise how quickly his father recovered from his confrontation and thought maybe that was part of his strategy. Slowly taking a long swallow of iced tea, he realized for the first time that he didn't fear his father any more. He looked straight into his father's eyes and calmly said, "I've always wanted to be in the military, but I also wanted to be a lawyer. Some of my credits transferred from North Bridge to Harvard. As for the money, I plan to take care of that myself. I'd never ask you for anything."

Vernon leaned forward, pointed his finger at Jack, and snapped, "You're absolutely right about that! I won't support you and you'd better not ever talk to me like that again! Do you understand?"

Jack's temper reached the boiling point again and words spewed from him like a volcanic eruption. He threw a fork across the room, slammed his fist on the table, and yelled, "God-damn it, I wasn't asking you for a damn thing. I've gotten along all these years without you, and I don't need your help now!"

Infuriated, Jack rose from his chair, shoved it aside, and stormed out of the kitchen to the front porch.

Sarah followed Jack and sat down in a chair next to him and whispered, "I understand your feelings. I've wanted to hit him many times, but I was afraid he'd kill me. At least you're big enough to fight back."

For the first time Jack saw the look of despair and weariness in her eyes. "Mother, if he ever hits you again, call me. I'll fix him so he'll never hurt you again. I'd leave this minute, but my flight doesn't leave until tomorrow morning." He patted his Mother's hand. "It's been good to see you, and I hope you will come to the wedding."

"You know I'll be there, Son. I'm so glad you came to see me. I know the wedding will take extra money. I've been saving some in case I needed it, and I would like to give it to you."

"That's okay, Mother. Don't worry. We'll get along." Sarah got up to get the money but before she walked away Jack said, "Oh, by the way, Lauren asked me to bring back some pictures. Do you have any?"

"I think I can find a few. You know how your father was about taking pictures. He detested the idea of wasting money on such foolishness. The ones I have are some our neighbors took."

When Sarah came back, Jack started looking at the pictures and five $100 dollar bills fell out of the photographs. He picked up the money, "Mother! Where did this money come from?"

Tears welled up in her eyes as she said, "I can't think of anything more special than giving this to you as a wedding present."

"I can't take your money," he said trying to put the money back into her hands.

"Please, I want you to have it. It would mean a lot to me knowing that I could help just a little. Take it."

Jack reluctantly put the money in his wallet and said, "Thank you...I really appreciate it. It will come in handy. I know it must have been hard for you to save money knowing how strict father is with the money he gave you. Someday I'll pay you back."

The next morning, before his parents were up, Jack tiptoed down the steps and slipped into the kitchen. He looked behind the door where his father used to keep the wooden paddle, and there it was. His father had used the paddle on him as a child, but then as he grew older, he used a leather belt. Jack took it off the hook and stuck it in his suitcase, called for a cab, and walked out of the house. His mother came running out just in time to say goodbye to him.

As the cab drove across the same bridge where he dropped the medal years ago, he stopped the driver, took the paddle out of his bag, got out, leaned over the rail, and dropped it in the river. It disappeared into the murky waters below.

CHAPTER 6

I'd better call Lauren, he thought as he reached for his cell phone.

At first Lauren didn't recognize who it was and asked, "Who is this, please?"

Jack laughed, "How soon one forgets. Have you already forgotten the sound of your future husband's voice?"

"You sound different," she cried.

"I'm in an airplane. I took a chance that you would be home."

"I've only been here for about two hours."

"Well, you were right about my parents." Then he dropped his voice in a pathetic way to play on her sympathy. "They aren't in favor of our getting married, and they won't give me any financial help. I don't know how we'll make it."

Lauren cried out, "Don't worry, Honey. We'll make it. I'll help you get through law school."

Jack faked disappointment, "I don't like the idea of you supporting me, and I can't bear the thought of not marrying you, but…if you think we can make it…"

"I told you not to worry." Lauren laughed nervously as she exclaimed, "We can do it."

A smirk spread across Jack's handsome face. In a contrived amorous tone he said, "I can't wait to see you, Doc. Meet me at the airport. I'll be coming in on Flight Number 940, Midway

Airline, at five o'clock this afternoon."

As soon as Lauren stopped talking with Jack, she looked at her watch. "Good Lord, I don't have much time to get to the airport." On the way, she thought about her conversation with Jack. He really sounded despondent. Lauren's thoughts were interrupted as she wheeled into a parking space. She made her way through the terminal just in time to hear the airport loud speaker announce Flight 940 would be landing in five minutes.

Lauren's heart beat faster when she saw the large passenger plane taxi up to the ramp. She stood at the opening of the tunnel, and watched the people trudge along dragging their bags. Her head bobbed back and forth trying to get a glimpse of him. The crowd thinned out but still no Jack. Her arms dropped limply to her sides and her eyes filled with tears. Disappointed, she turned to walk away, but suddenly she heard her name being called. She looked back over her shoulder and saw Jack running toward her. He dropped his bag, caught her in his arms, and kissed her hard. "Why were you leaving?"

As she wiped away the tears, she exclaimed, "Oh, honey! I'm so glad to see you. What took you so long to get off the plane?"

"I was sitting in the last seat. When I got up to get my bag out of the overhead storage, the latch was stuck."

"I can't wait to tell you about the wedding plans and to hear about your visit with your parents."

"You can tell me about the plans later, and then I'll tell you about my trip. Jack took off and Lauren had to jog to keep up with his long strides down the corridors of the airport.

As they hurried along, Lauren tried to talk. "Are your parents coming to the wedding?" Jack grabbed Lauren's hand and walked even faster. Lauren said, "Jack, what's wrong?"

"Lauren! I told you I would talk to you about my visit when we get home. I'm in no mood to discuss my business in public."

"Okay...okay. I've been thinking about it ever since you

called. I'm just anxious." Nearly out of breath, she dropped Jack's hand and followed him to the car.

Jack was silent until he drove out of the parking lot. When he got on the freeway, he opened the conversation about his parents. "My parents plan a trip to Kiawah Island. Father said they will stop by for the wedding. Isn't that a hella'va note, Lauren? He made it sound as if he were doing us a great favor."

Lauren's face burned with anger. She cried out, "Do you mean to say that is the only reason they're coming is because it's on their way?"

Jack gripped the steering wheel, stared straight ahead, and replied, "That's the way my father thinks...not my mother! Father and I had a disagreement while I was there. He made it a point to tell me that he wasn't going to support me in school if I got married."

Lauren saw an opportunity to get Jack to open up about his family, so she pushed on. "Jack, what is the problem between you and your father?"

"Damn it, Lauren, I've already said enough about my family." Jack stared straight ahead oblivious to the cars whizzing by or the landscape changing from farmland to shopping malls. He drummed his fingers on the steering wheel and glanced over at Lauren and saw that she was hurt by his remarks. "Okay, I'll tell you about an incident that happened at Kiawah." Jack paused and said, "Lauren, I'm sorry I yelled at you. When I hear about Kiawah Island I get very upset. I was about six years old, when we went on a vacation there. Father wanted me to learn to swim the old-fashioned way. So he took me out into the deep water and let me go. I fought as hard as I could to stay up, but the waves kept knocking me down. I went under several times. He never pulled me up. A big wave came along and washed me towards the shore. When I came to, my mother was giving me mouth-to-mouth resuscitation. She had gone out into the ocean, and pulled me up on the sand. I was drowning, and he didn't give a damn because I didn't do what he wanted me to do."

"My God, Jack. I suppose you do hold a grudge against him. That was a frightening experience. I'm beginning to understand some of the resentment you have toward your father.

Please share your feelings about your family with me. I'm a good listener."

"Lauren, I've said enough. Let's talk about the wedding. Tell me what you and your folks have planned."

She smiled as she slipped closer to Jack and ran her hand along his thigh. "Camille Bloomfield will be my maid of honor because she's my best friend. I assume your father will be your best man."

Without saying a word Jack pushed Lauren's hand off his leg, pressed down on the accelerator, and wove in and out of the traffic recklessly. He noticed Lauren braced her feet against the floorboard. When they reached the parking lot in front of their apartment, he still hadn't answered her question. When they got there, Jack got out of the car, grabbed his bag and walked in.

He left Lauren sitting in the car completely exasperated by his mood swings. She unconsciously ran her fingers through her hair and thought, there had to be a way to deal with his volatile outbursts. Maybe he would agree to counseling. Maybe mom's right. I don't know Jack very well. As bad as I would hate to postpone the wedding for several more months, I could get to know Jack a lot better.

Ten minutes had passed when Lauren came into the apartment. She immediately started to pace around the room, halting in front of Jack and said, "I've been thinking, maybe we should call off the wedding for awhile. I get the feeling you don't really want to get married right now."

All of a sudden Jack realized his plans to marry someone with money was about to vanish. He jumped up off the couch and grabbed Lauren in his arms and cried out, "You really think I don't want to marry you? That's the craziest thing I've ever heard. I was taking for granted that you understood the situation with me where my parents are concerned."

Lauren pulled away and said, "If you'd tell me something about them, maybe I would understand. I still want to know if you are going to ask your father to be your best man? It would help if you acted more enthusiastic about the wedding in spite of your feelings about your parents."

"Doc, I'm trying to be patient with you. I don't want to hear or talk about my father anymore. I'm sure the wedding can go on without him." Jack walked toward the bedroom and said, "I'm going to unpack my clothes."

Her eyes blazed. It was all she could do to keep from lambasting him. The task of changing Jack was going to be a bigger job than she had bargained for. She had taken a pizza out of the freezer to cook for supper when she heard a noise coming from the bedroom. Lauren cried out, "What's wrong?"

He shouted back, "Why haven't you made up this bed! Just look at this room!"

The blue and white-striped coverlet lay piled up on the floor, the blue sheets rumpled up on the bed, and clothes were piled on the back of a chair. She yelled back, "For crying out loud, Jack. I've just gotten home from my trip. I didn't have time to put my clothes away, make up the bed, pick you up at the airport, and cook supper, too."

Jack's outburst continued as he yelled, "I've kept my mouth shut about the way you keep house, but as soon as we're married, I expect this house to be spotless and organized to perfection," Jack exploded as he threw a bed pillow across the room.

Lauren had been pushed to the limit. If it meant she would lose him that was the chance she would take. She bit her tongue and calmly stood in the doorway and said, "Mr. Harper, if you don't like the way I keep house, why don't you help or move out?" Lauren closed the door, walked back into the living room, sat down on the sofa, and stared at the TV, not caring what was on the tube.

An hour later Jack came out of the bedroom. He sat down

beside her and pulled her into his arms and said, "Doc, I don't know what's gotten into me. My world has been so different from yours. Everything I did was expected to be perfect."

Lauren's anger melted away. He sounded so pathetic. "I was afraid I had driven you away. I don't think I could stand to lose you. I love you so much. I'll try harder to make our home perfect." Lauren paused, stroked his face with her hand, and said, "I don't want to keep hounding you about the wedding, but there are things that we need to talk about. Have you forgotten we're leaving for Williamsburg Friday morning?"

"Oh-h-h, man. I had forgotten about it. My stressful trip back home blanked out my mind about our wedding plans. Speaking of wedding, where are we going on our honeymoon?"

"I don't know. I had hoped you would surprise me and whisk me off somewhere on a magic carpet." Lauren laughed as she waved her hand like a flying bird, "Take me anywhere. I love being surprised."

"Lauren, you can't be serious. Did you think I could pay for a honeymoon? I don't have enough money to go anywhere. The trip home took most of my money I had in savings. I don't think I can even afford one night in a hotel room."

Stunned, Lauren cried, "Jack! I was sure you had enough for a honeymoon. I don't have much money either. The wedding will take most of my savings." Lauren hesitated and hoped he was kidding. Since he didn't offer any money, she said, "Well...I suppose I can afford several nights in Williamsburg, or we can postpone the honeymoon until we can afford something really special."

Jack waited for a few minutes to let her suggestion sink in. He said as tactfully as possible, "Doc, the beach would suit me better than touring an old town."

"The beach! Okay, if that's what you want. It'll be all right with me, too. I've seen Williamsburg many times, but I never get tired of it. I just thought you might like for me to be your personal tour guide..."

"Jack broke in, "Now if you really want to know what I'd like, I would like to go on a cruise."

"That would be wonderful, but you know that's impossible." Lauren paused and said, "Oh, well, we can dream about it. Speaking of dreams, I'm tired and I'm ready to go to bed."

"Doc, before you go, I want to ask you something. When I was putting away my handkerchiefs I pulled open one of your drawers by mistake. I saw an insurance policy, and I didn't think you would mind if I looked at it. You have your parents as the beneficiary for your $500,000 life insurance policy."

"Yes, I sure do. If I should die before them, I feel that I owe them something for all that they have done for me."

"Are you planning to keep it that way even after we're married?"

"I don't know. I haven't thought about it." She tugged on Jack's arm. "Come on, Jack, let's go to bed."

He flipped on the television and said, "I'll be there after the news."

Jack waited until he thought Lauren had fallen asleep. His mind wasn't on making love, but getting the beneficiary changed. It was late when he slipped into their bed.

CHAPTER 7

They decided to leave at nine o'clock Friday morning, August 27th. During the week, Jack studied a map and detailed the route he would take to Williamsburg, Virginia. They finally got out of the main traffic and were on I-95 when Lauren laid her head against the back of her seat, yawned, and said. "Jack, I'm going to take a nap. I've had to work extra hard to make up for the days I'll be gone. Stop whenever you want to take a break."

Jack was glad to have the time to think about his future—especially the insurance policy. The wedding was something he hadn't planned on, but now he had to go through with it. He was trapped. Jack focused on the turn of events since he had met Lauren. All he had wanted to do was to live with her until he finished school, and then after graduation move on. He liked being alone without any responsibility for anyone else.

Suddenly he had a flashback about a television program he saw at Lauren's. It was about a man that married a woman with a large life insurance policy. He planned to get rid of his wife and collect the money. Since he had seen Lauren's policy, he was determined to find a way to get her to change the beneficiary to him. If he had that money, then he wouldn't need Lauren. Accidents could happen. How long could he go on pretending to love her? She wasn't hard to live with, but she would never be the housewife like his mother. Right now Lauren was his provider, and he would have to cater to some of her demands.

Lauren began to stir. Like a child waking up, she sleepily said, "Are we there yet?"

Jack glanced at her quickly and replied, "You've got to be kidding!"

"Yeah, I was. I am ready for a pit stop if you don't mind." Jack drove on for a few more miles until he came to a rest area. When they got out to stretch their legs, Lauren said, "It's almost lunch time. Let's get a snack here. This rest area looks neat and clean."

"Okay, but we can't waste any time." After they had eaten, Lauren cleaned up the trash while Jack went back to the car. When she came, he was clutching the steering wheel and was grumbling, "What in the hell took you so long? You know we have a long way to go." Lauren hardly had time to close the door when he sped out of the parking lot.

"I'm sorry. I was helping a little boy who had fallen down. His leg was in a cast and he couldn't get up." Lauren gazed out the window and thought about her little patients. She turned and looked at Jack and said, "I miss seeing my little friends at the hospital. They…"

Jack cut in, "I've been wanting to tell you this. I wish you wouldn't bring your feelings about your patient's home with you. When we are together, I just want to talk about the things we like to do or go out for some entertainment. I really don't care to hear about their aches and pains."

She managed to say, "You've never mentioned that you didn't like children. You know that's my whole life."

Jack realized that he had made a grave mistake. Something had to be done quickly to mend it. "Oh, Doc, (Jack always called Lauren "Doc" when he tried to be loving or sympathetic), I didn't mean it the way it sounded. I'm just tired, and we still have a long way to go." He patted her arm and said, "Since I've met you, my whole life style has changed. I need to get accustomed to one thing at a time." He looked at Lauren and with the best smile he could muster, lied as he said, "Getting married is the only thing I'm thinking about right now. You'll be Mrs. Jack Harper in one more day."

"Some how you always come up with the right thing to say. I can't stay angry with you. I just have a hard time understanding why you don't want a family. In time, I'm sure you'll look at things differently."

Jack didn't say anything, but he thought it would be a cold day in hell before he had children. In the meantime, Lauren dozed off and several hours later Jack nudged her, "Look! There's the city limit sign."

She rubbed her eyes, sat up, and peered out of the window. The sun was setting behind tall trees that looked like black lace against the orange sunset. The streetlights and storefronts gave a warm glow of welcome to the tourists and hometown folks. "I used to love this time of evening. Mom and Dad would bring me downtown and we'd eat at a sidewalk cafe. The smell of fresh-baked bread made my taste buds work overtime. Then we would look in all the store windows. Even in August the merchants displayed Christmas decorations."

"It's interesting what you're saying, but you had better tell me how to get to your parents' house. I don't have a clue as to which way to go."

"Okay...I forgot you haven't been here before. You just drive and I'll tell you where to turn."

"Don't wait until I'm nearly past the street before you tell me."

Lauren giggled, "I'm so happy to be home. I'm extra happy that you're with me and we'll be getting married tomorrow—OOPS! Turn left, Jack! I'm sorry. I was busy talking. Keep straight until you get to the end of this street. They live in that two-story white house on the corner."

Jack was impressed with the colorful appearance of the Fulghum's lawn. A row of bright red geraniums, planted in front of large boxwoods, was like a fringe of lace on a sleeve of a dark green dress. His father would have never considered planting flowers.

Lauren and Jack walked up to the front door and peered through the screen door to see if she could see anyone. She heard her mom in the kitchen rattling dishes in the sink. "Jack," Lauren whispered, "I'm going to tiptoe in and surprise Mom. You stay here until I get back." She carefully opened the door and quietly crept down the hall to the kitchen. Lauren walked up behind Polly and put her hands across her eyes.

"Ben!" Polly yelled, "Don't scare me like that." She whirled around and saw Lauren laughing at her. Polly hugged her and cried out, "Baby, baby, you're home. I was getting worried." In the next breadth she asked, "Where's Jack?"

"He's on the porch waiting for me to surprise you. I'll get him."

Jack came in with Lauren's suitcase and put it on the floor. He flashed a smile that would have melted ice cream on a freezing day. He reached out his hand to Polly and said, "I've been looking forward to meeting you."

Polly smiled. "Hello, Jack. We've been looking forward to meeting you, too." She shook his hand with a firm grip and said, "My goodness I'm glad you all are here safe and sound. I'll call Ben. He's out in the yard somewhere...wouldn't leave the house all day because he was afraid you'd come and he wouldn't be here." Polly called out, "Ben! Come here! We've got company!"

From the back of the house a voice yelled back, "Who is it, Polly? Has Lauren come?" Ben came around the corner of the living room and when he saw Lauren he rushed over to her and wrapped her in his arms. "Shugh, I'm so glad you're back home again. Last weekend when you were here was much too short. We had kinda' gotten used to your being gone but when you left we were sad all over again. We sure do miss you."

"Dad, I'll make a bargain with you. Let's split the visits fifty-fifty."

"That's a deal." Ben and Lauren smacked their hands

together in a high five sign.

Ben didn't see Jack when he first came into the kitchen. Lauren laughed, "Dad, we were so caught up in each other I almost forgot Jack." She motioned for him to come over.

Ben put out his hand and said, "We've heard a lot about you. I'm glad to meet the *wonder man* in Lauren's life."

Jack shook his hand like a limp fish. "I feel as though I already know you. Lauren talks about both of you a lot." He let go of Ben's hand, walked over to Lauren, put his arms around her shoulders, and kissed her on the cheek. "Mr. and Mrs. Fulghum, you have a wonderful daughter. I really love her and I'm looking forward to taking care of her the very best I can."

"J-a-c-k, you're embarrassing me." She was also astonished by Jack's sudden show of affection and wondered if this was an act to impress her folks.

Polly broke in and said, "Oh, Honey, let him kiss you all he wants to. When you get older, husbands forget those affectionate touches." She kidded Ben by saying, "Don't you, old man?"

Lauren said, "Folks, I've got some things I need to do. I'm going upstairs, unpack my clothes, and check my list. I'll see you later."

Polly said, "Jack, stay in here with me and we can talk while I finish washing these dishes. "

He picked up a dry dishtowel and said, "Here, let me dry them. I'm used to helping Lauren around the apartment."

"Thank you. It seems as if I'm always cooking and cleaning. A woman's work is never done." Polly paused for a moment and then said, "Jack, Lauren hasn't ever told us anything about your family. Do you mind telling me something about them?"

Faking a cheerful response Jack said, "Of course not. Father is a retired army officer and my mother cooks and keeps a spotless house for my father. Sometimes she volunteers to work at her church."

"So, she doesn't have to help with the household expenses.

That's good. I'm hearing all the time from Ben that it's hard to make ends meet when you have house payments, insurance, and 'Lord have mercy' along with many other expenses that come with keeping up a home."

"I'm definitely going to get a job. Lauren understands that I have to work extra hard on my studies to keep up a good grade average. I want to become a good lawyer so that we can both save for our own house." He tossed the towel to one side and thought, damn...I need to get out of here before her mother asks me any more questions. Jack headed toward the door and saw Lauren. He said, "Doc, I've been thinking I'd better go to the Inn and let you and your mother have time together. My parents should be arriving today about six o'clock. As soon as they feel like it, I'll take them out for dinner."

Polly spoke up, "I've cooked enough to feed all of you. Why don't you bring them around here and we can meet each other before tomorrow? I'd really like to talk to your mom about the rehearsal dinner party tonight."

Jack stammered for words, "I-I-I'm sure they aren't going to do anything about a rehearsal dinner party. She will be very tired from her trip, and my father is very particular about what he eats. I'll apologize for them now."

Polly touched his arm as if to stop him and said, "Jack, wouldn't you like to come back here and go with us to the chapel? You need to know something about the procedure of the wedding ceremony and to meet the preacher."

"That's okay. Lauren can fill me in with the details tomorrow. I think I need to stay with my parents as much as possible. They'll be leaving soon after the wedding. My visit with them last weekend was short, and we didn't have enough time to catch up on what has happened in the past eleven years." Jack walked over to Lauren and pulled her into his arms and said, "Just think, tomorrow afternoon at six o'clock, you'll be my beautiful bride." After he kissed her, he looked over Lauren's shoulder and said to Polly, "Mrs. Fulghum, I love your daughter, and I'm looking forward to being a part of your family." Jack released Lauren and crossed over to Polly, "I don't want you to feel left out, Mrs. Fulghum," and he gave her a sweet kiss on the cheek and said, "I'll be seeing all of you tomorrow. " Jack turned and made a quick exit.

Lauren watched her mother for her reaction to Jack's adoration. Instead she saw a quizzical expression on her face. Polly said, "Honey, he acts like he loves you." With a twinge of sarcasm she continued, "I hope he'll make you happy, but I don't understand why he doesn't want to rehearse for at least fifteen minutes."

Lauren was miffed at her mother's snide remarks. She thought Jack had acted unusually polite and affectionate. With an air of indignation Lauren tossed her head back and retorted, "Mom! I have the feeling you don't like Jack."

Her mother's voice was pitched higher than usual, "Now what in the name of heaven gave you that idea? You're just imagining something that's not there. Come on, and sit down at the table, and let me get you something to eat. You're just tired and hungry."

"I suppose you're right. It has been a long day." Lauren sat down and watched her mom prepare a meal with the ease of a professional chef. "By the way, my maid of honor, Camille Bloomfield, is coming tonight. I don't know if I told you that she was in med school with me and that's where we met. We work at the same clinic."

"That's nice. I'm looking forward to meeting her." While Polly put away the dishes she said, "By the way, where are you going on your honeymoon?"

"Well…that's a good question. We don't have enough money to do what we want to do, so I guess we'll either go to the beach or tour Williamsburg for the hundredth time."

"Where do you want to go?"

"We'd really like to go on a cruise, but that will have to wait."

"I don't mean to pry but didn't Jack save any money for a honeymoon? I thought that would have been on top of his list."

Lauren snapped emphatically, "No…no…no…he can't. Please don't put the pressure on me about our finances. I don't need to argue with you about it. We'll manage."

"Okay, Baby…okay." Polly walked over to Lauren and put her arms around her. "You know that I only want the best for you. I pray that you will have a wonderful and happy time on your wedding day. I'm sure, wherever you go, it won't matter as long as you love each other."

"Thanks, Mom. I'll see you in the morning. Good night."

CHAPTER 8

As Jack drove up the oval drive in front door of the Williamsburg Inn, he was instantly impressed with the grandeur of the two story, whitewashed, brick building. Three flags, accented by floodlights, fluttered lazily in the summer night air from the arched pediments. It was the epitome of an elegant Virginia country estate. Lauren told him that her mother had made reservations for the reception to be held there. Earlier in the week he called his mother and told her the time and place to meet him. It was no wonder Lauren didn't have much money left after paying for his room at this Inn, Jack thought, it's expensive. Her parents must be rich, too? His father would have researched the town for the best deal on a room.

Jack parked his car and went inside to register. His room was upstairs and when he looked around, a low whistle slipped through his lips at the beauty of the bedroom. He thought this is the way he wanted to live. After he meticulously hung up his clothes, refreshed himself, and dressed in his best green linen jacket and white pants, he went back downstairs to the dining room. He moaned when he looked at the menu, there wasn't a price that matched what he could afford. He wondered how he could manipulate his father into paying for their meal. Of course, he would have to make an attempt to pay. Immediately he thought of a scheme. He'd bribe a waiter to pretend he had a call from Lauren and to stall long enough for his father to be obligated to pick up the tab. Prompt as always, he saw his parents coming in the front door. He stood up and walked over to them and hugged his mother. "I see you made it right on time, Mother. You look wonderful." Then asked his father, "How was the trip?"

"Okay, I suppose. There were too many people on the road," Vernon said with disgust.

"It's about time for dinner. Would you like to go out to eat or stay here? The food here is highly recommended."

Sarah spoke up, "I'm very tired and would like to rest for awhile."

Vernon scowled and said, "We'll stay here. I don't want to get back in that traffic again. You can rest later." Sarah glanced at Jack and dropped her eyes in the manner she always did when Vernon gave orders.

Jack was quick to say: "Mother, we'll order something that can be prepared in a hurry." Sarah was overwhelmed by the beautiful ambiance of the dining area: flickering candles in crystal candelabras graced an elegant buffet table and red velvet drapes hung from arched window frames. She whispered to Jack, "I'm glad you're holding on to me. I'm getting dizzy looking at all the beautiful trappings in this room."

The headwaiter ushered them to their seats and handed everyone a menu. While they thought about their order, the waiter asked if they would like to order a cocktail. Vernon answered, "Water for me and my wife."

Jack wanted to impress his father with his knowledge of wine. "I'd like a glass of Pinot Noir. Mother wouldn't you like some wine?"

She looked at Vernon to see if he would approve. His expression said it all. "Son, I'd better not."

The waiter tried not to appear shocked, but his eyes widened as he commented to Jack, "Excellent choice, Sir."

Vernon picked up the wine list and studied the cost by the glass and bottle. Vernon whispered in astonishment when he saw the price, "Jack, do you know how much that glass of wine costs?"

"Don't worry about it, Father. I'm paying for the meal." The waiter came back with the drinks and took their orders. While they waited for the food to arrive, Jack made an attempt to tell his mother all he knew about the wedding plans. "We'll be married in an old church on the outskirts of town, the reception will be held right here in this Inn. We definitely have to be at the church by five-thirty tomorrow afternoon. Mrs. Fulghum wanted you to come and eat with her tonight, but I told her you would be too tired. I think you'll like Lauren's parents." Vernon sat tight-lipped and took in every word.

Jack was giving out of things to talk about just as the food was being served. Vernon had dropped his venomous tone and broached a subject he was most familiar with. "Do you think the men in the armed forces are as dedicated as they used to be ten years ago?"

Shocked by his father's question and that he had said it in such a civil manner, Jack took a few minutes to answer, "It depends on who is in charge of the unit they're in. I have seen some units that have loosened up on some of the restrictions." For an hour, they discussed the pros and cons of military discipline. Jack was amazed that the conversation with his father was actually pleasant.

He was almost sorry that he was going to put his father in the position to pay for the meal. Lauren would give him hell if he charged it to her credit card. Before his parents arrived, he had bribed a waiter to take part in his plan. He told the waiter when he dropped his napkin on the floor, to page him at once.

The friendly chatter between Jack and Vernon awed Sarah. The hour was getting late, and she was sorry to have to break up their conversation. Sarah forced a smile on her face as she said, "Men, I hate to break up this camaraderie, but I need to go to bed."

Jack made sure the waiter saw him drop the napkin. Right

on queue he came to the table and said, "There's a telephone call for a Mr. Jack Harper."

Jack signaled to the waiter and said, "I'm Mr. Harper."

"Sir, the telephone is at the far end of the lobby."

"Thank you." Jack got up and said, "It's probably Lauren giving me some more orders. I don't know how long this will take."

Ten minutes passed and Jack still had not returned. Their waiter stood by waiting for someone to pay the bill. Sarah was exhausted and she finally said, "Vernon, I know you don't want to do it, but let's take care of it. I can't stay up a minute longer."

Vernon shoved the bill under Sarah's nose and hissed, "Do you know how much this bill is?"

Sarah glared at Vernon and her voice tightened as she said, "If I have to, I'll pay the bill. I just want to go to bed."

Vernon snatched the bill away from Sarah and gave his credit card to the waiter. In minutes he was back with the receipt. Vernon threw his napkin down on the table and led Sarah out to the car.

Jack had watched the scene take place as he peeked around the side of the doorframe. When his parents were outside, he rushed outside apologizing, "I'm sorry it took so long. Lauren wanted to fill me in all the details for tomorrow. Give me the receipt and I'll send you the money when we get back from our honeymoon."

Vernon didn't hesitate as he pushed the bill in Jack's hand and said, "I expect to be paid back with interest. I thought you were treating us. I should have known better."

Sarah got in the car and rolled down the window. Jack leaned over and kissed her and said, "It was great to be with you again. I'll be seeing you tomorrow."

"Okay, son. Get a good nights sleep." She rolled the window up and waved good-bye.

After they had driven out of sight, he decided to go to the lounge for a drink. He made his way to the bar and ordered a whiskey sour. While he waited for his drink, Jack stared at the clear shelves with rows and rows of crystal glasses. He noticed in the mirror behind the shelves an attractive woman sitting in front of a large picture window. She was dressed in a bright green, linen shift with bright colored flowers embroidered on it. Her short, shiny, black hair was nearly as short as a man's style but most attractive. He thought, I wonder if she's waiting for someone. Ten minutes passed and no one showed up so he decided to go over and speak. She had been sipping on a glass of wine when Jack sauntered over to her table and asked, "Do you mind if I join you. I hate to drink alone."

With a surprised look and obviously caught off guard, she managed to say, "I suppose. I'll be leaving in a few minutes."

"Thank you." Jack sat down, looked out the window at the formal gardens. The sun had sunk below the horizon leaving the gardens illuminated only by lighted pathways and post lights. He remarked, "I arrived late this afternoon and didn't have time to see the garden."

"I'd like to see them, too. I got here about eight o'clock tonight, and all I wanted to do was to unwind from the plane trip and a hectic day's work."

"What brings you to this historical place?" He asked, as he looked deep into her brown eyes.

She tilted her head to one side to avoid his stare and replied, "I have a friend who's getting married tomorrow."

"Can I get you another glass of wine while we talk, Miss…?"

"It's Camille. About the wine, thank you, but no. I've had enough. I was just getting ready to leave."

Damn, Jack thought he wanted to delay her as long as possible. He touched Camille's hand as if to detain her, "Don't go. I need to talk to someone, I'm…uh…a little nervous. Tomorrow, I'm getting married. Can't we talk for a little while? I won't be single much longer. I was hoping you'd let me enjoy my last hours of freedom with a beautiful woman like you."

Camille pulled her hand away. "Who are you marrying?"

"Lauren Fulghum. The funeral...sorry...I mean the wedding is tomorrow at six o'clock."

Camille raised her eyebrow and shot him a look that could have cut Jack down to the size of a midget. She exclaimed, "So—you're Jack Harper?" She grabbed her purse, stood up, and said sharply, "I'm Lauren's maid of honor! I can't believe you would flirt with another woman the day before you're to be married. From some of the things Lauren has told me about you, I'm not really surprised at your actions. It's evident she hasn't figured you out yet. I hope you don't disappoint her after you're married." Camille whirled around and walked swiftly out of the lounge leaving Jack stunned by her outburst.

"Damn," Jack muttered. He had a dreadful thought. Camille could be his worst enemy.

CHAPTER 9

Camille came over to the Fulghum's house Saturday afternoon to help Lauren get dressed for the wedding. She was in the kitchen when she heard Lauren call, "Camille, come upstairs with me. I'll need you."

"Okay, Lauren. I'll be right there."

When Camille walked into the bedroom she saw Lauren admiring her wedding dress hanging on the back of the closet door. "Isn't it the loveliest dress you've ever seen?" Lauren gushed. She took her fingers and traced the French Alécon lace appliquéd on the white satin bodice. Amazed at the intricate work, she spoke reverently, "Can you imagine the patience it took for someone to sew on thousands of pearls." Then she delicately lifted the veil and fluffed it up in the air and watched it float down like a feather over the bouffant skirt. Lauren sighed, "It looks like icing on a wedding cake."

Camille was on the verge of telling Lauren about her encounter with Jack last night, but when Lauren turned around, beaming brighter than sunshine, she didn't have the heart to tell her. Instead she forced a smile and said, "Your dress is gorgeous, Lauren. It will blow Jack's mind when he sees you in it. Camille paused and said, "Okay, Mrs. **future** Jack Harper, what can I do for you? I feel helpless standing here doing nothing."

"Just sit and wait until I take a shower and put on my make-up. When I have done all that, you can help me with the dress. It'll take awhile to button all those buttons down the back." When Lauren had finished taking her bath, a clap of thunder sounded so loud that it actually shook the house. She threw on her robe and ran into the bedroom, looked out the window, and cried out, "Oh no! I can't believe a storm has come up so fast. It was sunny just a few minutes ago. Just my luck! It's going to rain on my wedding day." The skies darkened until it seemed that night had already fallen. Another clap of thunder rolled across the sky and rumbled like a bowling ball crashing into banks of clouds bursting them wide open. Above the thunder she heard her mom's voice.

"Lauren!" her mom called loudly from downstairs. "It's raining! Better bring down your raincoat and umbrella when you're through dressing!"

"Can you believe it? " Lauren cried out, "Rain! Not just a light shower but thunder, lightning, and gobs of water. I'll never get inside the church without getting drenched. My shoes, dress, and my hair will look like a wet dish rag."

Camille took the wedding dress down from the door and waited for Lauren to step into it and said in a consoling way, "Don't worry, Lauren. Your dad will make sure that you are covered from head to toe. Come on let's get your dress on. Time's running out."

"You're right. If I'm late, Jack might think I've changed my mind just like I thought he had when he came back from visiting his parents. It took him a long time to get off the plane. I hope he doesn't get cold feet today and back out."

"What makes you think he'd back out?"

"Oh-h-h, I'm not a good housekeeper or cook. He wants everything to be perfect."

"Do you know him well enough to know if he would ever be unfaithful?"

"Lord, no, Camille. That's the last thing I'd worry about. Why in the world did you say something like that?"

"I never told you that I almost got married…he left me at

the altar. So you see, I don't trust men at all." Camille buttoned up the satin bodice, straightened out the net underskirt, and attached the long train to the bodice of the dress. With a hint of jealousy Camille said, "I hope one day I'll wear a wedding dress as beautiful as yours."

Lauren realized she hadn't expressed any sentiment about Camille's tragedy and stammered, "Camille, you never told me about being jilted. I'm so sorry. When I get back to work, please tell me what happened."

"Okay. But for now be glad you have your wonderful parents to care for you." Camille stepped back and looked at Lauren. Her eyes filled with tears as she sniffed, "You are beautiful. Jack's a lucky man." She bent down and picked up the bottom of the dress and said, "Dr. Fulghum, it's time to go."

Polly was dressed in a light blue, silk, two-piece dress with a beautiful white orchid pinned on her left shoulder. She leaned on the banister post and called again from the foot of the stairs, "Hurry, honey. We don't want to be late." Step by step Lauren descended the stairs. Her veil rippled down the steps like a cascading stream, and when she was halfway down, Polly looked up. Tears welled up in her eyes as she choked out the words, "You're beautiful, darling. When your daddy sees you, he's going to be blown away with your beauty."

"Thanks, Mom. You look lovely, too." Lauren then kidded her by saying, "Something's missing, and I believe it's your apron."

Polly giggled, "Oh Lauren, I can dress up sometime."

It didn't bother Ben if his basic black suit got dusty or not. He had work to do gathering plastic sheeting, umbrellas, and rubber boots for all to wear when they got to the church. Since the van was in the garage everyone could pile in without getting wet. He put the last umbrella in, bounded into the kitchen, and yelled, "You know the old saying," 'It's raining cats and dogs'." He crossed over to the hallway to call Lauren. His mouth dropped open and his eyes widened when he saw her standing at the foot of the stairs. After the shock of seeing her, he walked over, gently took her hand, and said, "Honey-bun, you're the most gorgeous bride I've ever seen. It's going to be tough giving you away. I suppose all fathers think there isn't a man good enough for their daughters." He batted the tears back and in a thunderous voice said, "Come on, folks! We're going to a wedding." He held the door open and helped Polly and Camille into the van. Then he went back to get Lauren. Ben laughed at her as he exclaimed, "Gee, Honey, I might have to get a truck for you and your dress." With both hands he held it tightly to keep it from billowing like a parachute when she sat down. He ran around to the driver's side and backed out of the garage. It was like someone had opened the floodgates as the rain poured down in torrents. Everyone tried to talk but the noise of the rain drowned out all conversations. Ben backed the van out into the street and drove toward the chapel. He strained to see through the windshield as the wipers whipped the water back and forth.

Lauren fell silent as she watched her dad lean over the steering wheel to get a better view of the road. A feeling of foreboding crept over her as the dark ominous clouds sank lower in the sky blacking out everything in its path. A sudden flash of lightning lit up the road like a beacon just in time for Ben to see the narrow road leading to the chapel. As Ben drove along the curving road, bordered by pine trees and hedges of wax myrtle, streams of sunlight made their way through the fleeting clouds. He let out a lengthy sigh of relief and said, "I'm mighty glad to see some daylight. Water is standing everywhere. If it wasn't for those stone benches in front of the chapel, I'd drive right up to the front door."

Camille joked, "It takes a storm to keep three women from talking. I was really worried for a while. I thought we might get washed off the highway."

"I was too! We're here and there's nothing going to stop this wedding!" Polly cried.

Ben chuckled, "I think we'll need a boat to get to the

church door although it looks like the rain is tapering off. I'll get the boots and stuff out of the back of the van. You ladies sit tight for a few minutes, and I'll be right back."

Lauren gazed out the window and asked her mom, "What made you pick this chapel?"

Polly said, "When I first came out here with the director of the church, he told me it was designed to replicate a miniature cathedral. It was built in the 1600's. Although the green moss and ivy has about covered the hand-chiseled stones, it is still beautiful."

Lauren peered out the window and looked at the huge black wrought-iron hinges on the oak doors and said, "Mom, those hinges must've been there for years and years." She sighed, "It looks rather dismal to me. It's bound to be dark inside with those small stained glass windows."

"Honey, don't you worry. We'll turn on all the lights. You're going to love it." Polly stopped talking and waited for Ben as he came sloshing through the water.

Ben sang out when he opened the side door, "Here we go, Honey. Poke your feet out the door and I'll put on the boots. Then I'll wrap you up like a basket of fruit in this big piece of plastic." Lauren couldn't help but laugh at him. As long as she could remember, her dad always knew how to calm her fears and make light of adversities. He carefully held her dress up and led her through the ankle deep water into the foyer of the church.

Lauren cried out, "Dad, it's so dark in here!"

"Don't worry! When I come back with Polly and Camille, I'll turn on all the lights in the sanctuary." Ben took the boots and plastic and repeated the same procedure with Polly and Camille. After he had gotten everyone safely inside, he took the flashlight and felt his way down the center aisle. He stepped up on the wide altar, searched for the electrical panel, and found it behind black, heavy curtains. He looked out into the sanctuary and cried, "Good Lord, I believe lightning bugs could put off more light than those wrought iron chandeliers."

Lauren cried out, "Mom! It's still dark."

"Don't worry. When Ben lights the candelabras it'll be brighter," Polly said as she rolled her eyes looking at the dimly lit room.

"Lauren," Camille said encouragingly, "It's fashionable to get married in a candle light atmosphere. Don't look at it as being gloomy but as being romantic. Just think bright lights could take away from the reverence of the occasion."

Lauren flashed an impish grin at Camille and said, "You always make the best out of the worst possible scenario. At work you always see something good in your job even if it's emptying bed pans."

There was a knock on the door. When Ben opened it, a man from the florist burst in with a tall basket of white calla lilies. He asked, "Is the Fulghum's wedding still on?"

Ben replied, "Of course. A little rain won't stop this wedding!"

"Just checking." He rushed to the altar, pulled a kneeling bench from behind the curtains, and placed the flowers behind it while leaving a narrow space for the preacher to stand. "Good night," he said and dashed out the door. Ben followed the man to the altar and lit the two sixteen branched candelabras.

Lauren let out a cry of joy, "Oh my, what a difference the candles make. Now, it does look romantic."

Polly peeked out the front door and saw car lights coming into the parking lot. She excitedly said, "Honey, it might be Jack. You'd better leave before he sees you." Lauren and Camille made their way down to a damp and musty smelly room in the basement. Over the years, water had seeped through tiny cracks in the wall and black mold had found a home in the dark corners of the room. Camille searched for the light switch while Lauren stood still, and held up her dress to keep it off the floor. She was afraid to move for fear she would get it dirty.

Camille flipped the switch and yelled, "Hallelujah! That helps! We won't be down here very long." She glanced at her watch, "Only ten more minutes and you'll be walking down the aisle with Jack."

"Ten minutes is a long time in this musty basement. My skin is already beginning to feel clammy. I'm expecting to see green mold sprout anytime. I'd sure like to have one of my surgical mask to keep from breathing this stale air."

"Sh-h-h," Camille whispered, "I hear a lot of moving around upstairs. Maybe we had better not talk anymore. Someone might hear us."

"Okay, but I can't keep my knees from knocking."

In the meantime, Ben had been a stalwart valet trudging back and forth from the parking lot holding an umbrella as he ushered guests to the chapel. Vernon, Sarah, several aunts, uncles, and neighbors filled three of the pews on the grooms' side of the chapel. He didn't want the Harpers to feel uncomfortable with more people on the bride's side than on the groom's.

The rain continued to beat down on the roof, like a crazed drummer, but the organist attempted to play his music loud enough to drown it out. Conversations among the guests became futile because of the noise.

Polly stood at the back of the chapel and welcomed the guests as they arrived. She noticed that Ben was extra polite to a man and woman as he ushered them into the church. He came over to her and said, "Polly, this is Mr. and Mrs. Vernon Harper."

Mrs. Harper held out her hand and said politely, "I'm so glad to meet you, Mrs. Fulghum, and it would please me if you'd call me Sarah."

"I'm mighty glad to meet you too, Sarah. You can call me Polly."

Vernon grunted and without shaking hands said, "Glad to meet you."

Ben stretched out his hand and forced Vernon to shake it, and then he shook Sarah's hand. She readily squeezed his warmly. "Come with me. I'll take you to your seats." Ben led the way and ushered them to the second row of pews on the right side of the sanctuary.

Polly craned her neck as she watched the Harpers take their seats. When Ben came back she muttered, "It's plain to see why Jack didn't want his father to be his best man. You must've been confused when Jack asked you to be his best man and not his own father. I hope Mr. Harper doesn't mind."

A bolt of lightning crashed to earth, hitting a transformer nearby. The lights went out. It frightened everyone. They crouched down in the pews afraid something might fall on them.

Lauren screamed from below. Ben rushed down the steps with a flashlight to tell her what had happened. She cried, "I don't care if Jack sees me or not! I'm getting out of here." All three of them made their way back up the stairs. Lauren peeked around the corner of the doorway to see if Jack was there before she stepped into the foyer. Lauren whispered anxiously to her dad, "Have you seen him? It's late and he should be here by now."

"The Harpers are here but Jack didn't come with them. Do you want me to ask them where he is?" His cheerful personality had been stretched to the limit.

"Yes! I'm getting worried."

He groped his way down the aisle and asked, "Mr. Harper, do you know what's keeping Jack?"

Vernon replied, "No, I don't! All I know is Jack said he would leave ten minutes after we left. I suppose you want me to call him at the Inn?"

Although it agitated Ben, he still responded politely, "No, that won't be necessary. We'll wait a little longer before we call anyone. Maybe he had trouble getting here in the storm." Without any further questions, Ben walked back to the foyer.

Lauren grabbed her dad's arm and frantically asked, "What did they say? Where is Jack?"

"Sorry, Lauren. They don't know...don't you worry...he'll be here." Ben opened the front door and looked out. He let out a sigh of relief when he saw car lights break through the thick veil of rain. When the car stopped, a man with a hooded raincoat rushed into the foyer. In the event that it was Jack, Lauren backed into a small hall, out of sight. Her hands clasped her throat as she let out a loud gasp when the man threw back his hood and took off his coat. He wore a black suit that hung loosely about his tall, lanky frame. His dark eyes sank deep in their sockets. His long thin hair was combed to one side with the intention of covering his balding head. Through thick lips his voice was deep and articulate. "I will be performing the ceremony. I apologize for being late due to the storm." Then he glanced at Lauren and said, "It's obvious you're the bride, and I must say you are exceedingly beautiful. If everyone is here, we'll begin the ceremony. The minister you met last night was taken ill, and I'm filling in for him."

Ben frowned and said, "We're missing the groom. We decided to wait a little longer before calling the Inn or the Highway Patrol." Ben's voice sounded like the voice of doom and everyone in the foyer fell silent. "Maybe he had trouble getting here in the storm."

Vernon's curiosity got the better of him. He got up from his seat to see what was happening. When he saw Ben, he said in a rude way, "I'm going to find Jack." Just as he opened the door, car lights shone through the darkness.

Ben caught his arm and said, "Wait! That might be Jack." Vernon stepped back and waited. Someone splashing through water made Lauren duck back into the hall. Jack burst through the door.

Vernon said through clenched jaws. "Where in the hell have you been?"

Jack kept his anger under control and responded coolly, "I'm here and that's all that matters." Vernon turned in a huff and stomped back to his seat. Lauren felt the tension in the air.

The lights still had not come on and the guests shuffled their feet back and forth with apprehension. Twenty minutes passed. The preacher approached Jack and said quietly, "The organist can't play the organ without electricity, but I can perform the ceremony with just the candlelight. Maybe you and Lauren should decide what you would like to do if the lights stay off much longer."

Jack's face lit up. "I've got all night, but maybe again, we can call off the wedding."

The preacher looked startled at his response and said, "Dear brother, I hope you are joking. If you're not willing to wait, maybe you shouldn't get married."

Jack hunched his shoulders forward and said, "I was just kidding."

Like the dawn of a new day, the lights came back on. The preacher took his place in front of the altar and announced, "Ladies and gentlemen we're all sorry for the delay. We are finally ready to begin the ceremony." The organist fingers nimbly played "Cannon in D" to give Jack and Lauren time to prepare their walk down the aisle. When Lauren walked into the foyer, Jack's eyes opened wide with admiration. He had never seen her with her hair pulled up in a crown of curls with waving tendrils framing her lovely face. Her veil was like a white cloud drifting over her hair and falling softly over her bare shoulders all the way down to the hem of her dress.

Jack crossed over, kissed her on the cheek, and said, "Doc, you look sensational. In fact, you're so pretty I think I'll marry you."

Lauren trembled with excitement when he touched her. "Thank you, sweetheart." She stepped back and her eyes traveled up and down as she looked at him. "My, my, Mr. Harper, you cut a mighty handsome figure yourself in your tuxedo. Yes, I'd like to marry you, too."

The organist looked for a sign from Mrs. Fulghum to start the wedding processional. Polly raised her hand for him to begin. "Trumpet Voluntary" rang with gusto up through the rafters and down through the sanctuary. Polly couldn't be seated earlier because she was directing the wedding. Ben escorted Polly to her seat. After that, he walked to the end of the kneeling bench, and waited for Jack and Lauren to come down the aisle.

Lauren hooked her arm into Jack's as they stood in the arched doorway, and waited for their cue. Since the wedding was delayed, seven chimes marked the hour rather than six. Camille led the procession and she took her place opposite Ben at the kneeling bench.

Loud rumbles of thunder competed with the music. The humidity slowly thickened like jello. It seemed to intensify the aroma of the Calla Lilies. The scent drifted through the air and it reminded Lauren of funerals. The music swelled as they processed down the aisle. Lauren looked up with adoration into Jack's eyes and he returned a weak smile. So far, Lauren hadn't read the signs of discontent in Jack's expressions or actions. The music stopped as soon as they stood before the preacher. At first, Lauren thought this man before her was the ugliest person she had seen in a long time. As he read the scripture and then went into the homily, she forgot how he looked. His voice was soft, gentle, and serene as he explained the marriage vows. He emphasized they should commit themselves totally to each other. Jack tried to keep from yawning from boredom. He glanced at Lauren and saw that she was captivated by the words the weird looking man was saying. His eyes shifted to Camille. He winked at her. She was aghast at Jack's brazenness. Camille tried to remain composed to keep Lauren from noticing her reaction. Jack went back to shifting from one foot to the other.

The preacher took the rings from Camille and Ben and blessed them. Jack pushed the ring on Lauren's finger and repeated the preacher's word without emotion. When it was time for Lauren to give Jack his ring, the words she repeated brought tears to her eyes. She had waited a long time for this day. At last she could start planning the family she had always wanted. The preacher whispered to Jack to kiss his bride. For the first time Jack showed some emotion as he kissed her.

The organist blared forth with the recessional, "Trumpet Tune." When they opened the front door they were relieved that the storm had slacked up.

After the wedding, they all went to the Williamsburg Inn. The bridal party and guests entered through French doors into a room that resembled a formal living room. Lauren took her parents' hands and said, "I can't thank you enough for all you have done for our wedding and reception. You have made my dream come true."

"Sweetheart, it was our pleasure. We wanted it to be extra special, " Polly said as she hugged Lauren.

At the far end of the room, Lauren saw Jack saunter over to Camille. "Excuse me, Mom, I'm going to get Jack and get something to eat. I'm hungry now that the wedding is over."

"You go on. Your dad and I had better greet the guests. We need to introduce them to the Harpers."

Before Lauren reached Jack, he spoke to Camille. She scowled at him, and said, "You are a real S.O.B." She saw Lauren coming and made a quick exit. She was afraid she was going to show her dislike for Jack in front of her.

When Lauren reached Jack she asked, "Honey, what happened to Camille? She seemed upset about something."

Jack said casually, " I don't know. I tried to be sociable, but for some reason, she wasn't interested."

"Maybe she's tired. I've kept her busy since she has been here. I'll go talk to her and see if she's all right."

Jack grabbed her arm and said, "Come on, let's get something to eat."

"Okay, but I'm still worried about Camille."

Just as they were getting ready to fill their plates, Lauren saw her mom coming toward her, pointing to the wedding cake. When she got closer she said, "Lauren, you had better cut the cake before all the guest leave. They're afraid the storm might blow up again."

Lauren and Jack stood by the white, two-tiered cake with pink rose buds circling each tier. The top tier was adorned with a pair of dolls dressed like the bride and groom. The videographer jockeyed around the people for a good spot to video them as they cut the cake.

They sliced two small wedges and they each fed them to each other. He whispered, "Doc, this has been an exciting day for me. I'll never forget it." Jack thought to himself, you'll never know just how much I'll remember this day.

Ben walked over to Jack and Lauren and said, "Ladies, gentlemen, bride, and groom, I want to make a toast. Raise your glasses to my beautiful daughter and her handsome husband." He laughed in a jesting way and said, " I don't mean to rush things but we would like to be grandparents as soon as possible." A light laughter came from the guests. Jack looked down at the floor without smiling. Lauren blushed and gave her parents a big "thumbs up." Ben continued, "Polly and I want to give you both a gift we know will be a surprise." Ben pulled an envelope out of his pocket and handed it to Lauren.

When she ripped it open, she saw two tickets for a week cruise that included Cozumel, Mayan Ruins, and Key West. Lauren threw her arms around her parents and shouted with joy, "Thank you! Thank you! I never dreamed we would be able to have such a wonderful honeymoon."

Jack walked briskly over to Ben and shook his hand hard, like he was pumping water from a well, and said, "That's where I wanted to take Lauren, but we couldn't afford it. Thank you both so much." After Ben's toast, the guests departed. Jack's parents were the last to leave. Polly and Ben followed them to the front door and asked, "Are you going back home to White Plains?"

Vernon responded, "No, we're going to Kiawah. That's where we like to take our vacations. We love it down there." Sarah smiled and thanked the Fulghums for their hospitality.

The Fulghums waved goodbye as they drove out of sight.

They were still standing on the porch when Lauren came out and announced, "We're going to spend the night here at the Inn and leave early in the morning. Arrangements have to be made in order for me to get off work, and Jack will also have to get excuses to cut his classes. Anyway, we're too exhausted to drive in this rain."

Ben said, "That's a good decision. I understand." Ben hugged Lauren one more time and said, "We will miss you and Jack. Try to get down this way more often. Have a safe trip tomorrow."

Lauren hugged her parents and thanked them again for everything they had done to make their wedding perfect. "We'll pack our gifts in the Bronco tonight and be ready to leave in the morning."

As soon as Lauren walked into the bedroom she said, "Jack, let's take a shower together. We aren't in a hurry and we can enjoy a long, leisure shower."

"Mrs. Harper, that's the best suggestion you've had all night." Both of them raced to see who could get undressed the quickest. After they finished their shower, they immediately went to bed and consummated their marriage. The next morning they got up, ate breakfast, and left Williamsburg about nine. After Jack made all the right turns to get out of town. Lauren was anxious to talk to him about the wedding. "Honey, you really scared me when you were so late getting to the church. I didn't know what had happened." Before Jack could reply, she said, " That preacher was most unattractive, but after he started talking I didn't notice how he looked." Lauren waited for Jack to reply. Since he didn't respond, she continued. "I wish you could have been there when the lightning hit a transformer. It nearly scared me to death."

Jack reached over to the radio and flipped it on. He slapped his hand on the steering wheel and said, "Lauren, I've heard all I want to about the wedding. That's all you've talked about for the last four weeks. Give me a break! I've got a lot more on my mind than rehashing the wedding. I've got to find a way to cut classes. If you want to talk about something, talk about the cruise. Okay! Or…why don't you just go to sleep." Lauren slumped down in her seat heartbroken.

Jack thought, oh, damn, I've done it now. With a flourish of animation he said, "Oh, Doc, I'm sorry for being so angry. I'm tired and we've got a long way to go. Someday I'm going to give you a wedding ring that will knock your eyes out. After I'm out of school, things will be different."

Again, Lauren succumbed to his charm. She held her ring in the sun light and said, "Sweetheart, all the jewels in the world couldn't make me love this ring more than I do right now. " Since Jack didn't want to talk about the wedding, Lauren leaned back in her seat and thought about all the things that had happened in such a short time.

CHAPTER 10

It was Sunday afternoon when they arrived at their parking space in front of a row of identical apartments. The only thing that made a difference from each other was a large number nailed to the door. He punched Lauren and said, "Wake up sleeping beauty. We're home."

Lauren sat up, rubbed her eyes, and sleepily said, "I really zonked out. I didn't realize how tired I was. My adrenaline finally gave out and I just collapsed."

Jack remarked, "We made good time. Maybe I can get in touch with someone at the administrative office about cutting classes." He motioned for Lauren to hurry up and help him with the presents and luggage.

"Okay, okay. I'm coming. I've got to call Camille, too. She's going to flip when I ask her to cover for me next week." Lauren picked up an armful of gifts and headed for the apartment.

As soon as Jack walked inside, he went straight to the bedroom and immediately unpacked his clothes. He yelled, "Lauren, you'd better get your things out to be washed. We don't have much time before we'll have to pack again."

"All right, all right. I wish we could look at some of our presents."

"For God's sake, Lauren, put those gifts down and make your phone call to Camille."

She cut her eyes at Jack as if to tell him to go to hell, but instead she stacked the wedding gifts in a corner of the bedroom. Lauren didn't stay miffed long. She knew he was right. It was about six o'clock Sunday afternoon when she dialed Camille's number.

After a few rings a voice said, "Hello."

"Camille! We just got into town after a long and hard drive."

"Lauren! I thought you would be coming home Monday."

"You'll never guess what my parents gave us for a wedding present. You had already gone when they made the announcement. By the way, I was worried about you. You seemed upset about something when I saw you across the room at the reception. What was the matter?"

Camille hesitated and with a guarded response replied, "Oh...I didn't tell you that I had a flight to catch. Sorry I missed the toast. What are you so excited about?"

"My parents gave us the most wonderful gift. We have a week cruise to Mexico and Key West. There's only one hitch to keep us from going." Lauren hesitated.

"Well! Tell me. What's the hitch?"

"Camille, we can't go unless you can cover for me that week. We hope we can get a flight out of here in the morning. Please forgive me for asking you to help me again. I'll be forever indebted to you."

"Wow! Not that I mind covering for you, but you're cutting it mighty close. You know I'll do it, Lauren. Have a good time. I'll be looking forward to hearing all about your trip."

"Thank you, Camille. You're a real friend. I'll tell you all about the trip when we get back. Bye"

Jack came stomping into the room yelling, "I thought you'd never get off the phone. I've got to see if we can get reservations and then call the administrative office." Lauren flipped her head to one side as she walked past him without saying a word. She went into the bedroom and unpacked her suitcase.

Jack called the airport. Luckily, a flight was available to Miami in time to board the ship, *The Royal Majesty*. As soon as he hung up, he dialed the administrative office. He paced the floor waiting for someone to answer. Without an excuse, his professors would give him a failing grade.

Finally there was a click and a female voice with a southern drawl said, "May I help you?"

"I sure hope so. I've just gotten married, and we were unexpectedly given a week cruise as a wedding present. We've made our plans to leave in the morning. As you know, I need a good excuse for cutting classes. Can you notify my professors why I won't be there for four days?"

Again in her sweet syrupy voice she responded, "Suh, I understand pur-r-fectly. Please give me your name and the classes you'll be missing. I'll notify the professors and explain your situation."

He gave her the information and said, "Thank you very much." He slammed the receiver down and let out a loud, "W-H-O-O-P-E-E!"

Lauren popped her head in the doorway and cried, "What happened?"

"Doc, we're on our way. Let's get packed again. We're going on a cruise." Exhausted from the trip home, and making arrangements at the hospital and school, they both fell into bed.

* * * * *

Monday morning the alarm clock rang at seven. Jack pulled open the blinds and the room was filled with sunshine. Lauren rolled out of bed sleepily and staggered to the kitchen and poured glasses of orange juice and toast two bagels. She called, "Jack, come and eat before the bagels get cold."

"Okay, okay! I'm getting my clothes out to wear on the trip."

"I'm not waiting for you. I've got to take a shower and then get dressed." Lauren had finished eating when Jack walked into the kitchen.

"You'd better hurry, Lauren. We don't have a lot of time to get to the airport."

"I'm going as fast as I can. I'm glad we packed our bags last night." She hurried to the bathroom and showered. She put on her make-up, dressed in a white linen suit, flipped a turquoise silk scarf around her neck, and glanced in the mirror. Her image brought a smile to her face.

Jack gulped down his food and walked into the bedroom. When he saw Lauren, he exclaimed, "You really look like you're going on a cruise. I don't know if I can compete with you or not." He decided on a yellow paisley sport shirt and a pair of navy linen pant. The color combination enhanced his olive complexion even more. He touched his black wavy hair to be sure it was combed perfectly and checked his shoes to be sure they were polished to perfection.

They raced out of the apartment. Tossed their bags into the Bronco. Jack drove like a madman. Lauren closed her eyes fearful he would hit someone. When they got to the airport, he let Lauren out with the luggage while he looked for a place in the vast parking lot. With long rolling strides Jack dashed into the airport, grabbed Lauren's hand in time to board the ten o'clock flight to Miami. Once seated, Lauren squeezed Jack's hand with excitement beyond words.

Later, they were awakened by the monotone instructions from the Captain, "Ladies and Gentlemen, we will be landing in ten minutes." Jack and Lauren readied themselves to leave the plane. Jack hailed a cab to take them to the port where the cruise ship, *The Royal Majesty,* was docked. Lauren held on to Jack's arm as they walked up the boarding ramp. They stopped momentarily for the ship's photographer to snap their picture; then they stepped into the main lobby of the ship. Lauren's eyes sparkled with excitement. The decor was like an Egyptian palace: gold marbleized floors and white stone columns rose to a star-studded ceiling. Jack caught a glimpse of Lauren, with her head tilted back, gawking at the beautiful painting of the sky. He walked over to Lauren and whispered, "Stop acting like you've just gotten out of the jungle. People are staring at you as though you've lost your mind."

"I'm sorry, Jack. It's all so beautiful. I can't hold in my excitement."

He yanked her by the arm and said, "Come on! We have to get ready for our evening meal. We have the first seating."

When they got to the cabin, he opened the door, picked up the bags, and dropped them on one of the twin beds. Jack stood looking around the room. In a few minutes he said, "What in the hell is this kind of a room? Twin beds for a honeymoon! There's not enough room for two people to turn around in, much less get dressed. This room looks as if it were decorated for a teen-ager: pink bedspread, pink floral carpet, and pictures of dancing fairies hanging over each bed." He snapped open his suitcase and immediately unpacked his clothes. He glanced up to see a frown on Lauren's face as she stood watching him and asked, "Why the long face?"

"Jack, you haven't acted the least bit excited, happy, or thrilled since we boarded the ship. All you've done is criticize this room and me. As far as the room, you should be happy just to have a hole in the wall. Dad told me he tried to get a nice room, but everything was booked. What else is wrong?"

He continued to unpack his clothes while ignoring her. Finally he said, "Lauren, I reckon I have acted like a jerk. So much has happened this past week, I feel like I've been on a roller coaster ride."

Lauren walked over to Jack, turned his face to hers and said, "Honey, I just didn't realize that all the activities about the wedding and the cruise would bother you. I took for granted you had taken everything in stride. Maybe after dinner we can both relax."

" That's a good idea. Come on Doc; let's take a shower together." Giggling unabashedly, Lauren undressed and followed him into the small enclosure. Jack laughed, "This is really togetherness. I can hardly move."

While the water ran down their bodies, Lauren kissed Jack and said, "I love it. Let's make love and forget about dinner."

"Not now. We'll have plenty of time for sex tonight. I'm starved." A chime, like a doorbell, sounded in their room. "Uh-oh. I hear the signal for dinner. Come on Doc. We'd better hurry."

Lauren stood in awe at the elaborate decorations. Every table had a bouquet of fresh flowers, and the buffet table was like a galaxy of every flower imaginable tucked in every conceivable place among the exotic food. Table after table of mouth-watering dishes of meats, seafood, and vegetables of all kinds lured one to want to sample everything. Even the staunchest dieter would forget about calories.

"Aren't you impressed with the elegance and attention the stewards give to every passenger? You seem so…indifferent." Lauren whispered as she punched Jack's arm.

"Sure, I'm impressed, but we don't have to act like we just came out of a cave. Let's eat and then take a walk around the ship. I'd like to see where the action is."

"C'mon, let's go to the buffet. I'm really hungry," Lauren said as she walked over to the food. After they had laden their plates with an assortment of appetizers, Jack ate like a man who hadn't had a meal in days. Lauren touched his arm and said, "Jack, slow down. We've got plenty of time. I want to savor every bite. Anyway, what's your hurry?"

"I've been trained most of my life to eat fast no matter how good or bad the food. I'm only interested in seeing what's going on outside this room. So…finish your meal." Jack waited a few more minutes for Lauren to finish part of her meal. He washed down his last bite with a swallow of wine, pushed back his chair, and escorted Lauren out onto the deck. A yellow stream of moonlight appeared to connect itself to the ship. Stars twinkled like millions of fireflies lighting a fantasy stage. He put his arm around Lauren's shoulders and pointed with the other hand out across the ocean said, "If our cruise is as fantastic as that view, we're going to have a spectacular time."

"Oh, I do hope you mean that. It's also unbelievable. It's like being in another world. We really need this time together. It's been a mad rush for two months: dating, moving in with each other, working, and getting married." Lauren snuggled closer to him as they strolled along the deck.

In a dimly lit lounge, a large shiny, mirrored ball hanging over a small dance floor, caught Jack's eye. "C'mon—let's go in here. Who knows, we might even dance a little."

"Great! I haven't danced in years. Before we sit down, I need to powder my nose. I'll be right back."

Jack walked over to the bar and ordered a vodka and tonic. A mirror behind the bar reflected his image. Jack looked at it, raised his glass, and muttered, "To you, you lucky stud, you've got it all, but…you're bored as hell. You want something exciting to happen." He spun around on the barstool and at the far end of the counter; he caught sight of a beautiful, sexy looking lady. Her long black hair hung loosely around her face. His adrenalin rose a notch or two especially seeing her figure in a low-cut, tight fitting, red sequined dress. A long slit in her skirt exposed her shapely legs right down to her red sandals, one of which dangled provocatively on the tip of her toe. Her sensuality moved Jack to recklessness. The lady sat with her back against the bar observing the dancers. In a casual manner, Jack moved to the barstool next to her and spoke, "Excuse me. I hope you don't mind my sitting here while I wait for my wife?"

She turned at the sound of his voice. Her emerald green eyes reached deep into his and said, "Not at all. I saw you and your wife come in." She paused, looked around and asked, "Where is she?"

"In the powder room. She should be coming back any minute."

"That's too bad." With her finger, she rubbed the stem of

the glass seductively, and said in a sultry voice, "You can call me Rita…Rita LaBaron."

Stunned for a second by her forwardness, Jack stammered, "A-h-h…I'm Jack Harper." He glanced quickly over her shoulder to see if Lauren was coming. What a surprise, he mused. Here's a chance to have some excitement, but damn it, Lauren's in the way. Oh well, he didn't have anything to lose talking to her. After all, the lady made the first move. He regained his composure and said, "I'd like to get to know you, but I have a slight problem…my wife."

"Oh-h-h, there's always a way to get around that obstacle. You heard what the captain said at dinner didn't you?"

"I'm afraid not so tell me…Rita LaBaron. What did the captain say?" Jack leaned closer to her face and the fragrance of her perfume intoxicated him.

She reached over and touched his hand and with a teasing smile said, "He specifically said he wanted his guests to be friendly." Rita took her long polished fingernail and pressed it to Jack's lips and said, "I'm just following orders."

Jack's testosterone rose to an all time high. With a flirtatious grin he asked, "Just how far will you go to be friendly?"

"Well, I'm a very friendly person, and I'll go as far as I think necessary."

Jack leaned forward to make her a proposition when Lauren appeared. Instead he said, "Don't go. I'll be back. Somehow I'll slip away." Jack slid off the stool and met Lauren as she came through the doorway of the lounge.

"I'm sorry it took so long. The world's a small place. You never know whom you'll run into. A mother of one of my patients was in the powder room. We started talking about her little girl and time slipped away."

"That's okay. I didn't mind waiting. I enjoyed listening to the music, but now I'd like to dance." Lauren fell into his arms with a loving embrace. As they moved around the floor, Jack wondered how he could get back to Rita. He glanced over Lauren's shoulder and saw Rita looking at him. He winked and then pulled Lauren closer, bent down, and kissed her softly from her lips to her neck. He hoped Rita understood the message he was sending to her. She winked and puckered her lips in response to Jack's demonstration. Lauren had closed her eyes, drinking in his affection.

The music stopped and Lauren said breathlessly, "Sweetheart, I can't wait any longer for us to make love. Let's go to our room."

"That's a good idea, but I would like to finish my drink. Here, you take the key and I'll be there in a minute. Put on that pretty gown you showed me before we left for the cruise."

Lauren looked perplexed and said, "You're not coming with me? I don't mind waiting for you to finish your drink."

"I thought it would be nice if you had some time to get ready for our first night as husband and wife."

"Oh, Jack. I didn't think of it that way. That's sweet of you." When she got to the door, she turned and said, "Hurry, darling."

As soon as Lauren was gone, Jack walked swiftly over to Rita. "I'm assuming you understood what I was doing with Lauren, didn't you?"

"Your actions were loud and clear. I don't quite understand your relationship with your wife. You do love her, don't you?"

"I don't have time to tell you the whole story. What are you doing tomorrow?"

"I'll be lounging around the pool."

"Great! I'll make sure I see you." Jack picked up her hand placed a kiss in the palm of her hand, and walked away.

As soon as Jack walked into their cabin, Lauren threw her arms around him, and cried, "Honey, I thought you would never get here. You haven't been that affectionate to me in a long time." Lauren started unbuttoning his shirt.

"Wait just a minute, Doc. I want to take a shower." Jack was still feeling the effects of his encounter with Rita. He showered again just in case Rita's perfume still lingered on him. When he got out, he looked in the mirror and splashed his face with his best cologne. He thought, no one had ever come on to him as fast as she did. There was a mystery about her and he wanted to find out what it was. Right now, he had to take care of Lauren. There was one way to do it and that was to make love to her like he had never done before. With the cunning of a fox, he quietly stepped out of the bathroom, and slipped into Lauren's bed. He whispered, "Honey, I'm sorry that I was rude to you today. I don't know what was wrong with me." Without another word, he took her in his arms and snuggled up close. Her nakedness brought back the arousal he had had for the lady in the red sequin dress. All the time he had sex with Lauren, his mind was busy making plans to get to know Rita a lot better.

CHAPTER 11

The next morning, a bird-like sound woke Jack from a deep sleep. He fumbled for the telephone and groggily answered, "Hello...thank you." He pushed up on his elbow and reached for the wall lamp over his bed.

The light woke Lauren. She propped up in bed and rubbed her eyes to get used to the brightness in the room. She exclaimed, "Why are you in that bed?"

Jack looked at her, smiled, and said, "You wore me out! I needed some rest. Sometime during the night you mentioned there were one hundred and one ways to have sex. I believe you tried every one of them."

"I'm mighty glad I pleased you. I realize we've had sex before, but it seemed different now that we're man and wife. By the way, who was that on the phone?"

"I left word with the desk clerk to wake us up."

"You're right. We've got things to do. It's time to get the show on the road. After we eat breakfast, we need to go to the Theater Palace Room at ten o'clock for an orientation about an excursion to the Mayan Ruins. You do want to go, don't you?"

"Sure, I do. I'm ready for some excitement," Jack said as he climbed out of bed and dressed in Bermuda shorts and a short-sleeve shirt. Lauren fumbled around in her suitcase to find a pair of red shorts and a multi-striped blouse.

After breakfast, they made their way to the Theater Palace

Room. It had rows of seats in a semi-circle in front of a small stage. The Director, who was tall thin and rather swarthy, strolled out in his starched white pants and shirt. He stood in the middle of the stage and quickly began his speech about the excursion. The Director droned on about the box lunches, snorkeling, and the two hours for shopping. Most importantly, they had to be on the tender Wednesday morning at six o'clock, or they would be left behind. Lauren and Jack went back to their room and changed into their swimsuits. Lauren wanted to relax in the sun, but Jack wanted to walk around the deck. While he strolled he heard Calypso music floating through the air from the swimming pool. He remembered Rita and scanned the swimming area for her. Jack rushed down the steps only to run into a hodgepodge of people in all shapes and sizes. Stepping over and around them, he made his way around the pool where she was sitting. She was even more beautiful today than last night in the bar. Her skimpy, kelly green bikini barely covered her tanned figure, and her black hair was pulled back and fastened with a bow. Jack slipped up behind her, and as she stretched her slender arm up over her head, he grabbed and kissed it. Startled, Rita jerked it away. Jack laughed, "Hope I didn't frighten you?"

"Yes, you did! Where did you come from?" Rita asked surprised.

"I was up on the sun deck. I told Lauren I wanted to walk around, but she didn't want to come—thank goodness." Jack's eyes followed every curve in her body and then he remarked, "I thought you were beautiful last night but today in your...barely-nothing bathing suit you're fabulous."

Rita teased him with a smile, "Well, I'm glad I meet your approval. I feel as though I'm under an x-ray machine with those penetrating eyes of yours."

"I told you I was going to think about you all last night. Lauren didn't know I imagined you were the one I was having sex with. Fortunately for her, it was the best she had ever had because of you."

Rita gave a soft moan and wiggled her body sensually to make Jack have a hard time controlling his emotions. "Damn it woman, I've got to have you. Somehow I'll find a way." Jack paused, "I've got an idea. Are you going on the excursion to the Mayan Ruins?"

"I haven't decided."

"Please go! I'll try to find a place to slip away. Please say you'll go."

"You make it hard for me to say no. What the hell, I need some excitement."

"Great! I'd better go. Lauren will wonder what's happened to me." Suddenly, Jack bent down and kissed Rita. She kissed him back with the same fervid action. "Damn, Rita, I'm on fire. I need a cold shower." He turned and dove into the pool. When he came up, he called out, "I'll see you tomorrow." When he got out, he looked up and saw Lauren waving to him. Oh my God, I hope she didn't see me kiss Rita. He wrapped the towel around his wet body, and climbed the steps to where Lauren stood. When he saw the expression on her face, he was sure she had seen him or else she was in pain. "What's wrong with you?" Jack grumbled.

She shivered as she folded her arms across her chest and said, "I think I have motion sickness or too much sun. I really don't feel good." At that moment she clutched her mouth and began to heave. She tried desperately to hold back the nausea. Without another word, she ran back to their room.

Jack went to the deck railing and looked down to see if he could see Rita. She was gone. Jack rushed to their room and when he opened the door, he saw Lauren curled up in a fetal position with the bedspread pulled around her shoulders. She groaned, "I shouldn't have stayed out in the sun so long. The nausea…I don't know…I can't remember when I have ever had motion sickness…I could be pregnant."

Her words stunned Jack with such an impact he was speechless. Lauren peeped out from under the spread to see

Jack's eyes blazing with anger. As the impact of her words registered he yelled, "Pregnant! How could that be? Haven't you been using the pill?"

His voice frightened Lauren. Before answering him, she waited for him to calm down. "Do you remember the night I had a romantic dinner waiting for you, and I told you I wanted to get married right away?"

"Yeah! I remember." Jack yelled.

Scarcely speaking above a whisper, "I was so sure that you were going to move out, I didn't take the pill."

"Damn it, you've ruined everything for me! If you have a baby, I'll never get through school. I'll have to work like a common laborer." He stopped abruptly and with renewed anger, yelled, "If you're pregnant—you *will* have an abortion!"

Lauren gathered all her strength, sat up, and stared into his fierce eyes and defiantly cried, "If I am pregnant, I will not have an abortion whether you like it or not." With those words stinging in his ears, Jack walked out of the room and slammed the door. With another wave of nausea rising in her throat, Lauren staggered to the bathroom.

Jack headed for the nearest bar, ordered a drink, and walked around the ship until he found the casino. He strolled around tables of roulette, black jack, and poker, thinking what a waste of money. He watched hordes of people playing the slot machines. He even watched old ladies play bingo, but that couldn't make him forget the word PREGNANT. It was late. He was tired. There was nothing else for him to do but to return to his room. Lauren heard him come in and get into the other bed, but she pretended to be asleep.

The wake-up call Jack had requested rang at five o'clock. He answered it grumpily and rolled out of bed. He mumbled, "I don't know whether it's worth it or not to get up so early."

Lauren asked weakly. "Who was that?"

"The Director. He said anyone going on the excursion better get ready. The tender would be leaving at 6:00 a.m." He looked over at Lauren and asked, "How do you feel this morning?"

She was glad his anger had subsided. His voice was almost pleasant. Lauren replied, "Not too good. I'm sorry to disappoint you, but I don't think I'm going."

"You're not! That's too bad." Jack's voice trailed off with satisfaction. He thought, what a lucky break. I can be with Rita all day without Lauren knowing about it. I wasn't excited about going, but I'll go now. Faking disappointment, Jack said, "Last night I decided I really wanted to go. It would be good to get off the ship for a few hours; but if you're not going, I'll stay here with you. "

Lauren slowly sat up in bed and said in a sorrowful voice, "I want you to go. Don't worry about me. I'm pretty sure I'll be all right by the end of the day. I'll get one of the stewards to bring me something for nausea and I'll be just fine."

"You really don't mind if I go alone?"

"Of course not. It would be a shame for you to miss the Mayan Ruins."

"Well, if you're sure you don't mind...I'll go, but I'll miss you." Jack bounced out of bed and dressed. On his way out, he lingered at the door and asked, "Can I bring you something to eat or drink?"

"That would really be sweet of you, Hon. I'd like some dry toast and orange juice."

"Okay. I'll be right back." Jack scurried down the corridors and up the steps to the tenth deck. He picked up the toast and orange juice and as he turned to leave, he saw Rita sitting at a table overlooking the water. He walked over to her and said, "Good morning, beautiful lady. I don't have time to talk to you right now. I'll be back in a few minutes. Don't go away." A rabbit couldn't have run any faster as Jack dashed back to the room. He flung the door open and practically threw the food at Lauren. "I'm sorry I have to leave you, but I've got to eat and be ready to go." He looked at his watch and exclaimed, "You're sure you don't mind if I go without you?"

"Of course not. I wish I felt like going. I'll be thinking about you while you're gone. Have a good time, I love you."

In a last minute attempt to act concerned, Jack kissed Lauren on the cheek. As he dashed out the door, he said one more time, "You'd better not be pregnant."

At first Lauren was elated over Jack's sudden attention; but with his last remark, her joy was short lived.

* * * * *

Rita was waiting for him. He picked up his breakfast and walked over to her table. "Thanks for waiting. I have some good news to tell you. How would you like to be my partner on the excursion?"

"Your Partner? What about Lauren?"

"She's sick with a sunburn, motions sickness, or is possibly pregnant. There's one thing for sure, she'd better not be pregnant."

"Don't you want to have a family?'

"Hell, no! Let's not talk about Lauren. All I can say right now, it's a lucky break for us. We'll be together for a whole day."

"I can't believe Lauren would let you go by yourself. She must really trust and love you."

"She does, but that's her problem."

Rita leaned over the table and said seriously, "I'll go…but you'll have to promise me to be discreet."

"Discreet! Hell, nobody knows us. They wouldn't know if we were married or not. We're going to have a great time. When we get on the tender, I'll be discreet until I'm out of sight of the ship."

"What's a tender?"

"Large cruisers can't dock close to the ports because the water is too shallow, so a tender is a boat that ferries passengers to the docks."

Rita looked at him with a mischievous smile and said, "You really like to play on the wild side. You're intrigued by the adventure of having an affair almost in the presence of your wife."

"So-o-o, look who's talking. You're willing to take a chance, too." Jack looked at his watch and said, "Are you ready to go? We have to be ready to shove off in a half hour."

"Good heavens, no. I've got to change clothes. I'll meet you at the tender. Please don't act like you know me until we're out of sight."

Taking her hand, Jack smiled and said, "That'll be hard to do, but I'll try."

* * * * *

In the meantime, Lauren gained enough strength to dress and make her way to a deck where she could see Jack board the tender. All she could see through the dense fog was a mob of people gathered around the loading ramp. Lauren gazed longingly out over the sea for Jack. All she could see was the sun burrowed beneath the horizon and the fog.

CHAPTER 12

Jack perused the crowd for Rita until he saw her standing in the mist of other passengers. She was dressed in a stunning floral beach outfit with a matching straw hat. She carried a yellow canvas bag that hung from her shoulder. A challenge, like never before, filled him with desire to seduce her and to bend her to his will. Why did she come on to him so fast? Why was she alone? Hell, why should he care? Whatever the reason, he was glad he'd been in the right place to connect with her.

The clouds were rimmed with gold sunlight as the sun nudged its way up over the purplish-gray horizon. Tropical fish fluttered beneath the now brightening waters. *The Royal Majesty* was soon out of sight of the tender, which was a blessing to Jack. He immediately wove his way through the crowd and made his way to Rita.

"It was all I could do to keep away from you. I wanted to be next to you and claim you as my partner. You're an exceptionally beautiful lady."

"Thank you. That's the nicest thing I've heard all morning. I'm flattered. Now stop talking like that, you're embarrassing me." Rita played with her hat, and then she swooped it up and placed it on her head. She peeped out from under it and with a sheepish grin said, "It feels good to be admired." Rita paused and asked, "By the way, how was Lauren feeling this morning?"

In a lackadaisical motion he waved his hand in the air and replied, "Oh…she was sleeping like a baby when I left." Anxious to get Lauren out of the conversation, he leaned over the rail of the boat and cried out, "Look at those fish."

Rita leaned over the railing and let out a delightful squeal, "It's fantastic! They look like small bits of rainbows that have fallen from the sky. Before I came on this trip, I studied all kinds of brochures. It's like a dream come true."

"When I look at that crystal clear water, the multi-colored shells, and those strange fish, all I want to do is jump in and snorkel." With a hearty laugh, Jack banged his hand down on the rail of the boat. "But I don't want to talk about the landscape. All I want to do is just hold you in my arms." Jack stepped closer to Rita and pulled her against him.

With a lilting laugh, Rita gently put her hands against his chest and said, "Whoa, big boy. These people might think you're going to seduce me right here on the deck."

"Well...that sounds like an excellent idea. Want to give them a show?" Before Jack could kiss Rita, the captain of the tender announced they would be docking in five minutes. He reminded them not to be late for departure, or they would be left behind.

The tender docked and dropped a gangplank and Jack and Rita left the boat. They strolled along the cobblestone streets, peeking into the shops filled with colorful souvenirs. Rita tried on some jewelry while Jack admired some unusual clay pots. They continued walking along the crowded sidewalks filled with vendors selling everything imaginable and chanting that their prices were the best in town.

Rita commented, "The Cruise Director told us that we should not pay the first price but to bargain. Usually, if I see something I want, price doesn't matter. It works the same way when I see a man." Rita took off her glasses and winked at Jack. "Do you think I need to bargain for you?"

Jack twirled her around, took her by the shoulders, smiled and said, "Babe, I'm very expensive, but you'll get your money's worth when you're with me."

Rita tilted her head back and with a broad grin quipped, "You are confident, aren't you?"

"Miss Rita, you're going to find out just how good I am on this trip. You might even want to pay more than I'm really worth." Jack pulled her in between two buildings, took her hands and put them around his neck. Then he ran his hand down to the small of her back and pulled her as close as possible into his arms and kissed her savagely.

He was on the verge of running his hand under her blouse when a small native boy, dressed in dirty and ragged clothes, begged, "Please give me a dollar. I'm hungry."

Jack growled, as he tried to brush the boy out of the way, "Go away, boy. Go find your mama."

Rita laughed as she reached in her bag, and pulled out a dollar and said, "Here little boy, go buy yourself some candy." Rita looked out on the street and saw a lot of the passengers walking toward the bus terminal. "Jack, we'd better go! They'll leave us if we don't hurry. I certainly don't want to miss seeing the Mayan Ruins."

The expression on Jack's face was one of disappointment because he had finally gotten her in his arms. He thought, by damn, somehow or other he'd screw her today. He reluctantly grabbed her hand as they caught up with the crowd. The bus appeared to have used up its best years. The yellow paint was sparse between the dirt and dents. Jack held Rita's arm as they boarded the bus. Then he guided her to the rear of the bus.

Rita asked, "Why are we sitting in the back? I'd like to sit up front so that I can hear what the guide has to say."

Jack gave her a quick kiss on the cheek and said, "You'll not care what he says when you're with me."

"My goodness, aren't you conceited," Rita quipped.

Before Jack could respond, the guide introduced himself as Alexandros Maureil. Everyone listened very attentively as he told them about the Mayan culture which started back in the 11th century.

When Rita had taken her seat, she placed her yellow bag in her lap. The bus rumbled so loudly Rita had a hard time hearing the guide's talk. Suddenly she felt something moving under her bag. She looked down and saw Jack's hand working its way under her pants. Rita frowned, cut her eyes at him, and snapped,

"Jack, I really want to hear what the guide has to say. I've been looking forward to this trip for a long time. Now I'm actually going to walk around places of historical interest. Don't ruin this trip for me."

"Okay, I'll be a good boy but not for long." He reluctantly withdrew his hand.

The bus pulled into a parking lot surrounded by white stucco buildings with red terra-cotta roofs and arched doorways. Souvenir and gift shops filled every available space—luring the tourist to buy their wares. The guide, wearing his wide sombrero with a red scarf tied around the brim, often called the group to hurry up. He had a tight schedule to keep.

Jack held Rita's hand as they walked over the rocky terrain up to the Mayan City built by the sea. It was about ten o'clock in the morning when the guide began his lecture. The tourists were hot and sweaty, but they listened as he told the story of El Castillo, a lofty pyramid temple. Alexandros expounded dramatically about the civilization of the Mayan tribes and how they had reached considerable heights in the arts and sciences.

Jack was actually intrigued by the story. He guided Rita over to one of the temples and examined the frescoes and commented, "It's hard to believe how those uneducated people sculptured art in this clay and it's lasted for years."

Rita rubbed her hand over the drawings and commented, "I've read about their history and now I'm seeing their art with my own eyes."

The tour continued to a tropical location called, Xel-Ha. Jack and Rita got off the bus and walked along the winding stone walkways. "My God, this looks like an oasis in the middle of a dessert." They came to a large open shelter with a thatched roof. Tables and benches were lined in rows to accommodate the tourist and their box lunches supplied by the ship, *The Royal Majesty.*

Rita said, "So far this cruise has been exactly what I needed. You'll never know how it has psychologically benefited me."

"That's a mystery, Rita. How psychologically has it helped you?"

"Oh, I can't tell you now. Maybe later."

"Okay, Miss Rita. I'll keep after you until you tell me all about yourself. Right now, I want to go snorkeling."

CHAPTER 13

Lauren woke to a voice over the intercom system announcing that lunch was being served either in the Epicurean dinning room or on Deck Ten. The room was dark when she tuned on the bedside light. She squinted and rubbed her eyes.

Slowly she swung her legs over the side of the bed and cautiously stood up. With a sigh of relief, she found that she wasn't nauseated. She made her way to the bathroom to take a shower. The tepid water washed over her tear-stained face and sunburned body, which soothed her skin. She hastily slid on a pair of pale pink linen slacks and a long-sleeve white voile blouse. She stepped out onto the deck, and a cool breeze embraced her. Lauren tested herself by strolling along the deck to see if she would get nauseated again. Fortunately, the sea was calm as a mountain lake. She scrambled around in her bag for a bottle of Dramamine tablets just in case she did get seasick.

The buffet brimmed over with all kinds of spicy food, pastries, and salads tempting her to indulge, but common sense told her it would have to be a fruit salad and crackers. She picked up her tray and looked for a place to sit. The luncheon area wasn't crowded as most of the passengers were on the excursion. Even though she was starved, she controlled her food intake. Her thoughts returned to Jack as she remembered the look of anger when she said that she might be pregnant. Why doesn't he want children she thought? They were both getting along in age. Her thoughts were interrupted when she noticed a woman waving her hand frantically. At first, Lauren thought she was waving to someone else until she saw her clutching her throat.

Lauren cried out, "My God, she's choking." Jumping up from her seat, she rushed to the lady. She jerked the lady up, placed her arms under her breasts, and performed the Heimlich maneuver. The food popped out of her mouth, and she gasped for air.

When the lady caught her breath, she said, "Thank you, thank you, you saved my life. I'm Doctor Ann Goodman but please call me Ann. If you're by yourself, please come over and let's finish our lunch together." Then she grinned, "I promise not to choke again."

Lauren laughed, too. "All right. I'll get my tray and join you." Lauren thought how charming Ann was. She's probably in her forties, judging by the gray highlights in her short brown hair and a few wrinkles of wisdom creasing around her lips. Her soft hazel eyes expressed a genuine feeling of sincerity. When she reached Ann's table, she said with an outstretched hand, "I'm Doctor Lauren Harper. Please call me Lauren and thanks for asking me to sit with you. I don't like to eat alone."

Ann's smile broadened as she remarked, "I'm so glad you were here, Lauren. I'm forever indebted to you. Are you traveling alone?"

With a look of embarrassment Lauren responded, "No…my husband and I are on our honeymoon. I became sick yesterday. We planned to go on an excursion today, but I didn't feel well this morning. I insisted that he go anyway, which he did without any resistance. Thank goodness, I feel better now, and maybe I'll be able to enjoy Key West tomorrow. Are you traveling alone?"

"Yes, I am. It seems good to be away from my stressful job. I have a tendency to let my patients' lives weigh me down. I'm a psychiatrist."

With a smile Lauren remarked, "I'm in pediatrics." Lauren looked nervously at her watch and said, "Excuse me, I keep looking for the tour group that left this morning. They should be returning around six o'clock this afternoon. I hope he had a good time. All he was interested in was snorkeling, but I wanted to see the Mayan Ruins. Oh well, maybe I'll get to see them one day." Lauren looked out over the water, paused and said, "I think I'd better go back to my cabin and rest. I'm beginning to feel a little woozy again."

When Lauren rose to leave, Ann stood up, hugged her, and kissed her on the cheek and said, "Thanks again, Lauren. If you need me for anything, I'm in cabin 336. I hope we can get together again on this trip."

Lauren walked back to her room and stretched out on the bed. As she stared at the ceiling, she wondered if Jack would still be angry with her if she were pregnant? There isn't anything he could do or say to make her have an abortion.

CHAPTER 14

Jack and Rita left the picnic area to find a secluded place to change into their bathing suits. As they walked along a sandy path, weaving through scrubby live oak trees battered by many hurricanes, Jack's eyes probed through the maze of sea oats and tropical flowers. He stopped short and pointed to a thatched hut about fifty feet away, which was barely visible from the path because a cascade of wild vines had obscured it.

He pointed to the left side of the path, "Look, Rita. Let's check it out." He grabbed Rita's hand and led her through the thicket.

Rita cried, "Slow down, Jack. I'll be scratched to pieces."

"Sorry. I can't wait to go snorkeling." When they reached the hut, all that was left of it were four bamboo walls and a roof that would surely fall down the next time a hurricane passed through. Whoever lived in this hut, left a small, crude, wooden bench in the middle of the room. Jack poked his head into the opening, turned around, and laughed, "I don't see any snakes or spiders, but it's a perfect place for us to change clothes. You change first while I keep a watchful eye in case someone comes this way."

While she was dressing Rita called to him, "I didn't see you carrying a suit."

With a sassy grin, Jack replied, "I have it in my pocket."

Rita laughed, "This secret place makes me feel very naughty."

Before she could finish her sentence Jack rushed in and said, "Snorkeling can wait. Never in my wildest dream did I think you would make the first move to have sex." They sat down on the bench and kissed each other. When their sexual appetite had been satisfied and they had cooled off, Jack wondered why Rita had changed her mind about having sex with him.

Rita lifted herself from Jack's lap and put on her bathing suit. A suit that was even more miniscule than the one she wore by the pool.

"My God Rita, do you call that a suit?" Jack teased. "I thought the one you had on yesterday was skimpy. Don't get me wrong. I love it! You have a fabulous figure."

When Jack put on his thong suit, Rita clasped her throat, "Talk about skimpy suits, why are you wearing one at all. That's about as near nothing as I've ever seen. But—I'm not complaining. Come on, Jack. Let's go swimming. Maybe that will cool us off."

Jack and Rita put their clothes in her bag. They walked to the lagoon, put on their snorkel gear, and plunged into the crystal blue water. It was clear enough to see an array of tropical fish near enough to touch. The underwater scene of white and pink coral, embellished with streaks of sunrays, cast pastel prisms throughout the water. Jack motioned to Rita to surface.

When they came up, Rita exclaimed, "I've never seen anything any more beautiful."

"You got that right." He looked at his waterproof watch and sighed, "As bad as I hate to leave, we'd better change our clothes. I'd like to walk down to the ocean just for one last look." It wasn't the ocean he wanted to see, he just wanted to go back to the hut.

Rita realized that Jack really wanted to go back to the hut and she didn't want to. She needed an excuse. Suddenly she cried out, "Look Jack, over there in that clump of trees is a bath house. We could have used that to change our clothes."

"Are you kidding? Just think what we would have missed."

"Yeah...that was special." When she stepped inside the shelter, she was glad to see a shower and towels supplied for the visitors. After she dressed, Rita stepped outside. Jack grabbed her hand and pulled her toward the path that led to the hut. Unexpectedly, she jerked her hand away and headed briskly down another path toward the ocean.

Jack's stride stretched longer to catch up with her and he said angrily, "What in the hell is wrong with you."

"Nothing." Neither one said another word until they came to a cement bench overlooking the ocean.

In an irritable tone, Jack said, "Why the cold shoulder? What's wrong with you?"

Rita stood up and gazed out over the turquoise water for a few minutes. She turned slowly and faced him and said, "I've used you."

Before she could explain, Jack yelled, "What do you mean—used me?"

Rita waved her hands in front of Jack trying to calm him down. "Please...just hear me out. Then I hope you'll understand my actions." Twisting her fingers nervously, Rita began her story. "My parents were very poor. They did everything possible to give me the best education they could afford and made many sacrifices to get me through law school. After I passed the bar, I was able to get a job in a small law firm. One night, the office staff threw a big party. That was the night I met Gerald LaBaron. I was completely swept off my feet. He was everything a woman could want: handsome, good personality, wonderful physique, and rich. We courted for about a year."

"Gerald's occupation was selling and buying antiques. He traveled out of the country and would be gone for a month or two. When he was in town, we were inseparable. We were both afraid to make a commitment to marriage, but we decided to try living together. At that time, my career and being the perfect girlfriend for him was all I wanted. He took great pleasure in taking me to important functions. Whenever we entered a room, all heads turned our way." Rita hesitated as if the memories were beginning to be painful.

Jack said impatiently, "For God's sake, Rita, don't stop now!"

Rita put her hand on his arm and said, "Don't worry, I'm going to tell you everything. In time we were married with all the fanfare a bride ever dreamed about. We bought a beautiful home in the best neighborhood and continued with our life the same as we had before we were married. We never talked about having children. I assumed he didn't want a family, and I was happy with my career. We'd been married for seven years, when by accident, I discovered a terrible secret he had kept from me. Somehow our bank statements were mixed up. We had always kept separate accounts. The statement was addressed to Mrs. Gerald LaBaron and not Mrs. Rita LaBaron. Being addressed to me, I had the right to open it. There were many checks written with Mrs. Gerald LaBaron's name on them. I was puzzled. When he gave me money, he always deposited it in my account, Rita LaBaron."

Jack was in no mood to show sympathy. He had been tricked into thinking it was his suave and handsome looks that had beguiled Rita into this affair. With a forced smile, he asked, "Rita, do you want to continue?"

"Oh, yes. I need to get this story out of my system." She gathered her composure and continued, "I called the bank's accountant to find out where these checks had come from. To my utter amazement, he told me that they'd come from overseas, which seemed natural at first because he had bought a villa in the south of France for business purposes. I still couldn't understand why was my name on the checks? I immediately took the next flight to France, rented a car, and drove to his villa. My knees nearly buckled as I walked to the door. When I rang the bell, I could hear children calling in French, 'Mama, someone's at the door!' The door opened and standing before me was an attractive lady, average height with short, curly auburn hair. In a thick French accent, she said politely, 'Madame, may I help you?' Instantly, three small children—one boy about five years old and twin girls probably three years old came along with her. They persistently tugged at their mother's dress, demanding her attention. I stared at the little boy. He resembled Gerald as he might have looked at that age, with thick wavy blond hair and big blue eyes. Curly ringlets, the color of their mother's, adorned the heads of twin girls. Their eyes—the same as Gerald's."

Rita stopped talking and walked to the water's edge. Jack followed. While they stood in the shallow fringe of the shoreline, the water lapped lazily across the tops of their feet. She lifted her head and faced the sun as if to gain strength to go on with her story.

With a deep breath, she began again. "I asked the lady if she was Mrs. Gerald LaBaron. She responded defensively, 'Why do you want to know?' I was caught off guard and thought frantically for some excuse. I hesitated and then said, 'I buy antiques from Mr.LaBaron while I'm in France; I want to discuss, in person, items I need for my business.' Mrs. Labaron apologized for having me stand outside and invited me in. She told me that her husband had stepped out for a few minutes but would be right back. She offered me some tea and a small pastry while I waited. It wasn't long before I heard Gerald's voice calling his wife's name, 'Bridgette. I'm home.' When he walked into the room, he walked nervously across the room to Bridgette. After he recovered from the shock of seeing me, he greeted me cordially and asked who I was. I had already decided how I would keep up the pretense that I was there on business. Bridgette would never know that her husband was also my husband. I introduced myself by my maiden name, and told him what I had come for. He looked at me with a blank expression before answering. I immediately saw his frustration and quickly told him the items that I needed, and that he could ship them to the same address as usual. I said goodbye to all of them. He mumbled a weak reply. I let myself out of the house without waiting for Bridgette to take me to the door. When I arrived in New York, I cleaned out all of his possessions. I didn't want to see any of his belongings in my home. Then I started divorce proceedings. He agreed to everything I asked for in order to keep his reputation from being ruined—especially the legal matter of being married to two women."

Jack's face remained expressionless as he watched Rita struggle with her story. He expected her to break down and cry for his sympathy but that wasn't going to happen. His ego was still crushed and, by damn, he wasn't going to pamper her. Rita still hadn't answered the question 'why she had used him.' Jack got up and kicked at the water a few times and then reluctantly asked, "Rita, what did you mean, you used me?"

Rita stared down at the water watching the tide flow to and fro over shells and muscles as they dug into the wet sand. After a few minutes she replied, "I feel like Paul Harvey saying, 'Now, for the rest of the story.' I had to get away, and that's why I'm on this cruise. The reason I responded so readily to your flirting was…I needed someone who would restore my self-confidence and someone who would make me feel desirable. I wondered if I would ever be able to have sex again and not be reminded of Gerald. When you came on to me, it was much more than I expected. I never dreamed it would be with such a handsome man like you. My only regret is that you and Lauren are on your honeymoon. I tried not to take advantage of you, but it was too tempting. Thanks to you, you made me feel like a desirable woman again. I'm very grateful. From this moment on, what has happened between us is in the past. I prefer that we remain only friends and I definitely mean—just friends." Rita took a deep breath and let out a cry, "Wow! I've talked enough. Now, it's your turn. Tell me about yourself."

With indignation Jack put his hands up in the air and said, "Well, if you really want to know, I'm studying to be a lawyer—if that makes any difference to you?" Before he could continue, off in the distance the sound of the bus horn echoed through the air. "Hell fire, we'd better get back to the bus. I don't want to be left behind." He grabbed Rita's hand, and they ran back down the path to the bus. The only seats left were behind the driver. Jack was glad the other passengers talked and laughed so loud that a conversation with Rita was impossible. When the bus pulled into the parking lot at the pier, everyone hurried to board the tender.

Rita tried to make light conversation, but Jack stared out over the ocean. Finally, she said, "Jack, I'm sorry that I've hurt you. I really would like for us to be friends and I really want to meet Lauren."

Jack's response was tinged with sarcasm, "You've gott'a be kidding, Rita. After what we've done—no-way!"

"I'm sorry that we have to part with such bad feelings." Without another word, Rita walked to the opposite end of the tender.

CHAPTER 15

Lauren leaned against the rail of the ship and took a deep breath as she felt the gentle wind blow against her face. She shaded her eyes and searched the horizon for a sign of the tender. The sun bore down on her as she strolled along the deck. She looked for a cool shaded area to sit while waiting for Jack. Lauren found a comfortable lounge chair, sat down, and began to nod. She was awakened by the sounds of a little girl begging her mother to read her a story from the book she was pushing under her mother's chin. The little girl, about five years old, had long red hair hanging down to her waist. From where Lauren sat, she could see her doll-like face with rosy, bow-shaped lips, and brown eyes pleading for her mother's attention. Since Lauren had had a lot of experience with small children, she knew that the child's mother would succumb to her daughter's wishes. Lauren's heart tightened at the sight, as she longed to have a child of her own.

A blast from the ship's horn jolted her out of her thoughts. She got up quickly and made her way to look over the side of the ship. Lauren pressed her hand against her forehead to shield the evening sun from her eyes. As the tender approached, she saw Jack waving in her direction. A feeling of anxiety welled up in her throat. She couldn't blot out her physical attraction for him and neither could she forget his verbal abuse. Lauren found herself waving to him, too.

Jack bounded up the steps two at a time. He pulled Lauren into his arms and crushed her lips into his. When he let her go he said, "Doc, I really missed you. I wish you could have been there with me."

Confused and bewildered by Jack's action, she finally caught her breath and exclaimed, "I can't believe you really missed me after the way you talked to me last night."

"Doc, I'm really sorry about that. You really floored me when you said you might be pregnant. I can't take that kind of news right now." Jack turned and signaled a waiter and ordered drinks and sandwiches for both of them. He launched into a narration of his day, "Lauren, you just can't imagine the beauty of the water and sea life. It was breathtaking. The tour took us through the quaint market place, down south to the Mayan Ruins, and then we had lunch in a tropical paradise. It was another whole world." He stopped momentarily when he noticed the sadness in Lauren's eyes. "Oh, damn!" He exclaimed, "Here I'm rattling on about the wonderful time I had, and you were back on the ship feeling miserable. Tell me how you're feeling."

"I'm feeling a lot better now. Not long after you left, I got up and had breakfast. That's when I saved a lady's life. I'm glad you had a good time. At least one of us is enjoying the cruise."

"Wait a minute! You what? You saved a lady's life? How?"

"Yes, I saved Dr. Ann Goodman from choking. After she recovered from the Heimlick maneuver, I sat with her while we finished our breakfast. She's a very charming lady. I hope to see her again."

He glanced at his watch, sprang from his chair and said, "Come on, Lauren. It's time for the entertainment to begin in the Palace Theater. We're here to have a good time! I don't want to hear you say anything else about having a baby." Lauren stared at the performers as though it were an empty stage. It was hard for her to believe that she still loved Jack, but she did. Regardless of her feelings, whatever the consequences, she'd never have an abortion.

Jack punched Lauren on the arm. "Get up, the shows over. I don't believe you even saw it. Your mind was somewhere else."

While they walked to their cabin, neither one spoke. Jack didn't make the slightest attempt to apologize nor did he even say good night as he climbed into the other twin bed. He was still fuming over Rita for making him look like a fool and angry with Lauren for wanting a baby.

The next morning Lauren made up her mind that she wasn't going to mope around any more. She'd make the best of a bad situation. She heard Jack stirring in bed and asked abruptly, "Are you going to breakfast with me?"

Still half asleep, he grumbled, "I suppose so."

They went up to Deck Ten for breakfast, and Lauren led the way toward the stern of the ship. She wanted to sit next to the windows so that she could see the morning sun shimmering over the tranquil sea. Just before they sat down, Lauren saw her friend, Dr. Ann Goodman, waving and walking toward her.

When she got to Lauren's table, she laughed, "This time my waving isn't because I'm choking."

Lauren got up and hugged her and said, "I'm so glad to see you again. Ann, this is my husband, Jack."

Ann smiled graciously and said, "Jack, I'm so glad to meet you. I suppose Lauren has told you about how she saved my life?'

Jack immediately put forth his best manners to impress her and responded, "Yes, she told me all about it. I'm glad she was there. It was too bad she couldn't have been in two places at once." He wavered slightly, cocked his head in Lauren's direction, gave her a fake smile, and lied as he said, "I really missed her."

Ann changed the subject. "Please, come to my table. I've just met another lady that was alone and I asked her to join me, too. This is what a cruise is all about meeting new people and having fun."

Lauren turned around and asked Jack, "Is it okay with you?"

"Sure—I reckon I can handle that." The lady with Ann was hidden from view by a potted palm. Jack was walking behind Lauren and Ann, and didn't see her. As soon as they got to the table, Ann motioned to the lady and said, "Rita LaBaron, this is Lauren and Jack Harper. Lauren is the lady I told you about that saved my life."

Luckily, Lauren couldn't see the shocked expression on Jack's face but Ann noticed it. Rita nodded to both of them, extended her hand to Lauren, and said with reservation, "Thank goodness you were here to save her. I'm very glad to meet you."

"Sit down everybody," Ann said brightly. A few minutes lapsed when Ann asked, "Jack, how did you like the excursion?"

He kept his eyes away from Rita as he summarized the events. When he finished, he cut his eyes at Rita for a split second, but she looked away. Jack continued, "I want to do everything I can on this cruise. It'll be a long time before I'll have another vacation."

"Lauren, Jack, and Rita," Ann exclaimed, "I have a suggestion. Let's all go shopping as a group when we dock at Key West tomorrow morning. Jack, you can be our bodyguard."

He replied with a grin on his face, "I'd be delighted, but I think you ladies can take care of yourselves."

Lauren spoke up. "If I feel as good as I do now, I'd like to go shopping."

"I hear you can save money on jewelry in Key West," Rita added.

Ann laughed and jokingly said, "As the Director of this shopping excursion, we'll meet at the boarding deck in the morning at nine o'clock. As soon as we dock, we'll take the Conch Trolley, and ride through the historical landmarks of Key West. After that, we'll shop till we drop." Ann looked at her watch and said, "Oh, my! It's getting late. Rita and I planned to lie out in the sun for about an hour and then go swimming. If you need to get in touch with me, call my room number 301 and leave a message if I'm not there."

As soon as they were out of sight, Lauren picked up her straw bag and stared steadily at Jack and said, "We should act like we're in love. After all, it is our honeymoon. Rita and Ann will suspect something if we don't talk to each other."

Under his breath he cursed, "Hell fire, Lauren…you've made this trip a disaster! All you can talk about is having a baby! You don't even know whether you're pregnant or not. I'll tell you one thing, I'm still going to have a good time."

It took a little while for his remark to sink in before Lauren responded cordially, "Okay, Jack, I'm sure you'll behave as long as you have an audience. What are you going to do the rest of the day?"

Because Lauren didn't blast back at him, Jack was caught off guard, he stammered, "I-I-I don't know."

"Well, do what you want to. I think I'll look for Ann and Rita and chat with them," Lauren said calmly as she walked away from Jack not asking him to join her. His mouth dropped open in surprise at Lauren's newfound courage. *The Royal Majesty* didn't have to anchor out at sea. The slips had been dredged deep enough to oblige large ships to unload passengers directly onto piers. Jack, Lauren, Ann, and Rita met promptly at nine o'clock at the boarding deck. As they stepped onto the sidewalk, it was difficult for all to walk side by side because it was crowded with tourists.

Ann took Rita's hand and took the lead. She raised her voice over the honking horns of cars to tell them something one of the guides said about Key West, "Except for the large number of people that moved in, the town remained the same as it had been for many years. The town kept the historical homes repaired and painted constantly, not only for preservation, but to keep them attractive for the tourists." They walked about a block when they heard the bell coming from the Conch Train. Ann called to them over the noise, "Let's hurry!"

The four of them climbed on and settled down for the tour. The train chugged along on its fourteen-mile route. The engineer spoke with an accent familiar to the islanders as he methodically chanted, "The inhabitants on the island suffered many occupational defeats in their survival to become a thriving community. Finally, they solved their economic problems by becoming a tourist attraction." The guide pointed to a house and said, "That's the Curry Mansion Inn, over to the left is Hemingway's House, and a little further is Mel Fisher's Maritime Museum. You'll notice that a lot of the old houses have gingerbread trim, but now it isn't used as much in the newer houses." The engineer stopped talking and clanged the bell as it came to a stop at the station. "Have a good day!"

"Come on folks." Ann called as she walked rapidly along the sidewalk, "We've got a lot of ground to cover in a short period of time, only four hours."

Rita chimed in, "Ladies, I don't want to slow you down while I look for jewelry. Why don't I meet you some place in an hour and a half?"

"That's a good idea, Rita," Ann replied.

Jack spoke up, "I'm going to "Sloppy Joe's Bar." Why not meet there. I sure as hell don't want to shop."

Lauren looked at Ann and asked, "Would it be okay if I tagged along with you?"

"Of course. I'd love it. Let's go. We've got money to spend."

Rita waved good-bye as she headed down Duval Street. Jack wanted desperately to follow Rita, but instead he began to look for Sloppy Joe's Bar.

Lauren and Ann found a department store and started shopping. It wasn't long before Lauren took Ann by the arm and said, "I would like to go to a drug store and get a pregnancy test. I think I'm pregnant, I just want to be sure. Do you mind going with me?"

"You're pregnant! Oh, that's wonderful," Ann said with delight.

"No longer than I have known you, Ann, I feel that I can trust you with my feelings. We don't have enough time for me to tell you my problems, but I will tell you this. Jack was furious with me when I told him I thought I was pregnant."

"Lauren, you didn't have to tell me you were having problems. I saw a lot of hostility in Jack's eyes when he looked at you yesterday. I'm sorry." They walked on down the street until they found a drug store. While they looked for the test, Ann said, "I'm worried about you. I want to help you if I can. Here, take my card and any time you need to talk or to get away, just call."

"Thank you. It's wonderful to have found a friend like you. Later on we'll talk again. I had better find the test kit. I'll let you know the results tomorrow. If I'm pregnant, I'm not going to tell Jack until it becomes obvious."

"Please be careful." Ann looked at her watch and cried, "Look at the time! We have to hurry! I believe the bar is several blocks away." They rushed down the street dodging in and out of the crowd of people. "Look ahead, Lauren. I believe I see Jack leaning against a light post."

When they got to him he said in a slurred voice, "Where in the hell have you broads been? Did you buy out the town? I've been here long enough to talk to everybody in town and drink all their beer." Jack looked around to see if Rita was with them and groggily asked, "Where's the other musketeer?"

Just at that moment Rita came running up and breathlessly said, "I'm sorry I'm late. It takes forever to get waited on in these stores."

Ann didn't want Lauren to have to walk with Jack. "Come on with me, handsome, let's you and I walk together." He looked over his shoulder and glared at Lauren and Rita.

"Rita, we haven't had time to get to know each other. I'd like to know more about you."

"There's not much to tell. I'm a lawyer for a firm in Connecticut. I'm divorced and this trip was intended for me to get my life back in focus on what's really important. What about you?"

"As you know by now, I'm a newly-wed," Lauren laughed nervously. "I'm also a pediatrician at Massachusetts General Hospital. I love my work, but I have found it's hard to keep house, cook, and work, too."

They were almost at the ship and time had run out for them to talk anymore. Rita dug down into her shoulder bag and pulled out a card and said, "Lauren, if you ever need me, call this number on my business card."

"Thanks, Rita, I hope that won't be necessary. I would like to call just to stay in touch."

By the time they had reached the ship, Jack was nearly sober. He picked up Ann's hand and kissed the back of it like an English gentleman and, with a giddy laugh, expressed his pleasure in being with her. Then he kissed Rita's hand and pressed his tongue on her skin. She jerked her hand away. Lauren saw an expression on Rita's face that showed repulsiveness. Why did Rita act like that, she wondered? Ann saw Lauren's concern, but she couldn't do anything about it. The other passengers crowded around them and by pure force they were pushed aboard the ship.

Ann yelled over the crowd, "Good night all! See you in the morning!"

Lauren and Jack went to their room in silence. She undressed, put on her gown, and crawled into bed facing the wall, thinking she would be sleeping alone again. Jack took his clothes off and hung them neatly in the closet. Lauren was stunned when she felt him climbing into bed with her. She didn't know whether to fear him or to be thrilled. She began to tremble when his hands caressed her breasts. His foreplay aroused her unexpectedly. Her heart was beating wildly. She could not hold back her desire to make love with him. What had caused him to change? Whatever it was, it didn't matter now.

The next morning Lauren slipped out of bed, took the test out of her bag, and went into the bathroom. Her hands were shaking. She ran the test. Holding her breath, she waited for the results. Her whole life hung in the balance. If she weren't pregnant, how would she ever talk Jack into having a baby. If she were pregnant, Jack would make her life a living hell. She stared at the results— pregnant! Tears filled her eyes with joy. At last she would have the one gift she had wanted for a long time. Lauren looked at the test again and another thought came to mind. She would probably lose Jack if she didn't have an abortion. There wasn't a choice, as far as she was concerned, she'd have to take her chances with him.

Lauren stepped back into the room and started dressing. Jack stirred. When he opened his eyes and saw that she was getting ready to leave, he asked sleepily, "Where're you going?"

"I'm going to Deck 10 for breakfast. You were sleeping so peacefully, I didn't want to disturb you. I'll wait for you by the pool." She opened the door and was out of the room before he could say anything else. Lauren picked up a bagel and a cup of coffee and then eagerly looked for Ann as she climbed down the steps to the poolside. Lauren called, "Good morning, Ann. Please join me."

"Okay! I'll be back in a few minutes." When Ann returned, she asked, "Why is that big radiant smile on your face spreading from ear to ear?"

Lauren giggled, "You know why I'm smiling. I'm so thrilled I can't hardly stand it."

Ann's mouth dropped open and cried, "You're pregnant!"

"Yes! Oh, Ann, I wish I could share my happiness with Jack. Maybe by the time I begin to show, he'll want our baby, too."

"Lauren, I'm happy for you. I don't want to take away your joy, but I do advise you to be very careful when he finds out."

Before they'd said much more, Jack appeared with his breakfast. In a jovial mood he quipped, "Well, it won't be long before all of us will be putting on heavy coats and wishing we were back in this warm climate. I'd like to stay here forever." He sat down and sipped his coffee and turned his attention to Ann,

"I hope Lauren and I will be seeing you again when we get back home. By the way, where's your friend, Rita?"

"She called me this morning and told me she had some urgent business she had to attend to and to tell everyone goodbye."

Lauren smiled at Ann and said, "I'll always remember you. I'll call you when I get back home." She struggled to keep from crying. Ann walked over to Lauren, and they hugged each other. Lauren whispered in Ann's ear, "Thanks for being here when I needed a friend."

CHAPTER 16

The conversation was sparse between Jack and Lauren on their flight back to Massachusetts. Lauren wanted to tell Jack her good news, but she knew it wouldn't be good news to him. It was best that she remained quiet for fear she might let it slip that she was pregnant. Anyway, he was too absorbed in a magazine.

They arrived late Sunday night at their apartment. Jack carried the suitcases into the bedroom, unpacked his bag, and hung up his clothes. Lauren scrambled through her bag until she found one of her trousseau gowns with anticipation that Jack would make love to her. Maybe she could make a new beginning. She crawled into bed and waited. She peeked at Jack as he undressed hoping that he would come to bed nude as he usually did. When he put on the pajamas pants, she knew sex wasn't on his mind. Disappointed, she turned over on her side, faced the wall, and thought, either he's too tired or he's wondering if I'm pregnant. Lauren's lips turned up into a smile anyway, and silently the words came out of her mouth, "It's too late, Jack, I'm pregnant and there's nothing you can do about it."

Monday morning Jack stretched, yawned, and mumbled as he crawled out of bed. "It's going to be hard getting back to the books again. I hope my advisor received my message and notified the professors why I was absent."

Lauren sleepily said, "I hope she did, too. In a way, I dread getting back to my routine. It was nice sleeping late." She slipped out of bed, put on her blue cotton chenille robe and scuffs, went into the kitchen, and cooked breakfast.

"By the way, are you coming home early?" Lauren asked.

Jack walked into the kitchen, sat down, and said, "Why do you want to know my schedule?"

"Sometimes I have to work late. I don't always have time to get the house cleaned up before you get home," she snapped.

"That's just too bad!" Jack was through eating before Lauren even started. He jumped up from the table, went to the bedroom, dressed, walked to the front door and snarled, "See ya' later. Don't forget to get this place clean before I come home!" He opened the front door and slammed it behind him as he went out.

Lauren stared at the closed door. She sipped her coffee and muttered tentatively, "*For better or worst*, I made a commitment. I just pray that I will stick to it and he can too." Lauren finished her coffee with a big gulp, rinsed the breakfast dishes, and dressed. Although she enjoyed some of their brief vacation, it felt good to slip into her white jacket, get back to work, and see her friends at the hospital. Lauren shivered when she stepped outside. What a difference in the weather, she thought; it'll take some getting use to. She sped along the familiar streets weaving in and out through the early morning traffic. The parking lot was filled except for her personal space. Lauren walked up to the door leading to her office, stopped, put her hand on the nameplate, and read aloud, "Doctor Lauren Fulghum. Uh-oh, it looks like a name change is in order—from now on it should read—Doctor Lauren Harper on the door and parking space."

Before starting her day's work, she went to the gift shop and bought a bouquet of flowers and a box of candy for Camille. She wanted to give her something to show her appreciation.

Camille came bursting through the door before Lauren could take the gifts to her. She exclaimed, "Lauren, it's good to see you back! We all missed you so-o-o much. I can't wait for you to tell me all about your trip." Laughing, she said, "You act like a kid hiding something from your mother. What in the world do you have behind your back? "

Lauren thrust the flowers and candy into Camille's arms, grinned, and said, "I can't repay you enough for all the things you have done for me. You are the best friend I've ever had. Let's have lunch and I'll tell you all about the cruise."

The cafeteria was crowded and noisy as usual. They found a table away from most of the noise. Camille leaned forward with her hands clasped together, her eyes sparkling with anticipation, waiting to hear all the juicy story about Lauren's honeymoon. She began with a barrage of questions. "How was your trip? Did you like the ship? How was the food?"

"Okay Camille, just be patient. I'll tell you everything." Lauren went into elaborate details about the luxurious ship, including the exquisite food, and the great entertainment. She told her about the two new friends she made and especially how she saved Ann Goodman's life. The excitement in her voice trailed off, and her eyes took on a look of sadness.

Camille whispered, "Lauren, is there something wrong?"

Lauren looked up. "Camille, I have something very serious to tell you. Promise you won't breathe a word."

"You know anything you tell me will be kept a secret, if that's what you want. What in the world has happened to make you look so serious?"

"Let's go somewhere that's more private. I don't want anyone to hear what I have to tell you."

"Okay. Do you want to go to my office?"

"Yeah. That's a good idea."

They took their trays and put them on the conveyor belt and headed to her office. Camille eased down in her black leather chair behind her desk. Lauren sat opposite her in a straight back chair Lauren clasped her hands and held them in her lap. Her voice seemed taut as she started talking. "Everything was wonderful in the beginning. The ship offered an excursion to the Mayan Ruins in Mexico. Jack and I were excited about going, but I got sick. At first, I thought it might be something that I had eaten. Then I thought I might be pregnant. I told Jack that I didn't feel like going ashore, and for him to go on without me. He asked me what was wrong?

I told him I was either seasick or pregnant. He went crazy when I said I might be pregnant. Before I knew what happened, he was yelling and ranting like a mad man. His arms swung wildly as he screamed at me. He said he'd make me have an abortion. I cried back, I will never have an abortion!"

Camille sat up rigidly in her chair and said, "Oh my God, Lauren, he's crazy!"

"Strange as it may seem, Camille, I still love him. When we first dated, he was thoughtful; we had fun together; he made me laugh, and I'm still attracted to him physically. I must be the most optimistic person in the world, because I still believe we can make our marriage work. After all, it just takes time to get acclimated to a new way of life. In my business, I've seen many young couples have disagreements when they first start a family."

Camille sat with her mouth wide open, shocked, as she listened to Lauren. She gasped, "My God, you are an optimist. But…the main thing is, you say you're pregnant. Are you sure?"

"Yes, I found out when we were in Key West. I'm hoping by the time I start showing, he'll like the idea of being a daddy."

"Oh, Lauren! You really do have a problem. Are you quite sure that you don't want to have an abortion? It might save your marriage."

"I'm thirty-one. Even if I wasn't pregnant, I don't think I could ever talk Jack into letting me have a baby. This is my opportunity to become a mother. I'll never have an abortion."

Camille got up from her chair and put her hand on Lauren's shoulder, and said, "Honey, I don't want to frighten you, but you've already told me how violent he gets. It's obvious to me you're willing to give up your marriage to have a baby. So, whatever you do, please be careful."

"I want this baby more than anything in the world, but as I said before, I'm sure my love for him and having a baby will make him change. Thanks for being my friend, Camille, everything's going to be just fine."

* * * * *

Professor Ernest Herring, a teacher of Criminal Procedure at Harvard, towered over most of his students. His steely gray eyes were large and wide apart. At times, he could be kind and understanding, but he could also chill your very soul when provoked. The professor was at his desk, stroking his full reddish-brown beard, as he watched the students file into his class.

Jack was confident that the professor had his excuse, and was surprised when he said, "Mr. Harper, I would like to see you after class."

Jack ambled up to the desk. He was sure the professor was going to congratulate him on his recent marriage. He stood in front of the professor and saw that his eyes had a look that could pierce metal. "Mr. Harper," he said sharply, "do you remember when I informed the students the first day they came to my class about my rule for absenteeism? If not, I'd like to refresh your memory—an excuse from your advisor stating the reason for being absent is absolutely mandatory! Regardless of how good a student might be, I have rules and regulations that must be followed." The professor exclaimed, "I do not have such an excuse from you, and unless you can bring me a legitimate one, you will have to pay the consequences!"

Jack couldn't believe what he was hearing. He blurted out, "Sir, I called my advisor before I left on my honeymoon, but she was out of town. I talked to the secretary and asked her to inform my advisor to send an excuse to all my classes. She promised that she would take care of it."

The professor looked Jack straight in his eyes and said,

"Mr. Harper, I've been around a long time, and I know all the excuses. I'm quite aware that you can catch up in your studies, but I am a stickler for rules. Produce an excuse, and if it is acceptable, I will take it under consideration." It was all Jack could do to keep his temper in tact. He held his body erect just like he would if he had been in the army. He glared at the professor with his dark brown penetrating eyes as if to argue with him. His face reddened with anger. Before Jack could say anything, the professor said, "Mr. Harper, I think I have made myself clear. I have to go." Professor Herring got up from his desk and left Jack seething with anger.

*****

Lauren got home before Jack and rushed around the living room to get the papers off the floor. Before she finished straightening it, Jack burst through the front door shouting at the top of his voice, "Professor Herring is a sorry S.O.B. He didn't believe me when I told him why I wasn't in class last week! I can't wait to get hold of the advisor that was suppose to send the professors my excuse." Jack stomped around the room hitting the walls or anything that was in his way. He started toward Lauren but she ducked into the bathroom for fear he might take his rage out on her.

Sometime later, she pressed her ear to the door and listened to hear if Jack had stopped blowing off steam. She waited a few minutes and peeped into the living room. Softly she asked, "Jack, did something at school upset you? Please tell me what's wrong!" When he didn't reply, she eased the door open a little more. She could see him sitting on the couch looking at television. In a calm voice, she asked, "Jack, what's wrong?"

He put the TV on mute and answered in a disgruntled manner, "Oh, I just feel like killing that woman I talked to before we left on our honeymoon. She assured me my excuse would be sent to all my professors. In every stinking class I went to today, I was humiliated because that bitch didn't deliver my excuse."

Lauren was relieved and eased out of the bathroom. She thought, at least, it wasn't something that she had done.

Jack later said, "By the way, I'm sorry I blew up. I had to vent my anger on someone."

Without another word, Jack finished watching the movie.

H-m-m, thought Lauren, maybe things will get better. She leaned over and kissed Jack on the cheek and said, I'm going to take my shower and go to bed. I hope you'll be along soon."

Lauren was nearly asleep when she felt Jack slide into bed. Her eyes popped open when she felt his naked body curl up next to her back. She rolled over on her back and he started kissing her. She whispered in his ear, "Darling, I love you. I'm sorry you got upset. You'll get everything straightened out tomorrow."

Methodically, Jack said, "I love you, too, sweetheart. Lauren, I realize this is bad timing but speaking of straightening things out, don't you think we should take out an insurance policy now that we're married? I saw the policy you have on your parents."

Lauren turned over, faced Jack, cupped his face in her hands, kissed him, and said, "Let's not talk about insurance right now. I just want us to make love."

Jack pushed Lauren away, reached over to the bedside table, flipped the light on, and said sternly, "Lauren, I think we should talk about insurance, now! You never know what might happen tomorrow."

Throwing back the covers, Lauren sat up in bed and said peevishly, "Oh, Jack, you're spoiling my mood. Can't you wait until the weekend to discuss this?"

Exasperated, Jack insisted, "Not really! I have a lot of studying to catch up on, and I'll be spending a lot of time in the library. We should take care of it right away."

Lauren jumped out of bed, stomped over to her desk, and jerked open her desk drawer and shouted, "Well! You already know that I have an insurance policy." She threw the policy on the bed and said, "You see who the beneficiaries are! My parents! When I first started practicing, the hospital offered a deal I couldn't turn down. My folks have been wonderful to me, and I want to leave them something if I should die first. No doubt you're wondering why I haven't changed the beneficiary to you. To be honest, I wanted to give our marriage a year to see if it was going to work. I also wanted to start a family and include the baby in the policy. If everything worked out, you would be the first beneficiary, then the baby, and last, my parents."

Jack got out of bed and walked around to Lauren and put his arms around her and said tentatively, "$500,000, that's a lot of money." He hesitated for a moment and said with a wry grin, "O.K. You're right. We'll talk about it later. Let's start all over again."

Displeased with Jack's concern over insurance Lauren crawled into bed and said, " All that talk about insurance has gotten me out of the mood." Lauren lay awake and wondered about Jack's sudden concern in insurance and beneficiaries.

The next morning Jack walked over to Lauren as she was making up the bed, kissed her on the cheek, and said, "Don't worry about supper tonight. If you can, try to be home by six o'clock."

Her eyes widened as she said, "What's going on?"

"I can't tell you. You just be here on time." He checked the clock. "Wow! I've got to run. See ya' tonight."

Lauren stood looking bewildered as she watched Jack rush out the door. She muttered, "Life with Jack is full of surprises. I'll probably never understand him." The clock over the mantel chimed. "Oh, my goodness!" She muttered. "I'll be late for work if I don't hurry." On her way out the door, she grabbed her white jacket and drove to the hospital still wondering what Jack had in store for her tonight.

CHAPTER 17

It was Tuesday morning. It was also the second week in September, and the weather had changed over night. A light frost covered the ground. The leaves had already begun to change from green to an array of autumn colors, but Jack wasn't thinking about the change in the weather. All he wanted was to get to the administration building and find the person who had caused him so much trouble. He slammed his foot down on the accelerator as the tires on his Bronco squealed out of the apartment parking lot. He parked three blocks from the administration building. As he walked briskly along the sidewalk to the building, he thought about what he would say to that 'old bag' who was his advisor. She would be sorry for her negligence when he got through giving her a piece of his mind. Damn her, he thought, she'd better give him an excuse. When he got to the building, he entered it and moved rapidly through the halls looking for the advisor's office. Her office door was open. He poked his head inside and expected to see his advisor sitting behind her desk. The last time he saw her was when he had registered for school. She had motley gray hair pulled back in a bun, a pointed nose, and eyes that squinted through black rim glasses. She wasn't there. He was frustrated. Time was essential. He had to have an excuse in a half-hour. Just as he turned to leave, he saw a young lady coming through a side door with her arms loaded down with books. Her head was full of curly blonde hair framing her cherub-like face. Her large brown eyes and full red lips were almost too much for such a small face. What attracted Jack the most was her black knit dress that fell over her well-proportioned body like a magnet.

She didn't see Jack standing in the door and almost dropped the books. In a southern drawl she exclaimed, "Oh, you nearly scared me to death! I didn't expect to see anyone in here." Quickly she walked around to the back of the desk and said, "Just a minute, Suh. Let me put these books down." The single strand of pearls and oversized black-rimmed glasses helped make her look like a secretary in an administrative office, but Jack wasn't convinced that she was all business. What a difference in this advisor and that other old crow, he thought. After she had stacked the books like she wanted, she cocked her head to one side, batted her long eyelashes and asked, "Now, what can I do for you, Suh?"

Jack stared at her lips when she spoke to him. He faltered for a moment but with a broad smile managed to respond soberly, "I'm Jack Harper. I talked to someone over the telephone last week. An excuse was supposed to be sent to my professors telling them I would be away on my honeymoon. When I went to class yesterday, none of the professors had received my excuse. I'm in deep trouble if I can't prove to them I'm telling the truth."

Words as sweet as honey came out of her mouth, "I'm Candice Rodgers. I'm Mrs. Blackburn's receptionist. She's gone out of town for the day." Candice scrambled around to the back of the desk and sifted through some papers. With a nervous titter she said, "Oh, Lordy! I've been so busy, I may have thrown it away." She continued to flip papers from one side of the desk to the other and finally she slapped her hand on the exact spot where apparently the message had been. She let out a squeal, "Well, what do you know, here it is. It was lying right here next to the telephone." Candice fluttered her eyelashes again at Jack as she got up from the desk and sashayed, with an exaggerated movement of her hips, over to the filing cabinet. Looking over her shoulder, she said, "Most people call me, Candy." Jack followed her every move. With a girlish laugh, she walked back to the desk. "Why, Suh, I think I can give you an excuse right now and solve your problem." She handed him the excuse making sure her fingers touched his.

Jack caught her hand and said, "I really appreciate this. My professors gave me hell for not having it yesterday." He looked deep into her eyes and asked, "What can I do to repay you for your kindness?"

With a tilt of her head and a coy smile, Candy said, "You could take me out for a drink or lunch sometime."

"You bet I will! I'd like to do it right now, but I have plans that I can't break today. What about lunch tomorrow?"

"Oh-h-h, Mister Harper that would be scrumptious. Pick me up about twelvish," Candy purred.

Jack let go of her hand and said, "I've got to run. My classes start in fifteen minutes. I'll see you tomorrow. Thanks again." He dashed out of the office. Jack could hardly contain his jubilation over meeting Candy. What a lucky break. He had found a *sugar babe*. He was going to have some fun with this one. He wished he could see her tonight, but he had already made plans.

After class he'd go to the insurance office and get another beneficiary form for Lauren to sign. Then he'd run by the delicatessen and pick up something for a very special meal: marinated shrimp, pasta salad, fresh baked rolls, bottle of wine, and cheesecake for dessert. To add the finishing touches, he would buy flowers and candles for the table.

It was five o'clock. In one hour, Lauren would be home. Jack threw a blue floral tablecloth on the table, put the flowers in a vase, and put candles on each side of the bouquet. He set the table with their best china and crystal goblets. Proud of his accomplishment, Jack stood back a few feet and admired the table, but there was one thing missing—music. He skittered across the room to the CD player and selected an album by Barbara Striesand. The new beneficiary form was conveniently placed in easy reach when he needed it. He took a quick shower and splashed cologne on his face. There was just enough time to slip into his silk robe and a pair of back velvet scuffs when he heard the door open. Jack bounded out of the bathroom like a broken spring. He wanted to see the surprised look on her face when she saw the spread he had prepared for her.

When Lauren opened the front door, she stood aghast when she saw the table set with their wedding china, candles, flowers, and her favorite music playing. Her mouth dropped open as she walked slowly around the room. She was speechless. Soon her voice came back, and she cried, "Jack, what's going on? I can't believe my eyes. The table's beautiful."

"Hi, sweetheart," he called cheerfully. As he sauntered over to her, he put his arm around her shoulder and led her to the bedroom. "Here, let me help you undress and slip into something comfortable." He began to take off her jacket.

"Whoa, Jack! Let me catch my breath. I can't believe the change in you and what you've done tonight." She twirled out of his arms and stepped to one side and said in a tremulous voice, "I-I-ah-ah, I need to take a shower. I smell like the hospital. I'll make it quick." Before he could argue with her, she made her way to the bathroom and closed the door.

Jack called out, "When you're through, put on your sexiest trousseau gown. I want this to be an evening you'll never forget."

"Okay," she yelled back. Then she mumbled under her breath, "I can't believe the way he's acting. It's wonderful." She stood side ways and looked at her stomach. She muttered, "It's beginning to pouch a little. He might notice and start asking questions. I don't want anything to spoil this night." She made sure her makeup and hair looked perfect.

Then she slipped on a lacy peach-colored gown that wasn't extremely sheer and put on a matching robe to help conceal her figure. Quietly she eased open the bedroom door to see what he was doing.

At first, he didn't know that Lauren was looking at him, but as he turned around he saw her. "Lauren," he crooned, "You look beautiful but why the tears?"

"Darling, I'm so overwhelmed I can't help myself. Let me help you."

"My dear, you're my guest tonight. I have it all under control. Here, let me escort you to your seat." He took her by the elbow, led her to her chair, and pulled it out for her. Before he sat down, he flipped a towel across his arm, popped the cork out of the wine bottle, and said, "Madame, would you like to taste this wine?"

Lauren laughed and said, "Jack, you act just like the waiter on the cruise ship." Jack chuckled, "I thought you'd recognize the impersonation." He poured the wine, sat down, raised his glass, and said, "Before we begin to eat this delicious meal, I would like to propose a toast. Here's to my beautiful bride. I hope that we'll have a long and happy life together!"

Tears trickled down her cheeks again as she raised her glass and said, "Here's to you, darling, I'll always love you, and I'll try to make you very happy."

"Now—let's eat. Smelling the aroma of those rolls whetted my appetite. I'm starved. It's been a long day." Jack made it a point to keep Lauren's glass filled with wine. She told him to stop several times, but he kept her laughing with funny stories that happened while he was in the Army. After they finished their meal, Jack could tell Lauren was feeling the effects of the wine. She staggered slightly as she moved around the table helping Jack clear the dishes. He ran over to her and said, "Honey, you sit right here and I'll clean up." He finished as quickly as he could because she might fall asleep. Jack sat down, put his arm around her, nuzzled his lips close to her ear, and whispered, "Lauren, do you remember when we talked about changing your insurance beneficiary? Well, I picked up a new form today, and now that we're married, don't you think it's time for you to change it over to me?"

Lauren's voice was thick and slurred. "Oh, Jack, let's not talk about insurance tonight. We can do that later."

He was close to losing his patience. All his work would go up in smoke if he didn't get her to sign the form now. Mustering up his patience, Jack spoke in a solicitous way, "Honey, life is so unpredictable." He pushed the form in front of her. In a cajoling manner, Jack said, "Hell Lauren, if you love me, just sign the form, and then we can make love."

Feeling the effects of the wine, she started jabbering, "Baby, baby, come here and let me 'wove' you," Lauren giggled. "Give me that paper! I'll sign it right now. I want to make love with my sweetie-pie." She signed her name with a flourish.

The next morning Jack slipped out of bed without waking Lauren. He dressed quietly and left the apartment for school.

When the 6:30 a.m. alarm sounded, Lauren groaned as she reached over to the bedside table and reluctantly turned off the clock. She sat up but flopped back down on the pillows.

"Oh my," she wailed. "My head is killing me. I drank too much wine last night. I knew I shouldn't drink so much, but I was afraid I'd hurt Jack's feelings." She struggled to sit up again and when she did, she held her head in her hands for several minutes until the throbbing subsided. After a few minutes she got up, splashed water on her face, and went to the kitchen. When she finished eating, Lauren was amazed at how much better she felt. Tonight, she'd tell Jack again how much she enjoyed their wonderful evening. Right now she had to go to work. Just as she pulled into her parking space, Camille drove up beside her.

"Good morning, Lauren. Wait for me." Camille called as she got out of her car.

They walked toward the hospital emergency entrance at a fast pace. "By the way," Lauren said excitedly, "If we can have lunch together, I want to tell you what Jack did for me last night."

"Oh, Lauren, it'll have to wait. I've got a meeting that will probably last all day."

Lauren looked disappointed, because she wanted to share her happiness with her best friend.

CHAPTER 18

The morning after Jack got Lauren to sign a new form, he went by the insurance agency and gave the manager the form with the changed beneficiary. He checked his watch. "H-m-m-m, he murmured, "I don't have a class until two o'clock. Good, I'll have time to arrange a lunch date with Candy." He went to her office and saw her through the glass door. He tapped on the window.

Candy looked up and waved for him to come in. Today she was dressed more like the students on campus: a red mini skirt, black clogs, and a red and white-striped knit shirt. Every inch of her figure was revealed in detail. The Georgia accent was exaggerated as she cooed, "Hi, handsome! You're early for lunch."

"I hoped that you might be able to get off a little early."

She held up one finger and said, "Wait just a minute. I'll see if I can get another student to cover for me while I'm gone." Candy left the office and came back giggling, "I didn't really think you'd take me out for lunch since you're married."

"I told you I was indebted to you for getting me an excuse. I would have failed my classes without your help. I hope you don't mind me taking you to a place that's quiet? It's a few miles out of town, off the beaten path. I'd like for you to tell me all about yourself without any interruptions." When they got to the parking lot, Jack enjoyed seeing how her mini skirt skimmed above her thighs as she climbed up into his Bronco.

After riding for fifteen minutes, Candy asked, "Where in the world are you taking me? I've never been out this way before, and I thought I knew all the cool places in Boston."

Jack turned down a narrow street and said, "Pretty little lady, here we are. I told you I wanted a secluded place to talk."

"You weren't kidding." They got out and entered a quaint Italian villa. Murals of famous places in Italy were painted on stucco walls. Baskets of flowers and ivy hung from everywhere in the large room. An Italian gentleman, dressed in costume, entertained the customers with his violin as he walked from table to table. Jack asked the headwaiter for a private booth. They were escorted to one with a curtain. They slid into the booth as the waiter handed them a menu.

Jack glanced at it and said, "Candy, why don't I make it simple? Since we don't have a lot of time, I'll order a medium pizza, salad, and two beers. Is that okay with you?" When the waiter left, Jack closed the curtain.

Candy looked wistfully up into his eyes and said, "I like this. It's so cozy and private.

No one would ever know that we were even here." She leaned over and pressed her breasts against his arm and said, "I hope you don't mind if I sit close to you?"

Glibly Jack said, "Well, you know that I'm married, and you're probably wondering why I'm flirting with you. It isn't often that I reveal my feelings to just anyone but you're special. To be honest, I married out of necessity. I needed someone to support me through school. In order to get a benefactor, I had to marry her. When I graduate, I plan to divorce her. That should tell you how devoted I am. Now tell me something about your life."

Candy gushed, "Dahlin, you want to know something about me? You may be in for a real surprise. I was born in Georgia and my folks made lots of money raising cotton and tobacco. They gave me everything I wanted but the freedom to do as I pleased. Mama and Papa treated me like a fish. Every time I got out of their sight, they'd reel me in. I felt like a prisoner most of my life. I'm very bright, made straight A's all through school. I convinced them that I wanted to better myself by going to a prestigious school, like Harvard University. I really don't have to work in an office. I just like meeting people. Just think, if I hadn't been working, I'd never met you. I'm making up for lost time since I couldn't be wild in high school. My parents wouldn't let me date unless I had a chaperone. Now…I'm free as a bird. I make my own rules." Candy took a deep breath and said, "I've talked enough."

He had just leaned over to kiss her when he heard the waiter standing outside the curtain say, "Sir, I have your order."

Jack threw open the curtains and said sharply, "Thanks. Just put it down. Don't bother us unless we ring." He smiled at Candy and said, "I'll finish what I started after we've eaten." He waved a slice of pizza under Candy's nose. "H-m-m, just take a whiff of this." The aroma of hot crust, melted cheese, garlic, and pepperoni filled the air. " I hope it tastes as good as it smells." Jack turned to Candy and said, "I hope you don't mind being kissed with garlic on my breath, but I would like to finish what I was about to do when the food arrived."

With an innocent look, Candy purred, "Why by all means, Hon, finish what you started. We both ate garlic. We'll just mix it together."

Candy wriggled into Jack's arms as he slid his tongue between her parted lips. He pressed hard against hers, which made her passion rise like mercury in a thermometer. One of his hands slipped under her sweater and caressed her firm breasts. Then he felt her hand on his thigh. After a few minutes of heavy breathing and fondling, Jack said, "Damn, woman, you don't waste any time."

"I told you I'm making up for lost time," she said as she tidied her makeup and hair.

"Sweetie, any time you want to exercise your freedom, let

me know. What you did was fantastic." Jack checked his watch and exclaimed, "I've got to go! My classes start in thirty minutes." On their way back to the University, he asked, "May I take you out again?"

"Why sure, Shugah. Call me any time. I have my own apartment." She scribbled her phone number and address on a piece of paper and said, "Here's your passport to paradise."

"Babe, you're going to make going to school a pleasure. You'll be seeing a lot of me." Jack let Candy out a block from the administrative building. He waved goodbye and went to his classes.

CHAPTER 19

The front door opened and she heard Jack whistling as he came into the living room.

"What makes you so happy?" Lauren asked.

He walked toward her and put his arm around her waist and said, "I'm happy because it makes a big difference when the professors accepted my excuse."

"I'm glad you got that problem straightened out. I'll start supper and maybe we can talk about making some plans to go out this week. We haven't been to a show or anything in a long time." Lauren wanted to tell him about some of the incidences that occurred at the hospital. But Jack had already made it clear that he didn't want to hear about her patients. It left little for them to talk about. The only thing they had in common was eating and going to bed.

"I'm afraid I won't have time to do anything in the next few weeks. I've got a lot of work to catch up after school. I'll make it up to you later."

* * * * *

The next morning as Jack got ready for school, he said pleasantly, "I might be late coming home tonight. I have to go to the library for some research. I'll grab a sandwich somewhere. Don't wait supper for me." He threw her a kiss and walked out the door.

Another surprise, Lauren thought, that's the first time he's ever thrown me a kiss. Maybe it won't be too long before I can tell him that I'm pregnant. She couldn't keep it from him much longer. As soon as she got to her office, she called Camille, "Good morning! Can you meet me at lunch?"

"Okay! I'm anxious to hear what's gotten you so excited. The smile on your face yesterday was brighter than the sun. If you get to the cafeteria before I do, find a quiet place."

Lauren took her lunch early and waited in a remote corner of the cafeteria. When she saw Camille, she waved to her. Camille hurriedly got her lunch so she could hear Lauren's fantastic news. Nearly out of breath, when she got to the table she said, "Okay, okay, start talking. We don't have much time. You're probably going to keep me in suspense as long as possible."

Lauren put her hand to her mouth to keep from laughing at Camille. "You won't believe it when I tell you how Jack has treated me lately. Since you were busy yesterday, I couldn't tell you how Jack surprised me two nights ago." Lauren went into detail about the lovely table, gourmet food, romantic music, and how he amused her with funny stories all through the meal.

Stunned, Camille's big brown eyes opened wide as she asked, "Lauren, is this the same guy you're married to?"

"Can you believe it? At first I couldn't believe it either." Some of Lauren's enthusiasm wavered as she continued with her story. "I drank a lot of wine, and I don't remember everything that happened. I vaguely remember him insisting that I sign an insurance paper. I have no idea what it was, but whatever it was he was happy." Lauren paused and said, "Camille, why is that look of apprehension written all over your face?"

"I don't understand why Jack wanted to talk about insurance when he was having a romantic evening with you. That doesn't make sense to me."

"I don't know…I was having such a wonderful time…he could have said anything, and I would have thought it was marvelous."

Camille placed her hand on Lauren's and said, "My friend, I've been down the same road you're on, and it's easy to be fooled into thinking that he really cares. To me, it looks like you're heading for more trouble. I'm sorry to burst your bubble. Please don't let love blind you."

With a nervous twitter Lauren said, "Oh, Camille, you worry too much. I'll be all right. Thanks for caring and being such a good friend." Lauren didn't want to hear any more derogatory remarks about Jack, so she jumped up from the table and excused herself.

It was five o'clock in the afternoon. Time to go home. There wasn't any hurry to get there because Jack said that he would be late. Lauren strolled leisurely out of the hospital rather than in her usual hurried pace. Upon arriving at the apartment, she micro waved a dinner, and then took a nice hot bath. Feeling refreshed, she crawled into bed and read for a while. It was ten o'clock and Jack still hadn't come home.

The next morning, Jack dressed to go to school. He chuckled, "Doc, when I came to bed last night you were really snoring. I figured you were tired so I didn't wake you."

Groggily, Lauren asked, "What time did you get in?"

Jack shoved his hands in his pockets. "I should've called. I met up with some buddies, and we went out for a beer."

Lauren sat up in bed and said, "I'm glad you have some friends. You've never mentioned that you had any at school. Why don't you invite them over to watch football or play poker? I wouldn't care."

Without responding, Jack leaned over the bed, and gave her a peck on the cheek. As he started out the door he said, "By the way, I'll probably be late again. Since I went out with the boys, I didn't finish my research. I'll see you later."

For the next two weeks Jack came home late nearly every other night. There was an advantage to his lateness for Lauren; he rarely saw her undressed as she was always in bed by the time he got home. He had even stopped complaining about the way she kept the house. She never questioned him again about being late.

It was the second week in October and the signs of fall were still everywhere. The sun sank below the muted colors of orange and violet clouds. The dusk of the evening filtered through barren trees without their mantle of leaves. Lauren wrapped herself warmly in a quilted, jacket, but she still shivered unexpectedly as she walked to her car. A feeling of apprehension crept over her as she drove home. She hadn't given it much thought, but now —she began to wonder why things at home had become so pleasant. She didn't know whether to cook supper for him or not. It was beginning to feel like she was single again. "Darn it," she muttered, "I'll let him fend for himself." She'd treat herself to a quick snack and take a leisure shower. A glance in the mirror, on the bathroom door, made her realize she couldn't put off telling Jack about her pregnancy.

Jack had gone to his five o'clock class only to find out that it was canceled. As he drove home, he thought about Candy. He'd like to be with her, but she was still at work. When he entered the apartment, he heard the water running. Tiptoeing to the bathroom, he heard Lauren humming a child's lullaby. Through the fogged glass shower door, he faintly saw her silhouette. Slowly he opened it, reached in, and turned off the water. Lauren couldn't see who it was because of the steam, so she backed into the corner of the shower and started to scream. Desperately, she tried to cover her body with her arms. Jack threw the door open. The steam dissipated quickly, and he saw her figure glistening with water and her hair hanging in wet strands. His muscles tightened and his eyes widened like an owl's. He saw that her breasts were larger and her stomach fuller. Bursting into a rage he shouted, "What in the hell is going on? You look like you're pregnant!"

"I...I...told you I thought I might be when we were on the cruise," Lauren stammered as she moved away from him.

"You led me to believe you were only seasick! I don't want

a baby! I told you that! You will have an abortion!"

Lauren got as far away from him as she could. Her voice quivered as she cried, "I was hoping, in time, you'd feel differently. I want a baby more than anything in the world."

His face contorted into a hideous expression as he yelled and shook his fist at her. "I don't want a wife with a bulging belly that looks like a watermelon. I'm tired of your sniveling!" He thrust his arm into the shower. Lauren pushed his hand away. He reached in again. Lauren slipped out of his grasp. Jack stepped inside again and grabbed a handful of her wet hair and jerked her out. She broke loose and made a dash toward the bedroom. Catching her by the arm, he swung her around, slapped her again and again. With his fist, he punched her in the stomach shouting, "If you won't get rid of this baby, I will!" Lauren slipped and collapsed on the floor. She curled into a fetal position to protect her baby. She lay still sobbing. Jack looked disgustingly at her. With one more act of anger, Jack kicked her in her side and stomped out of the bathroom, slammed the door, and left the apartment.

After Jack left, Lauren struggled to get up on her hands and knees and to crawl to the bedroom. She locked the door and managed to pull herself up by the bedpost to climb into bed. After she covered herself with blankets, she still couldn't stop shaking. In her business, she had seen pregnant women in the emergency room after husbands had beaten them. It was hard to believe that it had happened to her. She thought, she'd take her own advice to them and stay in bed and rest. It was easier said than done. She wondered what she would do if he came back and hit her again? She had to find some way to protect herself. After resting for twenty minutes, she found the strength to get up. She took a pair of scissors out of her bedside table and put them under her pillow. Lauren stumbled back to bed and looked up at the ceiling and thought—how can one night be so fabulous and the next one be a nightmare? She was wrong for not telling Jack that she was pregnant, but she also knew he would have forced her to have an abortion. Lauren tried not to fall asleep, but exhaustion took its toll.

In the meantime, Jack drove around the city until he found an all night bar. A neon sign blinked on and off, advertising Joe's Bar and Grill. As he stepped inside, red lights glowed in random corners of the room camouflaging the dirt and grime on the tables and floor. It was 2:00 a.m. when he finally left the bar. Still fuming over Lauren's pregnancy, he arrived at the apartment, searched in his pocket for the house key, and opened the door. Without turning on the light, he fumbled around the living room until he found the couch. Immediately, Jack stretched out on it, flipped on the television, and stared at a late show until it went off the air. He made no attempt to see Lauren.

* * * * *

The next morning, Lauren felt extremely sore. Somehow she had to get to the hospital. Lauren staggered to the bathroom, started to step into the shower, but it was a bitter reminder of Jack's brutality. The tub would be better. The warm water inched up over her body. Bruises in a kaleidoscope of colors of purple and blue covered her legs, arms, and stomach. Lauren soaked in the water until she felt some of the soreness ease up. It was a struggle for her to get out, but she was determined to dress in a pair of black wool slacks, a thick red knit sweater, and her winter coat. Slowly she hobbled over to the bedroom door and opened it just enough to see if the coast was clear. She hadn't heard Jack come in that night and was surprised to see him asleep on the couch. Grateful that he was snoring, she left the apartment without his knowing it. Every movement of her body made her want to cry out in pain. It could be a matter of life or death to her baby if she didn't get out of the house now before he hit her again. The rain and a bone chilling wind made her pull her coat closer to her body. Painfully she got into her car and drove to the hospital.

Lauren parked and made her way to Camille's office. When she walked in, Camille shouted, "My God, Lauren! What has happened to you? Have you been in an accident?" Lauren pulled some kleenex out of a box on Camille's desk and dabbed her eyes. She told Camille how Jack had hit her hoping to cause a miscarriage. Lauren trembled and cried uncontrollably. Camille rushed over to Lauren and held her in her arms. She asked, " Why didn't you call me or the hospital to come and get you?"

Still shaking, Lauren uttered, "I didn't want anyone at the hospital to know that I was pregnant, at least, not right now. I just didn't want to bother you."

Camille patted Lauren on her shoulder and said, "I'm sending you to Dr. Carolyn Koss. Since she's a gynecologist whom you know, maybe you'll feel more comfortable seeing her."

In a few minutes, Lauren heard the gurney rumble down the hall. Before she knew it, the orderlies had her stretched out on it and headed for an examination room. She hoped this nightmare would all go away.

Dr. Koss, a tall attractive brunette, was waiting for her. With a big smile, she greeted Lauren, "Hello, Dr. Harper. Dr. Bloomfield informed me of your condition." Lauren felt better as Dr. Koss joked with her about putting on the grey unattractive gown. Lauren stared up at the ceiling for a few minutes. In a low voice she said, "Dr. Koss, please keep this confidential. I'd rather the staff didn't know about my condition. It'll be easy to hide my pregnancy under my jacket for awhile."

The doctor said, "You have my word. I ordinarily have a nurse to assist me, but I'll handle everything myself." When she had completed the preparation for the exam, she slipped on her gloves and proceeded. When the examination was over, Dr. Koss walked around to the end of the table and patted Lauren's arm and said, "So far as I can tell, you're going to be all right. I've seen women fall down a flight of stairs and never lose their baby, but sometimes they're not so lucky. I want you to work only a half a day for a few weeks and rest in bed as much as possible. If you have any bleeding or any other symptoms, let me know." She gave Lauren some medicine to relieve her pain.

Lauren thanked her for her service and confidentiality. She looked at her watch. 11:30. Jack's in school...now it should be safe to go back home. As Lauren was ready to leave, she called her supervisor, and told her that she had fallen down some steps. The supervisor understood and said she would work out a part-time schedule.

Before Lauren left the hospital, she stopped by Camille's office to tell her she was going home. When she opened the door she said, "Camille, I don't feel well and the doctor told me I should go home. It's important to me I get there before Jack. If you don't mind, call me at 9:00 o'clock tonight just to be sure I'm okay? If I don't answer, call 911."

"Lauren, why don't you come and stay with me?"

"Don't worry. I'm going to lock the bedroom door. Don't forget to call." Lauren walked away before Camille could say anything else.

When Lauren entered their apartment, newspapers lay scattered on the floor. She thought it would be a cold day in hell before she cleaned up. She took some food and bottled water to her bedroom to keep from coming out of her room when Jack was there. To make sure that the door was secured, she pushed a chair under the doorknob. With her warmest gown on and her medication on the bedside table, she went to bed. For several hours she tried to read to take her mind off Jack. When that didn't work, she took some of her medication and finally dropped off to sleep.

Promptly at nine o'clock that night the phone awakened Lauren. Camille asked softly, "Lauren, are you all right?"

"Hello, Camille, I'm okay," Lauren said sleepily. "I have the door secured. Jack hasn't come home but that isn't unusual. He's been coming home late for the past few weeks. He says he's been studying at the library. I really don't believe him, but I'd rather not argue. He may be afraid to come home after what he did to me. Anyway Camille, I don't know what I would do without you. Thanks for calling."

CHAPTER 20

The classroom bell rang loudly, wrenching Jack from his thoughts of what he had done to Lauren. Damn, he thought, he'd really played the fool now. She might report it to the police or even kick him out of the house. He could have just lost his meal ticket and money to finish school. Jack picked up his books and walked toward the parking lot. Maybe she's gone to the hospital since she wasn't home when he left for school this morning. How in the world did she leave without his seeing her? Maybe she had a miscarriage. At least, that's what he hoped had happened.

Five o'clock. Lauren should be home. If she isn't there, I'll call and find out if she has been admitted to the hospital. He dreaded seeing her. When he pulled into the parking lot, he spied her car. Once inside the apartment, he saw that the bedroom door was closed. There was everything to gain if he acted sorry and played the part of a loving husband. He walked toward the door and knocked softly and said apologetically, "Lauren, I'm sorry for what I did to you." Silence. It infuriated him when she didn't answer. Next, he became even angrier when he turned the doorknob and found it locked. He raised his fist ready to pound on it, but stopped in midair and thought, he'd never get her confidence back if he hurt her again. Taking a deep breath he said affectionately, "Honey, can I get you something?"

Lauren responded angrily, "No! I don't want anything. Leave me alone!"

Jack grimaced. She rarely rebuked him. He was losing control. With clinched fists and a hurt ego, he sulked the rest of the night. "Damn!" he muttered, "My strategy isn't working." For the next two weeks, Jack felt like he had been put in solitary confinement. Lauren went about her daily routine just as though he didn't exist. He slept in the guest bedroom, cooked his own meals, washed his own clothes, and picked up papers and magazines he had thrown on the floor. Sex with Lauren had been scarce but now it was never. Patience wasn't his best virtue. It was time to pay Candy a visit. It had been two weeks since he last saw her. A female companion might make his misery easier.

The next day he stood outside the glass door of the office and stared at Candy while she worked. Involved in her work, she didn't notice him. Finally, Jack opened the door and said, "Hello, beautiful. I believe I've seen you in my dreams."

Candy's head jerked up. "Lordy me! I thought you had vanished off the face of the earth." She blinked her eyes and fluttered her eyelashes and drawled a sexy, "M-y-y-y, it's good to see your handsome face again."

Jack leaned over the desk, "I'm hungry. Would you like to have supper with me?"

"I've a better idea, Shugh. How would you like to go to my apartment? I can throw something together real quick."

"Sounds good to me. When can you leave?"

"I can go now. It's nearly quittin' time. Come on, honey, we'll ride in my little car." Candy grabbed her long black winter coat and closed the office door.

They walked a few blocks until they came to a sporty, bright red Miata. Jack exclaimed, "My God, Candy, how does a poor working girl like you afford a car like this?"

"I thought I told you. I don't have to work. My sweet daddy gave this to me when I graduated from high school." Candy caressed the fender lovingly and said, "I hope it will last through Harvard."

As soon as Jack settled into the passenger side, Candy

started the car, pushed her foot down on the accelerator, and zoomed out of the parking space. Jack held on to the sides of the seat. "Are you practicing to be a race car driver? This car will never see three more years with your driving in the fast lane. You're gonna' end up wrapped around a tree."

"Why, honey, I just love to drive fast. It gives me a thrill and, besides, I want to hurry up and get where I'm going."

Candy pulled up in front of her apartment. It was very similar to the one that he and Lauren lived in. Instantly she jumped out of the car, dashed up to the front door, and motioned for Jack to follow. When he walked in, he was astonished at the way it was furnished. "Wow, you must have paid a fortune for this spread." Almost all her furniture was made of Lucite. Six geometrically designed chairs with thick cushions filled the room. Jack strolled around until he came to a soft white brocade couch and flopped down on it. He thought, one day he'd have the best of everything.

Candy stood by the fireplace and asked, "Do you like it? I did it myself."

"You decorated it? It's great! Fantastic!"

"I told you my folks didn't care how much I spent as long as I studied and made good grades." Candy watched Jack's eyes as he examined every detail. After a few minutes she said, "I've got an idea. Look at a book or something while I put on something comfortable."

It wasn't long before he heard a tapping. He looked up and saw Candy framed inside the bedroom door. The light from the bedroom shone through the black lace negligee. It didn't take long for Jack to get the message. He sprang to his feet and scooped her up in his arms and dropped her on the bed. After an hour of steamy love making, Jack slowly got up and said, "Well, Babe, it's late. I'd better get dressed and go home."

Candy purred, "Jackie boy, aren't you going to let me feed you? I do have other talents."

"Thanks anyway. I'll grab something on the way home."

"Don't you want me to take you to your car?"

"Oh, yeah, I forgot. You can make a man forget everything." Candy put a heavy coat over her naked body and took Jack back to his car. "Will it be okay if I come to see you again?"

"Honey, you can come as often as you like. I'll be right here waiting for you."

CHAPTER 21

Winter had set in and Jack's disposition matched the weather, which seemed to be perpetually gray. When he looked at Lauren, in her fifth month, getting fatter and fatter, it disgusted him. He watched her go through her chores like a zombie and hibernate in her room night after night. When, he thought, would she ever get over her anger?

About a month after he'd hit Lauren, he lost interest in his studies, and even having sex with Candy became irrelevant. One day as he sat down on the couch to sort the junk mail from overdue bills, he saw a letter that had been forwarded to him from his parents' home. There wasn't a return address. When he opened it, to his astonishment, it was from Lisa Mitchell. My God, he thought, it's been more than three years since he had seen her. That was when they both resigned from North Bridge. Before he read the letter, he had a flashback remembering how he had met Lisa.

* * * *

In the last two years of his tour of duty at Fort Bragg, Jack had been in charge of hundreds of soldiers. The day that he arrived at North Bridge, five years later, was an easy transition for him. He already had experience leading soldiers, so stepping into the position of being an instructor was easy.

Two years later he was still an instructor at North Bridge.

He wanted to be a Captain; after all he had four years as a cadet, five as a soldier, and now two years as an instructor. Jack remembered how he hated Colonel Hoffner. He disliked him immensely, not only because he had the job he wanted, but also because his physical appearance wasn't military. He was short and portly with a few gray hairs stuck out of his bald, globe-like head. Piercing steel blue eyes peered through a pair of wire-rim glasses.

The officer in charge of the Education Department called him to pick up class information at Office C rather than Office B. He went immediately to Office C and was about to raise his hand to knock, when he saw a female cadet standing at a filing cabinet. He scanned her figure from the back of her short auburn hair all the way down to her shapely legs. The cadet whirled around and saw him looking at her. He opened the door and asked if this was the office where he was supposed to get the new books? With a business-like manner, she said it was. They chatted for a few minutes as she gathered all the books and reports he needed.

He signed the acquisition form, and then he asked what her name was? She responded, "Cadet Lisa Mitchell."

On the way back to the office, he couldn't get her out of his mind. He made it a point to see her more often. It had been a long time since a woman had aroused his sexual desire. He wanted to make love to her but he knew if they were caught, it would be disastrous. One day as he was on his way to see Lisa, he passed by the Colonel's office. When the Colonel saw him, his look could have scorched the feathers off a chicken. He knew that the Colonel disliked him as far back as his cadet days. The Colonel wanted him kicked out of the academy, and all he needed was to catch him doing something against the rules.

When he got to Lisa's office, he told her of a plan for them to get together. He gave her detailed information about how they could rendezvous in the laundry room. Jack remembered how clever he was to obtain a key to the door. He also remembered how cold Lisa was when she took off her clothes in that cold and damp room.

After a month or two, their sex had become monotonous, and he wanted to do something different. Jack thought about how much he liked skiing and decided that he would plan a way to slip away from the academy and go skiing. With every detailed worked out, he and Lisa went to a cabin in the mountains where he used to go skiing. At the time, he didn't know the Colonel was suspicious of their being together. One day, the Colonel and Lisa collided in the hall. That's when a note fell out of her pocketbook and the Colonel saw Jack's name on it.

All cadets and staff members had to sign in and out on a designated register: stating time and place. The Colonel checked the register and learned exactly where to find them.

Jack thought about the good time they had while at the cabin; the Chippendale dance he did for Lisa and the fun it was having sex in a feather bed. The fun ended when there was a knock on the cabin door.

At the time, he didn't know it was the Colonel, because he disguised his voice. The Colonel said he had been trying to dodge a snowdrift, and had run off the road. Now he was stuck and would like to use their phone to call for help. When the Colonel came in, he took pictures. That was all he needed to court-martial both of us.

When the Colonel left, Jack was so angry that he took his frustration out on Lisa. He knocked her down on the floor and was ready to hit her in the stomach. She yelled for him to stop because she was pregnant with his child. From that moment on, he knew his career was over at North Bridge Academy. The only thing left for them to do was to resign rather than face a court-martial.

* * * * *

Jack stared at the letter for a few minutes to let some of the old hatred for the Colonel dissipate and the disgrace he brought upon himself be forgotten.

Now that he had calmed down, he read the letter with a great deal of interest. Stunned at the contents, he read it again word for word.

> Dear Jack,
>
> I'm sure you're surprised to be getting a letter from me. I've been thinking about you lately and wondered what you were doing these days. A lot has happened to me since I last saw you.
>
> I came back to my hometown and found a good job similar to the one I had at North Bridge. There was one rule that was different from the Academy. It wasn't against the rules to fraternize with the employees (you know what I mean, ha, ha). The man I worked for courted me. We fell in love, and within a few months we were married.
>
> Do you remember when we went skiing at Forest Hills Ski Resort? I had planned to tell you something very important but Colonel Hoffner came on the scene. Your hatred for him frightened me. I was afraid to tell you my secret. In your rage, you were about to hit me again and that's when I told you that I was pregnant. On the way back to the Academy, we both decided to resign from the Academy. Your son is a very handsome boy and is almost three years old now. He has red hair, the color of mine, and your good looks. His name is Travis Harper Cannon. Unfortunately, my husband was killed in an automobile wreck three months ago. I miss him very much. He knew Travis wasn't his son, but he loved him as much as if he were his very own.

In his will, he left me everything. I have a large estate, and I will never have to worry about money again. If you have time, I would like to hear from you just for old time's sake. If you're not married, maybe we could meet at a mutual place and have dinner together. It would be fun to talk about our days at North Bridge. I still hold a very special place in my heart for you. With love, Lisa

P.S. My address is Mrs. Lisa Mitchell Cannon—210 Lakeside Road—Lake George, New York
Phone: 201-398-4571

He jumped up from the couch and paced the floor, hitting his fist in his hand. He had to come up with a scheme to visit Lisa without Lauren knowing about it. His thoughts moved quickly as he tried to figure all the angles. All of a sudden he yelled out loud, "Hell fire! I'm between a rock and a hard place." He had a child he'd never seen and an unborn baby he didn't want. He couldn't delay his scheme any longer. Immediately, he went to the kitchen and started washing the dishes and whistling while he worked. He knew Lauren would be coming home soon, and he was going to surprise her by cooking supper. Just as he planned, Lauren came walking through the door and stood transfixed at seeing Jack in such a happy mood. With his best smile said, "Hi, Doc, I'll have supper ready in a jiffy. You sit down and relax. I'll call you when it's ready."

Lauren said nothing, but walked cautiously across the opposite side of the room. Then she went into the bedroom and locked the door. Jack heard the click. Uh, oh, he thought, he'd scared the hell out of her. Some clever maneuvering was necessary to convince her that he wouldn't hurt her any more. Maybe sweet-talking to her will work. He pressed his face against the door and said, "Honey, supper's ready. I know you have reservations about coming out. I promise I won't hurt you. I'm sorry for what I did. Please give me another chance to prove to you that I've changed. I don't know if you have a gun, but if you do, bring it out with you for your protection if you're afraid. Please Lauren, let's start over."

Lauren opened the door enough to see Jack standing in the kitchen. "Jack," she called cautiously, "I will report you to the police if you ever hurt me again."

"I wouldn't blame you, Doc. Come on out and let's eat supper before it gets cold." When she came out, Jack pretended to be a waiter with a towel draped across his arm while holding a bottle of wine. "Will you have a glass of wine, Mrs. Harper?"

Lauren was quiet. Jack panicked. What am I going to do now? An idea hit him. "Honey, after I clean up the dishes, would you like to watch a movie with me?"

Stoically she put the fork beside her plate, looked Jack straight in the eyes, and said with indignation, "Perhaps, but first, I want to ask you a question. Why did you beat me?"

Shocked at Lauren being so blunt about his abuse, he struggled for an answer. It was unusual for Lauren to be in control. He rose from his chair, ambled around the table to collect his thought, and stood behind her. He saw her hand go into her robe pocket and clutch something. Gingerly he placed his hands on her shoulders, bent down, and kissed her softly on her neck. But with trepidation in his voice said, "Doc, I was shocked when I saw your body getting larger. I went berserk. You had a beautiful body. I'm sorry. I promise you, I won't hurt you again, and I'll be a better husband from now on."

Lauren listened. Finally she looked up at him, "Jack, I know it was hard for you to apologize and I appreciate your effort. I need some space from you. I suppose you remember Ann Goodman, the doctor we met on the cruise. She said if I ever needed to get away for a weekend to come to see her. I'm going to call her tomorrow and see if the invitation still stands."

Jack couldn't believe his ears. What a break, he thought, now he could go see Lisa. He hid his elation the best he could and said sympathetically, "Honey, I'm sorry you're gonna' leave just when I thought we might be starting over. However, I can understand your apprehension."

"Well, maybe when I'm away for awhile, I'll feel like trusting you again," Lauren said without any emotion.

"Honey, I'll wait for you until you're ready. Would you like to watch a movie with me, now?"

"I don't think so. I've got a lot to do tomorrow and I'm tired." Lauren got up from the table, went to her bedroom, and locked the door.

CHAPTER 22

The next morning, Lauren was still confused over Jack's adulation and his apology. That was the last thing she believed he would do. She still loved him in spite of his violent temper, but she couldn't take a chance on his hurting her or the baby. Lauren lay in bed and thought maybe Ann Goodman could advise her on how she should handle her problem. With that in mind, she couldn't wait to get to work and to call her. She threw back the covers, slipped out of bed, and dressed. She didn't have much choice of cloths since she was close to being five months pregnant. Her basic wardrobe consisted mostly of a black skirt, different colored over-blouses, and her white jacket.

When she walked out of the bedroom, Jack said, "Good morning, sleepy head. I thought you were going to sleep the day away."

Bewildered again by Jack's change in his usual petulant personality, she kept her distance. Standing behind the kitchen table she said, "This is certainly a surprise. You were so quite. I didn't hear you stirring around."

The atmosphere was strained. Jack spoke first, "Doc, are you still going to call Ann?"

"Yes, I'm going to wait until I get to the office. She's probably not up this early."

"I'll clean up this mess and let you go on to work."

"I must be dreaming," Lauren laughed. "I can't believe

the change in you. I plan to enjoy this dream as long as possible."

Without sounding to eager, Jack said, "Do you have any idea when you might go see her?"

"Well, since this is Friday and if it's all right with her, I'd like to go tomorrow morning."

"While you're at work, I'll come by the hospital, get your car and have it checked over to be sure it's safe for you to drive."

"Why Jack, that's so thoughtful. I'd appreciate that very much."

As soon as Lauren left, Jack dressed, slid Lisa's letter into his pocket, and hurriedly left the apartment, allowing time to make his call before his first class. Absolute privacy was important when he called Lisa. His hands shook, but not from the cold, and then suddenly he heard the sound of Lisa's familiar voice, "Hello…hello…who is this, please?"

She was about to hang up when Jack cried, "Wait! Don't hang up. This is Jack."

"Jack! Jack Harper. What a surprise!"

"Lisa, I couldn't believe it when I received your wonderful letter."

"I'm glad you got it. I wasn't sure if you were still living with your parents."

"In your letter you asked me if we could get together. I have some free time this weekend. Would it be possible for us to see each other?"

"Of course, that would be wonderful! I'm anxious for you to meet your son. Where are you living?"

"Boston."

"I've got an idea. Tell me the name of the nearest airport and I'll send my company plane to pick you up. Then I'll meet you and drive you to my house."

"Wow, that sounds great. There's a small community-owned airport called Boston Airlines. I'll be there tomorrow morning at nine o'clock, but I'll have to be back home Sunday afternoon. I hope that won't be an inconvenience for you."

"Oh, no! We'll make the best of what time we have together. See you tomorrow morning."

"Okay. Goodbye! When Jack hung up, he could hardly contain himself. All he wanted to do was shout to the top of his voice. I've hit it rich! Just imagine her very own plane. Now it would be up to Ann Goodman to say it's okay for Lauren to visit her. What a mess he'd be in if she doesn't go tomorrow. But, that bridge can be crossed later. Right now he had a class, and after that Lauren's car had to be serviced.

* * * * *

Lauren went straight to her office and called Ann. "Hello, Ann, this is a voice from your past."

"I'd know your voice any time Lauren, my dear. Where in the world are you? I've been thinking about you for the last several days and wondering how you were getting along."

"I'm here in Boston, and I've been doing okay. I have a favor to ask. Would it be possible for me to visit you this weekend?"

"Why, of course. It's a perfect time for you to come. I'm between lectures, and I would love to have you. You won't believe it, but Rita called me last night and said she would like to come down, too. It will be wonderful for the three of us to be together again."

Lauren laughed. "Our minds must be in tune with each other. I was thinking about Rita a few days ago. It won't be long before my traveling days will be limited since I'm in my fifth month. I'll leave tomorrow morning about seven o'clock, and I should get to your house in about three hours. It'll be great to see you and Rita. Goodbye."

The last patient walked out of Lauren's office, and she left to go home. Once inside the apartment, she automatically picked up the mail that had been pushed through the mail drop. Tossing it in a basket on a small table next to the door, she went to the bedroom to slip into pajamas and a robe. Everyday she wondered what kind of mood Jack might be in when he came home. She was determined not to let her guard down in case he turned on her.

It wasn't long before she heard, "Doc, I'm home."

She stuck her head out of the bedroom door and called back, "I'll be out in a minute." She brushed her hair and checked her makeup.

By the way, did you have a good day?"

"I called Ann and she was delighted that I wanted to come. She told me that Rita would be there, too. I'll be leaving early tomorrow morning."

"Rita," Jack exclaimed. "Why is she going?"

"She must have wanted to get away, too. I'll be glad to see her."

"You gals will really have a lot to talk about. While you're gone, I'll concentrate on my research papers. By the way, what time will you be leaving?"

"I hope to leave around seven in the morning. That should put me at her house by ten. I'm really looking forward to this trip."

"Your car is in tip-top condition, and you shouldn't have any trouble."

"Thanks for taking care of it and thanks for the supper. I think I'll go pack since I have to get up so early." Before Lauren finished packing, she thought she'd better call Camille and tell her where she was going this weekend.

After a few rings, Camille answered, "Hello."

"Hi, Camille. You sound a little sleepy. I hope that I didn't wake you. I thought I had better call and let you know that I decided, at the last minute, to go visit Dr. Goodman in Falmouth. I'll be back Sunday afternoon."

"That sounds like a very good idea, Lauren. I'm glad

you told me because I would worry if I called and you didn't answer. Please be careful. If you run into any trouble, call me."

"When I get back, I'll tell you about some of the nice things Jack has been doing for me. He really has changed, but I'm still apprehensive."

"You're right about not trusting him. Just keep a watchful eye on him. Have a good trip and I'll see you Monday morning."

The alarm woke Lauren. She rolled over and smacked it. "Oh, my," she grumbled, "I feel like I've just gone to bed. I'm still sleepy." The shower revived her. A silk over blouse in a leopard print and black slacks were slenderizing. She wanted to look fashionable when she saw Ann. There was something missing. A gold chain and gold loop earrings were just the right accents to complete her outfit.

Jack was asleep on the couch, but just as she picked up her bag to leave, he woke up. "Here, let me help you with that bag. You shouldn't be lifting anything that heavy."

Lauren rolled down the window and said, "Good-bye. I'll be back home Sunday afternoon."

Jack put his head inside and kissed her on the lips. With affection he said, "Be careful, Doc. Don't push yourself too hard. Tell Ann and Rita hello for me."

Without any more delay, she drove away. She thought, Jack's thoughtfulness and attention was having an affect on her. Now, what was she going to do?

When Lauren was out of sight, Jack gave a high sign and yelled, "She's gone, and I'm going!" He ran back into the apartment, grabbed his bag out of the closet, and packed the new clothes he had bought with the money his mother had given him for his wedding.

* * * * *

Lauren enjoyed the scenery as she sped down Highway

93. All thoughts of Jack and what had happened in the last month were pushed out of her mind. Surprisingly, memories of her early school years surfaced. When she was a little girl, about eight years old, her dream was to be a ballet dancer. Rather than having fun with her friends, she spent many hours practicing. She had become quite an accomplished ballerina. Whatever she wanted to do, her parents always encouraged her to be the best.

Feeling tired, she stopped at a rest stop, which was about halfway to Ann's house. After another fifty minutes, a Falmouth city limit sign came into view. She was on time when she parked in Ann's driveway. Her house was a lovely Cape Cod style, built beside the Nantucket Sound. Lauren imagined how lovely it must look in the summer with flowers planted along the white picket fence. A welcome sign wasn't necessary; its appearance said it all. A cold blustery wind came off the sound. It made Lauren shiver as she got out of the car. She rang the bell and when Ann opened it, she immediately embraced Lauren and cried, "Lauren, my dear, you look beautiful! Pregnancy becomes you. I know you must be freezing. The wind feels like it's coming off an iceberg. Come, we'll go stand by the fire in the den."

"I'll be there in a minute. I'd better get my bags."

"Don't worry about that. My housekeeper will get them for you. Here, let me have your coat. Tell me how was your trip down here?"

"The trip was easy. I enjoyed getting out of the city and seeing the open spaces. I felt like I had been let out of a cage. Being cooped up in the hospital all day, one forgets what the outside world is all about. You'll never know how much seeing you means to me."

"The same goes for me, too. It was meant to be for us to meet, whether it was on the cruise or otherwise. While you thaw out, I'll go tell my housekeeper to get your bags."

Lauren backed up close to the fire and looked around the

room. The brown cobblestone fireplace extended all the way through the ceiling. Picture windows surrounded the fireplace, offering a view overlooking the sound. In one corner of the room was a handsome lady's desk cluttered with papers. A leather couch with a matching wingback chair sat nearby. Many framed pictures, most likely of family members and friends, had been placed wherever there was a space for them.

When Ann came back, Lauren spread her arms out as if enveloping the room and said, "I just love your home."

"Oh, thank you Lauren. It's a mess right now. I told my housekeeper not to tidy this room. If she did, I'd never find anything. Come with me. Let's have a cup of coffee in the sunroom while we wait for Rita."

Before Ann could serve the coffee, they heard a car drive up. She rushed to the door and there stood Rita. Ann welcomed her and they returned to the sunroom chattering like birds in a nest. Soon it was a three-way conversation. Ann laughed and said, "Time out. Let's take turns. Rita, you go first. I'll pour the coffee while we catch up on our past and present."

"Okay," Rita said, "Since the last time I saw you ladies, my law practice has been doing very well. I'm getting married next spring. I'll send you an invitation when I get all the plans finalized. I've enjoyed my single life, but now I'm ready to settle down." Rita laughed, "I could spend an hour talking about him but it's your turn, Lauren."

"Obviously you can tell what's going on with me by looking at my body. When I feel my baby move, it's the most exciting thing I've ever experienced. When I told my parents about the baby, you could have heard them all the way from Williamsburg. They even want to move to Boston to help take care of it."

"When did motherhood start? What does Jack think about it?" Rita asked with interest.

"Well, that's another story. I thought I was pregnant

when we were in Key West. I was afraid to tell anyone because I didn't know for sure. As for Jack, we see each other briefly in the morning and at night. Other than that, he spends a lot of time at the University library working on his research. That's about it. My life isn't very exciting." Lauren pointed a finger at Ann and said, "It's your turn."

"I have semi-retired and brought my practice home. It's good not to have to rush off in the morning and drive fifty miles to work. Sometime ago, I would have had you ladies make an appointment to see me, but here you are on the spur of the moment. That is one of the pleasures I'm beginning to enjoy. This afternoon after you have rested from your trip, we can go shopping, or I can show you some of the tourist spots. Take your pick."

Rita spoke up, "I don't know how you feel, Lauren, but I would love to see some of the historical sights."

Lauren laughed and quipped, "It isn't much fun for me to shop with this figure. I think we're fortunate to have our own personal guide to show us around this quaint old town."

"Great!" Ann said, "It sounds like the vote's in ladies. After we have lunch and rest for a little, we'll go tour!"

Ann amused them by imitating a tour guide's speech. She showed them the home of the Congregational Church where Paul Revere cast the first bell to hang in the church. They moved on to the Historical Society Museum Complex, enjoyed looking at many famous artifacts, and especially enjoyed seeing where Katherine Lee Bates wrote "America the Beautiful." After they finished touring the museum, Ann said as they stepped outside, "Would you like to take a ferry ride over to Martha's Vineyard? It's a cold and bumpy ride this time of the year, but I'm game if you are."

Lauren spoke up, "If you two want to go, I'll wait for you; but I'm afraid I might get motion sickness."

Rita said, "Ann, let's take a rain check on that trip and save it for the summer."

"Good idea. That will give you a good excuse to come back to see me."

Lauren spoke up and said, "I'd like to walk down to the water's edge. It's cold but the moon shinning off the water is beautiful."

Rita responded immediately, "If you want company, I'll go but I'm ready to sit by the fire."

"You go right ahead, Lauren," Ann said. " Rita and I will wait for you in the den."

While Lauren was gone, Rita said to Ann as they sat by the fire, "You probably have an idea that things aren't well with Lauren's marriage. Jack isn't to be trusted. He doesn't love her, and I'm afraid she's headed for some serious pitfalls with him. I wanted to warn her while we were on the cruise, but I didn't want to cause any trouble. Maybe she will open up to you. I'll leave early in the morning so that you can have time to talk to her without me around. I would like to stay longer, but she needs you now."

"Yes, you're right. He doesn't want a child, and I'm afraid of what he might do to her."When Lauren came back to the house, Rita, Lauren, and Ann talked for another hour.

The next morning, Rita joined Ann and Lauren in the breakfast room. Lauren said, "You surprised me, I thought you weren't an early riser."

"I've been on the phone for an hour. I'm working on a case and my partner called to tell me that we have a problem that has to be taken care of immediately. I'll drink a cup of coffee with you ladies, and then I'll scat."

Lauren said, "I'm really sorry you have to leave early. There's a lot more we have to talk about"

Rita finished her coffee, put her arms around Ann, and thanked her for your friendship and hospitality. "I hope we all can continue this friendship forever. If I can ever do anything for either of you, let me know. Don't get up, I've already put my bags in the car." Rita reached in her purse and gave Ann and Lauren her business card, waved goodbye, and walked out of the house.

"Now," Ann said as she turned and looked at Lauren, "Let's get that worried look off your pretty face."

Lauren sat her cup down, and the words tumbled out of her mouth. She went into detail about how abusive Jack had been to her, not only verbally but also physically. "Then Lauren said, "I don't understand why all of a sudden he becomes affectionate and even acts glad I'm pregnant. I'm confused by his actions. Last month he prepared a lovely meal, made funny jokes, and then pushed a form in my hand to sign, making him the beneficiary of my life insurance policy. Ever since that night, he's been very solicitous but doesn't make love to me. Other than not having any sex, he's been good." Lauren sighed with a confused look on her face and said, "Ann, I can't help loving him. I keep praying that when the baby is born, he'll love it. What should I do?"

Ann sat quietly thinking about the things Lauren had told her. Finally, she leaned forward and held Lauren's hand. "It's difficult to give you advice without talking with Jack, too. I know that will be impossible. However, I did observe him on the cruise. Probably all hell would break loose if you asked him to seek help. He has to want it before it will do any good. I don't have a clue about his background, but from similar cases that I have handled, he has all the signs of having been abused either by his father or his mother. Jack's parents probably put a lot of pressure on him to be perfect. He's carrying his upbringing over into his life with you. Has he ever talked to you about his mother or father?"

"Whenever he mentions his father, he becomes very angry. But I'm pretty sure he loves his mother very much."

"I would like to recommend a doctor in Boston to help you. I can be your friend, but not your therapist. In the meantime, keep a watchful eye on Jack and be careful what you say and how you say it. Jack's a perfectionist, and things have to go his way. When you say that he doesn't want to have sex with you, a case comes to my mind. This may not fit in with you, but this man loved his mother so much, that he didn't want to have sex with his wife because she reminded him so much of his mother."

After listening to Ann's advice, Lauren said, "I know you're probably right. I wish I could wave a magic wand and our life could have a happy ending." Tears filled her eyes and her voice broke. "If things don't work out, I guess I'll have to divorce him." Ann got up and hugged Lauren. "Dear, when someone loves a person like you do, it's hard to see his faults until it's too late. No human being is perfect. When you return home, please promise me that you'll keep in touch."

Lauren looked at her watch. "Oh my! It's twelve o'clock. I had better get on the road. I don't want to be driving after dark, and I told Jack I would be home around three."

Ann walked Lauren to her car and said, "Please be careful. Jack is unpredictable and may be dangerous. Don't let your love for him interfere with good judgment. I think I know what makes Jack tick but without further information about him, I might be making the wrong evaluation. Write down the things that you have just told me about Jack's behavior. Sometimes writing about your concerns makes you see things more clearly."

"I'll try to follow your advice. Again, thank you for caring," Lauren said, as she waved goodbye and drove away.

CHAPTER 23

Ten o'clock Saturday morning. The tan jet with Cannon Industries painted along the sides in black letters edged in red was parked in front of a hangar. As he stepped out of his Bronco, a blast of cold November wind swept down the runway and hit Jack in the face like millions of tiny needles. He tightened his leather coat collar around his neck, grabbed his bag, and dashed to the waiting plane. The pilot, dressed in a black company uniform, pulled down the steps and waited for him to enter. Jack took a step forward, and the pilot asked him for some identification. A driver's license convinced him that the passenger was okay.

It was like living in a dream. Never in his wildest imagination would he have believed that Lisa would ever have this much money. He was impressed by the luxurious interior of the plane. Every possible comfort feature had been installed. His mind clicked like a computer. There had to be a way that he could have all this luxury —only if he wasn't married to Lauren.

He tried to form a mental image of Lisa. Surely, he thought, she hadn't changed a lot in three years unless having a baby had changed things. He remembered that her hair was short and auburn, her eyes were the color of huckleberries, and she had a fabulous figure. It would be awesome if she was still as beautiful as she was at North Bridge and—wealthy, too!

There was a slight bump as the plane hit the runway and

taxied toward the large company hangar. Ordinarily, Jack could handle the unexpected, but this was extremely different. As cold as it was, the palms of his hands were damp. His heart raced with wild anticipation. Jack hurried down the steps and looked around for Lisa. Off in the distance, a woman stood in front of the hangar door. The woman started toward him and waved. There was something different about her. Her hair was still auburn but it was shoulder length now. As she drew closer, her face looked young and vibrant. She pulled her full mink coat closer to her body as the cold air whipped around her.

When Lisa reached Jack, she put her hand on his arm, leaned close to his face, and said, "Hello, Lieutenant, I'm glad you could come. It's been a long time. You're as handsome as ever," she purred, "Maybe even more so."

"Lisa! My God! I didn't think you could be prettier than you were at North Bridge but you're gorgeous."

"Oh, Jack, you're going to make me blush." She took him by the hand and said, "Come on, let's get out of this cold air. I hope you haven't made plans to stay at a motel?"

"I had planned to find something after I got here."

"You can stop planning. You'll stay at my home. I have plenty of room." She stopped beside a white Eldorado Cadillac with red leather interior and said, with a lilting laugh, "Climb into my carriage handsome prince, and I will take you to my castle." Lisa drove for fifteen minutes until she arrived at an exclusive neighborhood with a gated entrance. The security guard waved her through, and Jack noticed the houses were more like estates. She slowed down and turned into a driveway lined with trees.

Jack tried to hide his amazement when he saw her palatial estate and said in a joking way, "I might be able to spend the night in this little shack." Her house reminded him of a French chateau he had seen in *Architectural Digest*: steep slate roofs, detailed molding beneath the eaves, arched windows, bits of random mortar jutting out between old Salem bricks, and ivy that wound its way across trellised doorways. Jack teased, "I bet you mow your own lawn."

She laughed as she drove up to the front door, "Don't think that I couldn't if I had to. I've got all the right equipment. Well, anyway, this is where I hang my hat. Get your bag, and we'll go in and have a drink. The gardener will take care of the car."

Jack tried to act nonchalant and to pretend he was accustomed to such luxury. But, he wasn't prepared for the inside of an extraordinarily beautiful home. Marble floors, marble columns, a huge winding stairway graced the entrance. A mixture of exquisite French provincial and traditional furnishings was found throughout the house. Jack's mind was working overtime. He knew for sure that he would do everything in his power to live in this house.

"Come with me. I'll give you a tour and then we'll have a drink."

As Jack followed her, he overcame his pride and admitted, "Your house is absolutely magnificent. Your husband must have worked hard to afford this luxury. What kind of business was he in?"

Lisa's eyes misted over. "During his early years, he tinkered with computers. One of his ideas was patented, and it made him a millionaire. He worked hard, but he always made time to be with Travis and me. He showed his love for us every day, and we miss him very much." Lisa walked into the den toward an elegantly carved mahogany bar that was complete with every kind of liquor a person would want. To cover up her sadness she laughed and said, "Whoa! It's time to be happy. Let's have a drink and celebrate two friends reuniting. What would you like to drink?"

"A whiskey sour would be fine."

"Okay. I'll have a glass of wine."

When she handed him his glass, Jack lifted it and said, "I would like to propose a toast to the most beautiful woman in the world. Here's to a new beginning between two good friends." Their glasses clinked and their eyes met.

Lisa quickly looked away and replied, "I'll toast to that. I have someone I want you to meet. I'll be right back. Make yourself at home." She hurriedly left the room.

Jack roamed around the den admiring its masculinity. This, he thought, is the ultimate way to live and by damn he was going to have it. There were pictures of a little boy, who must be Travis. Other pictures were of Lisa and her husband. Seeing those pictures made him realize that he had to tell her that he was married. How was he going to let her know about Lauren? His thoughts were interrupted when he heard the sound of someone running into the room. A little boy with a head full of red curls, wearing tennis shoes, green pants, and a turtle neck sweater ran straight to Jack and jerked on his pants and said, "Hey, I'm Travis."

Jack bent down and took his hand and said, "Hello Travis."

At that moment, Lisa strolled into the room and called, "There you are! I've been looking everywhere for you." She glanced at Jack. "I see you two have already met. Lisa sat down in a chair and pulled Travis up into her lap. She stroked his hair and kissed him on the cheek and remarked, "He's a smart little boy." Lisa caught Jack staring at Travis.

"It's amazing. Mother has pictures of me at that age. Except for the red hair, we look exactly alike."

"I'll tell you more about him later. It's time for lunch. Two o'clock is his nap time." Lisa got up from her chair and motioned for Jack to come with them. She led him to the sunroom overlooking a lawn that sloped hundreds of feet to the water's edge. The room was so cheerful with a profusion of indoor plants that it made one forget that it was winter. The maid served lunch on a black, wrought iron table that had an arrangement of orchids in the center. Lisa put Travis next to Jack.

Searching for something he could say to Travis, he asked, "How old are you?"

Holding up three fingers, he counted, "One, two, three," and squealed with delight.

Jack tried again. "What games do you like to play?" It was hard for him to get his thinking down to a child's level. He was completely lost to know how much a child could communicate with an adult.

Between trying to talk to Travis and eating his lunch, he was glad when Lisa interrupted and said, "Come on, 'punkin,' it's time for your nap." She called the maid to take him and whispered in her ear, "I want privacy with Jack, so don't let anyone interrupt this weekend."

Jack winked at Lisa and said, "You got a big kick out of me trying to talk with Travis, didn't you?"

"I sure did. It was the first time I've ever seen you squirm. Who knows, you might learn how to understand him before the weekend is over."

"I can talk to famous people and any high official with the greatest of ease, but talking to a child is really a challenge for me. But I like the idea of being challenged by Travis."

"Well, you're already a father. What do you plan to do about it?"

Jack was caught off guard. The timing wasn't right to tell her about Lauren. He got up from his chair and walked over to Lisa and said, "Let's go back to the den." He wanted to stall for time and the right moment to break the news to her.

As soon as Lisa closed the door, he took her in his arms and held her tightly against his chest and whispered in her ear, "Lisa, I've been wanting to kiss you from the moment I saw you at the airport." She wrapped her arms around his neck and turned her face up to his. Jack couldn't hold back his desire and kissed her hard and sensually. Instinctively, her hands slipped around to his back and pressed him closer. Their hearts pounded against each other. Slowly he unbuttoned her blouse.

Lisa's breathing became erratic but without warning she pushed Jack away. "Oh Jack, as much as I would like for you to make love to me, I need time to get to know you again."

"Don't tell me you've forgotten what we meant to each other at the academy?"

"No, I haven't forgotten, but there is someone else that I have to think about and that is Travis. Try to be patient with me."

Jack's ego was totally deflated. He withdrew his arms and ambled back to the bar thinking how he could keep from showing his disappointment. Light heartedly he said, "Let's at least have another drink to our reunion. What would you like?"

"That's a good idea. I'd like another glass of wine." While he poured the drinks, Lisa said, "Jack, you seem to be a little edgy. Is there something wrong?"

"Not necessarily. It's taking me awhile to get over the shock of seeing you and Travis." He took the wine to Lisa. He returned to the bar and braced himself against it. Taking a deep breath he finally said, "Lisa, I have something to tell you. Please hear me out before you get angry."

She focused on his face and said, "My goodness, you sound serious."

Jack groped for words. "I thought I would hear from you after we left North Bridge. Since you didn't write, I assumed you never wanted to see me again. I entered Harvard Law School over two years ago." He paused for a moment to gather his thoughts because what he was about to say could ruin his dream of living with Lisa. He continued, "I was having a struggle to pay my way. The army's supplement helped, but it wasn't enough. One day, I was in a café and met Lauren Fulghum. I was studying to be a lawyer, and she was already a successful doctor of pediatrics. After we had dated for about two months, she insisted that I move in with her." Jack could see Lisa's mood change. Jack pleaded, "Please don't get upset until I have finished telling you everything."

Lisa threw her hands up and cried out, "I think I know what you are going to tell me. Damn it! You're married!"

"Lisa, wait! Hear me out!" He waited for her to calm down. "Yes, we did get married, and she promised to support me until I graduated. We've been married for about four months. I'm miserable living with her, and I'm going to get a divorce. When I saw you at the airport, I realized that I've always loved you." Jack paused again. He could see that Lisa's anger was subsiding. It was now or never to put up a strong defense. " You are every thing I ever wanted."

"My God, Jack, that's awful. How will you stay in school?"

" I'll get a job and work out a schedule for night classes. I'm determined to get my law degree. I just can't go on living with someone that I don't love."

"You certainly have surprised me. I had hoped we were going to pick up where we left off. But it looks like you are already tied up in a marriage knot."

"Lisa, didn't you hear what I said? I'm going to get a divorce. Then I'll be able to be with you and Travis. I want to be his father. I want to make up for all the hurt I've caused you. I'll do anything to be a good husband and father. Please give me a chance."

Slowly Lisa stood up, walked toward the window, and stared out for a few minutes. She turned around and said, "Well, maybe you can give me a second chance."

Shocked, Jack asked, "What do you mean?"

"I suppose I was partly to blame for our being caught in the cabin. I didn't tell my mother what to say, if anyone called, to cover for my being gone that weekend. I never dreamed that Colonel Hoffner suspected that we were going off together. I'm sure now that he must have read the note that fell out of my bag when I ran into him in the hall."

With a sigh of relief, Jack thought, he would seize this opportunity and use it for all it was worth. He walked briskly over to her and put his hands on her shoulders and said, "Let's compromise. Let's call it a draw. Why don't we make a new start and do it right this time?"

Before Lisa could respond, there was a knock on the den door. The maid opened the door and said, "I'm sorry to interrupt, but Travis was very insistent to see the man named Jack."

No sooner were the words spoken, when Travis ran in and grabbed Jack by the leg and begged, "Play with me."

Perfect timing, Jack thought. Then with a hearty laugh said, "Okay, big boy, let's play." He knelt down on the floor and pretended to be a horse and let Travis climb up on his back. He could see, out of the corner of his eye, Lisa loved seeing the two of them play. As they played, he knew that the key to Lisa's heart was through Travis.

After awhile, Lisa called time out, "Hey, you fellows, how about some cookies and milk?"

Travis took Jack's hand and led him to the kitchen. Jack said, "Okay, big boy, when we finish our cookies and milk, can we go outside and play?"

Lisa was exuberant, "That's a great idea. I'll take pictures with my camcorder and the Polaroid camera. I'll have something to remember you by after you leave." The three of them, with their dog Burnie, went outside. The wind coming off the lake was chilling to the bone, but Lisa had made sure that Travis had on plenty of warm clothes. In fact, he was so bundled up he waddled like a duck. Lisa taped and photographed them in everything: romping on the ground, swinging Travis around like an airplane, and kicking a ball to each other. Lisa put the Polaroid on the self-timer mode and posed with Jack and Travis. They played for a while longer until it started to get dark. Lisa gave a time-out signal. "Okay, boys, it's time to go in. We'll have a picnic inside by the fireplace!"

"Yeah-h-h!" screamed Travis. The maid had already prepared the food for the picnic: hot dogs, buns, chips, drinks, and cookies.

After they finished their picnic, Lisa said "Punkin, it's time for you to go to bed."

"Mommie, can Jack do it?"

"Is it okay?" Jack asked.

With a big smile she nodded and said, "Sure. Go on, Daddy, put your son to bed." Travis held Jack's finger as he led him up to his room. There was hardly any place to walk as his room was flooded with all kind of toys. Jack thought back to his childhood. He was lucky to have one toy and that had to be related to the army. Shaking that memory away Jack said, "Okay son, hop into bed and I'll tuck you in."

Travis said, "Okay. Good night. Can we play again tomorrow?"

"If your Mom says it's okay." Jack bent down and kissed him on the forehead.

Back in the den, Lisa greeted him with a big smile. "Well, Dad, how did it go?"

"I've never seen so many toys. He's a very lucky child. It didn't take long for him to fall asleep."

"Speaking of sleep," Lisa said, "I'm exhausted. I don't want you to take this wrong, but if you don't mind, I'll sleep alone. Since my husband died, Travis gets up in the middle of the night and crawls into bed with me. It might frighten him if he finds someone else there."

Jack was disappointed, but he definitely wasn't going to push his luck. "I understand. Show me where you want me to sleep." Lisa held Jack's hand and they climbed the winding marble stairway. At the top, she led him down a hallway that was covered with a thick Dresden blue carpet. She opened a door to a spacious room. It reflected the grandeur of the early Colonial period: elegant wood trim, a large fireplace and mantel with floor-to-ceiling windows overlooking the lake.

Lisa waited until Jack had surveyed the room. "Do you recognize anything familiar?"

It took a minute before he realized what she was talking about. "My God Lisa, the bed is exactly like the one at the cabin."

Lisa smiled, "It's as close to it as I could remember, even to the feather mattress."

Jack walked over to the bed and, with a big grin on his face, said, "You haven't forgotten."

"The decor is different from the cabin, but everything else is identical. Many times I've come up here and thought about you." Jack crossed over to Lisa, pulled her into the curve of his body, and whispered, "Lisa, it doesn't have to be a memory. We can have it all again, but even better. We have Travis." He brushed her face like a butterfly with his lips, kissing her until their lips met.

They clung together for a long time until Lisa gently pushed him away. "It's hard for me to leave you, but if I don't go now, my willpower will be gone." She turned around and vanished down the hallway.

Jack was awakened the next morning by a soft-spoken voice over the intercom system, "It's time for breakfast, Mr. Harper," and then he heard Lisa giggle. He looked at his watch and thought, damn, it was already ten o'clock. There wasn't much time left to be with her. He quickly dressed and hurried down to the sunroom where he was greeted by Travis and Lisa.

When Jack walked into the room, it was filled with sunlight shinning through the multi-faceted windowpanes. A rainbow of colors streamed across the plants and flowers.

"This is truly a beautiful sight. Where do you get flowers like this in the dead of winter?" Jack remarked.

"My gardener keeps me supplied from the greenhouse."

Lisa was about to say more, but Travis banged his spoon on the table and cried out, "Jack, we play today?"

"I'm afraid not, big boy. I'll be leaving soon."

Silence fell over the room. Lisa and Jack exchanged glances. Finally, she asked, "What time did you say you had to be home?"

Jack took Lisa's hand as he walked with her to the foyer and said, "It would be best if I got home before Lauren. She said to expect her by three o'clock this afternoon."

Lisa looked at him with a quizzical expression, "What do you mean, before your wife gets home? Doesn't she know you're gone?"

"Lauren drove to Falmouth to be with a friend for the weekend. If I had told her I was going off, too, she would have been furious and would have suspected something. My plan is to stay with her until the semester break. Then I'll look for a job and get my divorce."

Somberly, Lisa looked at Jack and said, "I don't want to be the reason for your divorce."

"Don't feel bad. I've already told you that I had planned to leave her before I read your letter."

Her eyes filled with tears as she said, "I don't want to be without you any more. I want to be with you again even though you aren't divorced. I know it isn't right, but I'll be miserable until I can see you again. I can fly in to see you, and we can meet at a motel for a few hours."

Jack smiled and said, "You've got a deal. I'll be in touch."

The grandfather clock chimed resonantly twelve times. Lisa said sadly, "Well, time has run out, and we have to part again. I'll call the airport and have the pilot get the plane ready."

Jack hugged Lisa and whispered in her ear, "Nothing will keep us apart this time, darling. I'll do everything I can to be with you as soon as possible. Jack dropped his arms from around Lisa and said, "Honey, before I leave, I would like to say good-bye to Travis." As quickly as he could, he went back to the breakfast room and told him good-bye. For a brief moment, Jack thought, it might not be so bad being a daddy. He might even miss Travis. When she drove up to the hangar, Lisa said, "It will be best if you kiss me good-bye here. You never can tell who might be looking. I don't want to do anything that will get in the way of your divorce."

Jack pulled Lisa close to him and said lovingly, "I'm going to miss you, sweetheart. You'll be in my thoughts every waking minute. I'll call as often as I can, although, my studies keep me very busy. It's my goal to be the best lawyer possible." He kissed Lisa passionately and hoped she would not forget him.

Before he got out of the car, she said, "Jack, take these five pictures of the three of us and this note. Keep them close to you heart. I'll make sure Travis sees pictures of you everyday, and I'll keep reminding him that you are his daddy. That way, by the time he sees you again, you won't be a stranger."

"Thanks, sweetheart. It will be a constant reminder of how lucky I am to have you and our son." He took the photos and put them in the inside pocket of his leather jacket. When he climbed into the plane, he sat next to the window where he could see Lisa sitting in her car. He thought, I can't believe my good fortune. I'll never have to worry about money again.

CHAPTER 24

The plane broke through the clouds and leveled out as it skimmed along the airwaves like an eagle in flight. Jack leaned back in his seat, took out the pictures of Lisa and Travis, and thought about his weekend. He was on the brink of having everything he wanted. "Except," he muttered as he looked at Travis's picture, "When I move into your house, young man, you'll do things my way. You will not sleep in our bed. You will go by my rules or feel the consequences." He pushed the picture down inside his leather pocket and checked to make sure they wouldn't fall out. Now it was imperative to make plans to get rid of Lauren. A fiendish expression spread across his face.

The plane touched down and came to a screeching stop not far from where his Bronco was parked. The pilot opened the door and let the steps down. As soon as he had done this, Jack made a dash for his Bronco. It was necessary to get home before Lauren.

Jack rushed into the apartment, slipped on a pair of jeans, and pulled on a fleece-lined sweatshirt. It wouldn't do if the house looked neat. After flipping on the television, scattering some books and newspapers around, he reclined on the couch.

* * * * *

The clock on the dashboard showed it was three o'clock when Lauren pulled into the parking lot. She got out and walked up to the door of the apartment. When she opened it, Jack sprang up from the couch and rushed over to greet her. "Doc," he said affectionately, "Here, let me take your bag. I didn't realize I would miss you so much. It seems like you have been gone for a month. What you said about, 'absence makes the heart grow fonder,' really worked for me. Come on, let's sit on the couch. I want to hear all about your trip."

Lauren followed him and said haltingly, "Well…hello, to you too. That was quite a warm welcome. I've never heard you talk so much." She glanced around the room, sat down, and asked skeptically, "What in the world has gotten into you? I've never seen you act like this before." She leaned over and gave Jack a quick kiss and said, "I can't believe you really want to know what we girls did, but if you do, here goes. First, Rita and Ann send their regards and wish you well on your research paper."

"That's a surprise. I didn't think they cared after the way I acted that last day in Key West. Anyway, I hope I'm successful, too. It's tedious work." Jack reached over and patted her hand, "Doc, let's not talk about me."

"Ann's home is very cozy and attractive. The view from her den windows is unbelievably beautiful. It overlooks Nantucket Sound." She went into detail about the tour of the historical places. Finally Lauren sighed and said, "I'm tired and I've talked enough about my trip."

"It sounds like you ladies had a good time. I found out I don't like coming home to an empty house and having to cook my meals. I realize now that you've spoiled me. I appreciate all the things you do for me." Jack took his hand, crossed his heart, raised it as if to swear before God and said, "I promise, I won't complain any more."

Lauren's mouth dropped open. She couldn't believe he was still giving her compliments. "Jack, you can't imagine how much I appreciate your telling me these things." She chuckled, "Maybe I should go off more often?"

"Just to show you how much I've changed, during my semester break, I'm going to start looking for a job to help out with the expenses. Please bear with me until I can get through the exams next month. By the way, I haven't looked through the mail. I just piled it up with the rest of the junk. If you want me to, I'll pop some TV dinners in the microwave while you look at it."

"Thanks, I am tired after that long trip." Lauren got up and crossed over to the mail basket, gathered it up, and returned to the couch. She separated the junk mail from the bills, picked up two catalogs, and was ready to toss them in the trashcan when a letter fell out from between them. It was addressed to Miss Lauren Fulghum forwarded from her parents' home. Her eyes opened wide when she saw that the name on the return address was David Williams. She was puzzled. Why would David be writing to her now? It's been four years since she'd last seen him.

Jack called from the kitchen, "Did we win the sweepstakes? I wish they'd save their postage and quit sending us those magazines entries."

"No, just the same old stuff we get everyday." Lauren stuck the letter in her pocket and decided she'd read it later.

"Come and get it!" Jack called from the kitchen. "It isn't the Tavern on the Green but Harper's Bar and Grill will have the honor of serving his 'lady love' a gourmet dinner right out of the microwave."

"My goodness, I didn't know you were a stand-up comedian." As she walked to the table, she thought, "Why had he kept this funny side hidden?" After they finished eating, Lauren got up and said, "I hate to break up this delightful home coming, but I have a heavy schedule tomorrow." Lauren went around the table, kissed him on the cheek, and thanked him for everything. Then she took a shower, put on her cotton nightgown, dashed herself with cologne, and went to bed. She thought that her night would be complete if they made love. She knew that wouldn't happen because he had slept in the guest room ever since he had found out she was pregnant.

Jack finished washing the dishes and put them away. After showering, he quietly tiptoed into her room, slid into bed, and put his hands across her breasts. When Lauren felt his hands, she screamed. Jack burst out laughing.

Lauren yelled, "What's so funny? You scared me half to death. I didn't expect you to get in bed with me."

"I'm sorry, Doc. I didn't mean to frighten you. I should have told you that I wanted to make love."

"Make Love! Are you kidding? I was wondering how long it would be before you wanted to try."

Jack tickled her breasts with the tips of his fingers. "You're really getting a big pair of knockers." Lauren smiled and waited, wondering what he would do next. His naked body sent shivers down her spine. Deftly, she removed her gown and cradled herself into his arms.

He pushed her gently over on her back and moved his hand down on her stomach, "Do you mind if I feel the baby? I've never wanted to do this before but I feel differently about it now." Before she could answer, Jack jerked his hand away and stammered, "W-w-what happened, Lauren? Something moved under my hand." Lauren began to cry. Jack asked, "What's wrong?"

"I'm not crying sad tears. Your actions have taken me by surprise. I can't control myself. I've never been happier in my life. I've prayed for the day that you would be happy that we were going to have a baby."

"Now I'm glad. I never thought I wanted to be a father, but you have changed my mind." Jack raised up on his side and said, "Doc, do you think it is all right if we make love?"

"Yeah, it's okay. The doctor said it would be all right for the next couple of months, but we should be careful." The next morning when Lauren awakened, she felt as though she could float out of bed. All her worries seemed to have disappeared. She slipped out of bed trying not to awaken Jack as she prepared to go to work.

Jack heard Lauren get up, but stayed in bed until she was through dressing. When he heard the click of the front door, he jumped out of bed, ran and caught her by the arm. "Doc, I love you. Last night was great." Jack leaned over and kissed her.

Lauren was spellbound. She couldn't get used to his new behavior. "You simply have amazed me by how you've changed."

Jack called to her as she walked to her car, "See ya' tonight, honey."

With a smile that went from ear to ear, she responded, "I love you, too." Lauren felt like she could fly to work. She was so happy!

On his way to school, Jack stopped by a public telephone and called the Forest Hills Ski Resort. When the manager answered, Jack said, "I would like to make reservations for the third weekend in December."

CHAPTER 25

Even if a blizzard had been raging outside, it would still have been an exceptionally beautiful day to Lauren. Nothing could mar her good mood as she jockeyed for the right lanes and ignored the rude horn blowers. On her drive to work, she checked to see if David's letter was still in her purse. Sometime during the day, she planned to read it. As she drove into the hospital parking lot, much to her delight, her new name had finally been painted on one of the slots, Dr. Lauren Harper.

Wow! Lauren thought, she couldn't believe so many good things happened this weekend. She still had a nagging feeling that things with Jack weren't as good as they seemed. The warning that Ann Goodman gave her still rang in her ears, 'Jack is unpredictable and dangerous'.

Lauren brushed the thought out of her mind. She was too happy to let anything spoil it now.

* * * * *

Camille was waiting for Lauren in her office and said in a jovial voice, "You look radiant Lauren. What did you do on your weekend to make you look so happy?"

Lauren spun around playfully in her chair and answered giddily, "I had a wonderful time with the ladies; but it wasn't what I did on the trip that has made me so happy. It was the way Jack treated me when I got home. He was fantastic! He called me all kinds of endearing names, hugged, and kissed me. And, the best news of all, he acted excited about the baby and we actually made love. You heard that, didn't you? We made love! There's a big difference between making love and having sex." Lauren got up from her chair, threw her head back, twirled around her office with arms outstretched, and said, "I'm so happy I'd like to sing and dance all over the hospital." She grabbed Camille's hands and said, "It's the first time my heart hasn't been laden with worry. I know now that happiness can mend a broken heart." Lauren finally calmed down and sat in her chair. She looked at the concern on Camille's face and asked, "You look so pensive. Are you afraid that Jack's actions are not sincere? Well, don't you worry anymore. You'd have to be there to see the change in him."

Camille got up from her chair and said, "Lauren, I hope he is sincere because he has a long way to go to repent for the way he has hurt you. I've got to get back to work. Do you want to meet for lunch?"

"Sure. I'll see you in the cafeteria at twelve o'clock." Lauren knew Camille well enough to know that she didn't believe Jack had changed. I suppose it's her right to believe what she wants to, but I live with him and I should know if he's sincere or not. A receptionist called Lauren on the phone and told her the 11:30 a.m. appointment was cancelled. Good, she thought, I'll read David's letter. When she opened it, old memories flooded her mind.

> Dearest Lauren,
>
> I'm sorry. This letter is long overdue. It's been four years since I last saw you at the airport. It was all I could do to keep from asking you to go with me. I should have written you immediately to tell you why I had to leave, but I thought it would have been unfair to ask you to wait until I could get

through my family problems. I wanted you to have the opportunity to follow your dreams without my being in your way.

Father was very ill, and there wasn't anyone else he could rely on to help run the business. Later, as it turned out, I was able to hire someone to work for me part-time while I finished my degree in family medicine. I had to attend night school and work my schedule around day classes. At last I can say, hooray! I have my diploma and have hung my shingle on a door in a quiet rural community.

You've often been in my thoughts, and I have wondered what our life would have been like had we married. I would like to know what you're doing and where you're working. If it's possible, I would like to pick up where we left off. I would like to make up for the stupidity on my part for not taking you with me. No one has ever been able to fill your place in my heart.

Please forgive me and give me a second chance, if you still care. I have a couple of wonderful ideas. The first one would be for you to become my wife. The second would be for you and me to work together in this pastoral community. We would make a great team.

Call this number 908-426-1234 as soon as possible. I want to hear from you.

With all my love, David

Lauren stared at the letter until the words blurred. Tears filled her eyes. She cried pitifully, "Damn you, David. It's too late." She wiped away the tears and thought how she would never leave Jack now, especially the way he had changed. Lauren folded the letter and put it back into her purse. She leaned back in her chair and wondered if she should call him to acknowledge the letter. Of course she would. They'd been good friends. She'd call him out of courtesy and curiosity. Lauren could hardly wait to tell Camille about the letter.

When Lauren came into the cafeteria, Camille had already eaten her lunch. "I'm sorry I had to eat before you got here. I have an appointment waiting for me in fifteen minutes," Then she took a real good look at Lauren and said, "What has happened to you since this morning? You were smiling all over the place and now you look like you've lost your best friend. Has Jack upset you again?"

"No-o-o," Lauren smiled. "I received a letter from David Williams. We were in medical school together, and we were also sweethearts four years ago. It's a long story, but I'll give you the short version. We were in love, but he broke it off unexpectedly. He has just written me a letter explaining the reason he left. Here...since you've already eaten, you read the letter, and then give me your advice as to what I should do?"

After Camille read the letter, she laid it down on the table. She carefully chose her words and said, "Lauren, you mean a lot to me, and I don't want you to get hurt again. Jack's been abusive, and it seems like his mood changes a lot. You can never tell when he might become violent again. I really don't think he can be trusted." Camille hesitated for a moment and continued, "This wonderful man, David, has the same outlook on life that you have. If I were you, I would get in touch with David and tell him what's going on in your life. You can tell him that after the baby is born, you're planning to divorce Jack. If he loves you enough and understands, he'll wait for you. Lauren, you asked me what I thought."

Lauren was surprised. "I can't believe you would say such a thing, Camille. You just don't understand Jack. I told you he has changed. It's his baby I'm carrying."

"I was hoping what I said wouldn't make you angry. I'm

your friend. I don't trust him. You're right about one thing—I don't know him like you do. I've heard enough to believe he'll hurt you again."

Lauren sipped her tea for a few moments before she answered. "I don't have to take your advice, but I do appreciate your concern. Right now, I see a wonderful future with Jack, and I don't want to lose it. I value your friendship, but I'm sure I'm doing the right thing."

Camille looked at her watch and said, "Lauren, I don't have time to hear about your trip. My appointment is due right now. Please think about what I've said."

Lauren wondered if she was so much in love that she couldn't see through Jack. Even Ann had bad vibes about him. She shrugged her shoulders and mumbled, "It's my life."

CHAPTER 26

Cooking and cleaning the apartment wasn't as much of a chore as it used to be. It was all because Jack appreciated her efforts. She didn't feel like a slave any more. When Jack came in from school, he had something behind his back. She cried out, "Jack! What are you hiding behind your back?"

"This! My love! Is a big bouquet of roses for a most beautiful woman!"

Overwhelmed with joy, Lauren laid the roses on the counter and threw herself into his arms and cried, "Jack, they're beautiful! What in the world possessed you to bring me flowers?"

"I've been thinking about you all day. Last night was very special, and again, I didn't realize how much I missed you until you were gone." Jack walked to the couch, sat down, and called to her. "I have something I want to talk to you about."

While Lauren arranged the flowers in a vase, she called back, "Can't you tell me now? You've aroused my curiosity."

"No...it will have to wait. I don't want to be rushed."

"My curiosity is killing me. I can't wait. I want to know what you're planning for us!"

"Okay, I'll tell you my idea. It's three weeks until Christmas. You told me you had to give two weeks' notice if you wanted to get off for a week or weekend. Is that right?"

"Yes, yes, go on."

"I've made reservations for us at the Forest Hills Ski Resort the third weekend in December. I used to go there to ski. You'll love the setting. The mountains are fabulous this time of the year. Skiing will be perfect. When we get to the log cabin, we can start a fire in the big stone fireplace and catch up on our cuddling. Later, we can go out in the woods and cut down a tree for Christmas. Of course, I've got to squeeze in a little time to swoosh down the mountain. What do you think of my idea?"

Lauren was ecstatic, "Oh Lord, I can't believe my ears! That's a great idea! Yes! Yes! I want to go." Her excitement suddenly trailed off. "I'm afraid we have a problem. Mom and Dad will be very disappointed if we don't go home for Christmas. She goes all out for decorating and cooking. They'll expect us to come home for the holidays."

"That's right. I forgot about going to your parents' house. I was only thinking that after the baby comes, we couldn't go places like that any more. Maybe we could bring in the New Year with them."

The excitement fell flat. Lauren propped her elbows on the table, cupped her hands around her chin and thought about what Jack had suggested. "Well, if I told them about our trip this far ahead, maybe Mom would understand. I'll call her tomorrow."

"I bet she'll understand. We'll make it up to her later."

* * * * *

In mid-December, a week before they were to leave for the mountains, Lauren decided to call David from her office. She dialed and waited. The sound of his voice was as familiar as if it had been yesterday when they last spoke. "Hello, this is Dr. David Williams."

Lauren felt a tingle of excitement run through her body. She composed her feelings before she answered. "David, this is

Lauren. I received your letter and needless to say, I was very surprised to hear from you."

He was elated. "Lauren! Oh Lauren, I'm so glad to hear from you! Tell me where you are, and what you have been doing these last four years?"

"A lot has happened, and it would take a long time to tell you everything. I'm not angry with you any more. Time has eased the pain. I finished my degree in pediatrics and began my career at Mass General in Boston about two years ago."

"Massachusetts General Hospital! Goodness, you've stepped up in the world."

"Not only do I have a good job, but I've changed my name."

"Why did you change your name?" He didn't understand.

"David, I'm married."

She could hear his gasp, "Married! I was a fool to think that you would wait for me after I had to leave you without a full explanation. I haven't forgotten that you are a beautiful woman, and I should have known that some lucky man would find you irresistible."

"Thank you, David. There's one more thing you should know: I'm pregnant."

There was a long period of silence and then he said, "I'm sorry, Lauren, your news has stunned me. I'm so caught up in my practice that it's hard to believe the time has passed so quickly. I was really foolish to think that I could walk back into your life just as though nothing had ever happened."

"David, I do wish you had told me more about your father's circumstances. I would have understood. As for me, in the beginning, my marriage was a disaster. When my husband found out I was pregnant, he was abusive and tried to make me have an abortion. I stood my ground and was ready to divorce him. Since then he has changed for the better, and I couldn't be happier. We're planning a weekend at the Forest Hills Ski Resort for the Christmas holidays."

David was quiet for a few minutes. "Lauren, you deserve the best."

"Thanks David. I will always keep a special place in my heart for you. It's been wonderful talking to you, but I had better get back to work. If it's okay with you, let's continue to stay in touch."

"Lauren, I will always love you." The line went dead.

Just as she hung up, a nurse came into her office and told her the next appointment was ready. Lauren put David out of her mind and took care of her patients.

CHAPTER 27

That same morning, after Lauren had gone to work, Jack drove his Bronco to school, parked, and looked for a public telephone. It was imperative that he call Lisa. He needed to hear her voice. His plan for Lauren wasn't working. His act of being an affectionate husband wasn't an act any more. Lauren had been so sweet and forgiving, he was actually enjoying being married to her. In some ways, she reminded him of his mother. But, in spite of the change in his feelings for Lauren, Lisa had a lot more to offer. He needed reinforcement from Lisa that she still wanted him. Jack walked down the sidewalk to a telephone booth and found someone using the phone. He pounded on the door. The man gave him a dirty look and waved him off. He pounded again and yelled, "This is an emergency! Please let me use the phone for just a few minutes."

The man gave Jack another dirty look and hung up. When he opened the door, he said, "Buddy, you better make it quick, or I'll bust your nose!"

"Thanks. I won't be long." Jack dialed Lisa's number. While he waited, he thought, damn it, Lisa's fortune means more to me than Lauren. The phone rang three times and then he heard her voice. "Lisa!" he shouted, "It's wonderful to hear you. I can't get you off my mind. I miss you so much."

"Jack darling, it's great to hear from you, too. I was afraid you had changed your mind about coming back. When will I see you again?"

"Sweetheart, please be patient. If everything goes as planned, I'll be a free man very soon, and I will be at your side forever. Honey, I can't talk any more. I've got to go to class. Just remember, I love you. I'll be back in touch. Good-bye, sweetheart." Lisa's voice was all the reassurance he needed.

* * * * *

Jack sat at the breakfast table feverishly looking at a map. Since all the arrangements for their vacation had been made, Lauren relaxed by reading a book. After fifteen minutes of studying the best route to the resort, he got up from the table and sat down beside Lauren. "Doc, I think it would be advisable to spend one night on the road. I don't think it would be good for us to try to make it in one day, especially in your condition. We'll pack today, leave early Thursday morning, spend the night at a motel, and be fresh Friday morning to finish our trip."

"That's sweet of you to think about me. I like your plan. We can enjoy the trip without being rushed." Lauren got up and headed for the bedroom. "Do you want to start packing now?"

"Sure thing!" They pulled out the suitcases and started packing.

"Do you want to take this leather jacket or your ski jacket?" Lauren asked as she pulled them out of the closet. Jack turned around and yanked the leather jacket out of her hands. If looks could kill, Lauren would be dead from the piercing look he gave her. "Leave my clothes alone! I'll do my own packing!"

"I'm sorry. I just wanted to help. I should have known better. You pack things a lot neater than I do."

But Jack continued to be irritable and impatient. Finally, he walked out of the bedroom and into the kitchen, opened a cabinet, took out a liquor bottle, and poured himself a strong drink. He gulped it down and thought, he had to calm down or he would lose everything.

Lauren called from the bedroom, "Jack, what are you doing?"

"I just poured myself a drink to celebrate our vacation." His hand trembled slightly as he lied to her.

"Honey, I believe you're looking forward to this trip even though I can't ski with you. I never could ski very well, and I really would be afraid to try it now."

Jack walked into the bedroom and said, "Don't you worry, Doc. I probably won't ski much. I just want to be with you and enjoy relaxing by the fire." Jack hung his leather jacket neatly in the suit bag and remarked, "Just think, I won't have to look at any more law books for several days and you won't have to deal with a bunch of sick children."

"You're right, we both need a break. It'll be the first time we've been together without any major interruptions since we've been married." Lauren tossed a few more clothes in the suitcase, looked at Jack, and said, "By the way, what time are we leaving?"

"Six o'clock in the morning. We can get something to eat on the way."

"In that case, I'm going to finish packing now."

"When you close your suitcase, I'll take the bags to the Bronco."

When the alarm clock sounded, Jack bounced out of bed like a kid on a trampoline. He was dressed before Lauren got out of bed. He cried out, "Get up, sleepy head. It's time to hit the road to paradise."

Sluggishly Lauren rolled out of bed. She checked the list of things that needed to be done: be sure the stove burners were off, the iron unplugged, timers set, counters cleaned, and the thermostat turned back. She had just finished when Jack came dashing into the kitchen yelling, "Lauren, hurry, we should be on the road by now. It snowed about four inches last night. Driving will be slower than I expected."

"Okay, okay. I'm coming. I want everything to be cut off. I'll get my purse. I'll be right out."

It was still dark when they drove out of the parking lot. The falling powdery snow made it difficult for the car lights to penetrate the darkness for more than a short distance. Jack turned on the radio and listened to the forecast for the weekend.

The announcer said, "Good morning, early risers. I bet you were surprised to see the snowfall. There will be snow flurries throughout the day. Christmas shoppers, be careful. The road and sidewalks are slippery with a thin coat of ice. Merry Christmas to all of you out there in radio land."

Lauren laughed, "I believe most weather announcers like to talk about the bad weather conditions. It must be boring for them when everything is pleasant. If you don't need me to watch the road, I'm going to sleep."

"Okay Doc." Jack tightened his fingers around the steering wheel and thought about his plan. It would take all day Friday to settle down and get adjusted to the cabin. Saturday, he'd go skiing. That afternoon he'd take her to the cliff that overlooked a majestic view of the mountain range.

Off in the distance, a flashing restaurant sign caught Jack's attention. He pulled into the parking lot. When the car stopped, it awakened Lauren, and she said sleepily. "Where are we? My goodness, I really must have been tired. I zonked out. How much farther do we have to go?"

Jack chuckled, "I know I drive fast, but we'll have to spend the night somewhere. We're stopping for breakfast. You can get out and stretch. I'll take the map in and show you how much farther we have to go."

The restaurant was a renovated log cabin with a stone fireplace at one end of the room. They ordered their breakfast and then unfolded the map on the table. "We still have part of Massachusetts, Connecticut, and a small part of New York to travel. When we get on the far side of Connecticut, we'll spend the night."

"I'll help drive if you want me to. I've had some experience driving in the snow since I moved up North."

"I'd rather drive than be the passenger." Jack stopped talking while the waitress served them their food, but as soon as she was gone Jack asked, "By the way, you never told me your mother's reaction about us not coming for Christmas."

"Mom was very disappointed, but she understood. I mentioned that we would like to go see them for New Year's if we could afford it. She said Dad would pay for our flight to keep us from having to drive."

"New Year's!" Jack's head twitched nervously. He thought, they'll never see us New Year's. "Excuse me Lauren, I need to go to the men's room. Hurry up and finish your meal. When I get back, we'd better get on the road again." When Jack entered the rest room, he took a deep breath and thought, this is getting harder than I realized. He'd have to get a hold of himself. The stakes were too big to let sentimentality get in the way. On his way back to the table, he thought of what he would say to Lauren about the New Year's at her parents'. "Doc, in response to your parents' offer, I appreciate their being so understanding. Yep, we would definitely have to fly. It would be too long a trip for us to drive." Jack stood up and helped Lauren with her coat and said, "Doc, let's go."

It was late. They were tired after driving until dark. Jack started looking for a motel. He thought it would be easy, but he had forgotten it was the Christmas season and vacancies would be difficult to find. He became worried. "Damn it! I thought I had everything figured out to the very hour. The snow has thrown my plans all to hell. I can't see a damn thing."

Lauren sat up and leaned forward to get a better view in case she could see a motel along the highway. The only lights to be seen were other car lights beaming down the road. All of a sudden she shouted. "I see a flickering vacancy sign just down the road on the right." As they got closer they could see half the letters had burned out, but at least it would be a haven for the night.

Jack's anger cooled off as he parked the Bronco. From what

they could see of the motel, it really looked like a dump. He and Lauren carefully made their way over an icy path and into the office. The fabric on the chairs was worn out, the fake leather couch had gashes ripped across the cushions, and there were cigarette butts scattered on the faded linoleum floor. Lauren looked scared. Jack whispered, "I know this isn't what we would like to have, but we don't have any choice tonight."

They walked to the desk to register but no one was there. A bell was on the counter with a sign saying, "ring for service." Jack popped the bell, and a short, stout woman waddled out of a door. Her hair was dyed bright orange and piled high in tight curls on top of her head. Owl-like eyes, outlined in black mascara, looked at them wearily. When she started to talk, her lips looked like red wax lips children buy in a candy store. In a twangy voice she asked, "What kin I do for ya'?"

Disgusted with her looks, Jack said with indifference, "We want a room."

"You folks are mighty lucky this time of night to find a place...been full all week." With a flick of her short fat fingers, she pushed the registration pad in front of Jack. She looked at Lauren and said, "Honey child, you must be dead tired. I'm goin'a do ya'll a favor. I'm goina' switch rooms and give you two love-birds a nice room. Come with me." She led them down a poorly lit hall. Her three-inch heels clicked like a typewriter and her hips swayed back and forth under a short, red and black, polka-dot dress, which was two sizes too small. The woman stopped at one of the doors, turned and asked Lauren, "Honey, have you had anything to eat?"

"No, ma'am. We didn't take time to stop. It was getting late, and we were afraid we wouldn't be able to find a place to stay. I was really getting worried. I'm expecting a baby and I needed to rest."

"Here you are, folks. This is the best I got. If you need me, just pick up the telephone and call for Edna Earlson."

Lauren smiled, took Edna's hand, and thanked her. When

Jack and Lauren entered the room, they were surprised to see how clean and attractive it was: a queen-size bed covered with a bright floral comforter with matching drapes. Even the bathroom had sparkling white fixtures.

Before they had settled down for the night, there was a knock on the door. Jack looked through the peephole. There was no mistaking who it was when he saw the flaming orange hair.

"Hello Edna," Jack said when he opened the door. "Is there anything wrong?"

"Lordy no. I have something for you." She walked in with a tray of food: hot coffee, sandwiches, and some homemade cake. "You both looked so tired, I thought you could use a little nourishment."

"Oh my goodness," Lauren cried as she walked over to Edna and hugged her. "You are so kind and thoughtful. We appreciate your generosity for this room and for bringing us something to eat. If we don't see you when we leave in the morning, thank you again and have a Merry Christmas."

"Honey child, you're welcome. Have a good night's rest." She closed the door and the last thing they heard was the clicking of her high-heeled shoes. Lauren wiped her eyes. "I'm touched by her kindness. It just goes to prove; you can't judge a person by the way they look. She has a heart of gold."

"Yeah," Jack said sarcastically, "She'll double the cost of the room when we pay our bill in the morning. She didn't do those things for nothing."

Lauren didn't say anything. She put on her nightgown and mumbled, "Good night." Jack didn't make any effort to change his remarks about Edna.

The next morning, Jack pulled back the drapes to see if it was still snowing. He turned to Lauren and said, "The driving conditions are going to be even more hazardous than yesterday. C'mon, get dressed. We need to be on the road."

Jack and Lauren made their way to the front desk to pay the bill. There was a gray-haired, elderly man, in a faded-blue wool shirt and worn-out overalls, slouched down in a swivel chair behind the desk. He looked at them over his glasses and waited for them to speak.

"Where is Edna Earlson?" Lauren asked.

The man grunted, "She took sick and had'a go home in the middle of the night. She done left dis note fer you."

Lauren read the note to Jack.

"Mr. and Mrs. Harper, you don't owe me for the night. You reminded me of the story of baby Jesus's mama and daddy looking for a place to stay at the Inn. I know you weren't ready to birth a baby, but it just reminded me of the story. You were real tired, just like them. I decided I would be different from that stingy innkeeper and give you the very best I had. I gave you my room. I hope you had a good night's rest. Think about me when your precious baby is born. Merry Christmas, Edna Earlson."

Lauren couldn't hold back the tears. "Jack, that was such an unselfish act of kindness. She knows the real meaning of Christmas. I wish she was here so I could thank her personally."

Sarcastically Jack said, "She must be crazy to give up sixty dollars to strangers."

CHAPTER 28

It didn't take long for Jack to forget about Edna Earlson. He got excited as they drew nearer to the Forest Hills Ski Resort. Every curve in the road took them higher up the mountains, which made Jack happy knowing he would be skiing down the white slopes in a matter of hours. On the other hand, Lauren's eyes were taking in the beauty of the snow-covered mountains—from high peaks that seem to reach to the sky and to far away villages tucked in snow-covered valleys below.

Jack said tensely, "Keep you eyes open for a sign, Forest Hill Resort. I've got to keep my eyes on the road because the snow has made it impossible for two cars to pass without stopping."

Minutes later, Lauren shouted and pointed to the right. "There it is! There it is!"

"Great! I can't wait to get to the cabin. It's been a long time since I've been up here." Jack drove on for fifteen minutes and then he let out a yell, "Hot damn! We're here at last."

"Oh Jack! It's beautiful. I can't wait to see the inside of it."

Jack laughed, "You'd better wait until I stop. You can't just run up the mountain.

The snow is deep and the path is slippery. I'm going to get as close as I can."

Suddenly, Jack had a flashback when he remembered how he and Lisa had to walk through deep snow because a tree had fallen across the road blocking their way. Quickly as the thought came, the memory disappeared. He stopped the Bronco and helped Lauren walk to the cabin and go inside. Grinning from ear to ear, Jack asked, "Well, how do you like it?"

"Like it! I love it! It's exactly like you described it." Her head was turning from one side of the room to the other taking in every rustic detail.

"I'm going to get a fire started, then I'll bring in the suitcases and the food."

Lauren watched how skillfully Jack started the fire. After he finished, she backed up close to it to get warm. Before long, the room was nice and cozy. When Jack came in with the food she asked, "Do you want me to fix something for us to eat now? It isn't exactly lunch time or supper."

"We're not watching a clock anymore for the next two days. I'd say let's eat when we want to."

"That suits me just fine. I believe it's warm enough now that I can take off my coat. Let me have your leather jacket and I'll hang it up with mine."

Jack's mood changed instantly as he glared at her. "No! I'll hang it up myself when I'm ready!"

"Okay, don't get in such a huff. I thought you might be getting warm wearing it in the cabin. I'll make some sandwiches while you do whatever you want to do about your precious coat." Lauren dismissed his curt remark and went about making sandwiches and heating some vegetable soup. About fifteen minutes later, she called out, "It's ready. Where would you like to sit?"

Jack poked the logs harder to get the flames to rise higher but; when he heard Lauren, he stopped and said, "Let's sit in front of the fireplace and have a picnic." This action reminded him of Lisa and Travis sitting in front of her fireplace having a picnic. Damn, he thought, I'm being pulled from one woman to the other. I've started this scheme and I intend to see it through.

Lauren broke into his thoughts when she said, "That's a

super idea. You clear the coffee table while I bring the food." She walked over to the table and giggled, "I like this kind of camping. I'm not much on roughing it outside in a tent."

It tickled Jack as he watched her struggle to sit down and cross her legs under the table. "Doc, it appears your flexibility isn't what it used to be. Had you rather sit in a chair?"

"Heck no. I'm having fun. I'm sure you'll have to get a crane to lift me when we're through eating."

Jack couldn't keep his eyes off Lauren. She never looked so beautiful as she did right then. The glow from the fire reflected in her face and her silky blonde hair fell softly around her shoulders. He couldn't stand it any longer. His willpower began to crumble. Jack sprang up from the floor and began to pace around the room. He frantically thought of what he could say to cover his restlessness. "I'm sorry Lauren, memories of my school days resurfaced. Some of my schoolmates used to come up here with me during Christmas break. I don't have a lot of happy moments from my childhood, but they were the best of times. My restlessness isn't any reflection on you."

"I'm glad to hear that. You were looking at me in such a strange way. I wondered what had happened when you jumped up."

"By the way, how would you like to hear about the history of this cabin?"

"I'd love it. You told me a little about it, but it's better than what you described."

"Okay, but you need to stand up and walk around the room with me." Lauren tried to get up but her legs were stiff. Jack laughed, "Maybe we do need that crane." After lifting her to her feet, she was okay. With a wave of his hand, Jack began his history lesson. "You are standing in the middle of a handmade room. The pine bed, trestle table, chairs, floors, and the twelve-inch thick mantel were all made from virgin timber cut off this very land. The only thing not made from wood is a fabulous feather mattress, which we will christen tonight." Jack put his hands on Lauren's shoulders and turned her around. "Doc, that's it for the house tour. Now, I hope you don't mind if I ski this afternoon."

"Of course, not. You go right ahead. I'll read or take a nap."

"While I'm gone, you might have to add some logs to the fire." He took her outside and showed her where the wood was stacked against one end of the porch.

"I think I can handle that chore all right. I'll miss you while you're gone. Have a good swoosh."

Jack put on his ski outfit and clomped out of the cabin. On his way out he called to her, "See you later, Doc."

It didn't take Lauren long to decide what she was going to do. Without hesitation she headed for the couch. A big, fluffy, navy-colored pillow was tucked in the corner of the couch. She grabbed it and stuck it under her head. The fire mesmerized her and before she knew it, she had fallen asleep. A loud stomping woke Lauren. Still half asleep, she pushed herself up and went to the window to see what was making the noise. Relieved to see Jack knocking the snow off his boots, she opened the door and let him in.

"Man! I had forgotten how cold it gets skiing. It isn't so bad going down the mountain, but I thought I would freeze walking from the ski lift over here to the cabin. Don't get me wrong. I'm not complaining. It's worth it to me. I can't remember when the condition of the snow has been so perfect. Tomorrow, I'm going back again—right after breakfast. It'll be a long time before I ski again."

"You know I don't mind. Wouldn't it really be great to stay up here for a week? You could ski all you wanted to; I could sleep and not have to listen to a ringing telephone. In fact, the only noise would be the wind whistling through the trees. It doesn't hurt to dream." Lauren walked over to the kitchen and prepared something to eat. When she was through, she called Jack, "Are you hungry? Come and get it!"

It didn't take him long to go bounding over to the counter like a rabbit. "Wow! It smells so good." Jack dove into the food like a starving prisoner. He didn't wait for Lauren.

"It's obvious that you liked your supper. I can't take much credit for cooking it. Everything came from the deli." Lauren looked at the clock hanging over the stove. "We really meant what we said about not caring what time we ate. I don't know whether this is supper or a late night snack. It's ten o'clock. When you've finished eating, why don't you lie down on the couch while I clean up the dishes. I'll wake you when I've finished."

"Mrs. Harper, I think that is an excellent idea. I'm bushed. First, I'll bank the fire for the night before I lie down."

Lauren swept up the last crumb, and tiptoed over to the couch and found Jack sound asleep. She didn't have the heart to awaken him. Disappointed, she put on her gown and crawled into the soft feather bed by herself.

CHAPTER 29

Jack shivered. He was cold. The fire was nearly out. He rolled off the couch and threw more logs on the smoldering ashes. He looked over at the bed and saw Lauren curled up in a ball, snuggled deep in the feather bed with blankets tucked all around her. "I've done it now!" he muttered. He hadn't made love to her as he had promised. The crackling of the dry wood woke Lauren.

"What are you doing?" Lauren asked sleepily.

"Damn it, I've overslept. Don't worry about fixing me any breakfast. A bowl of cereal will hold me." Lauren crawled out of the bed and started dressing. While he ate, he watched her dress in a pair of rose-colored pants, and a heavy white ski sweater He walked over to her and said, "You look beautiful this morning."

She slipped her arms around his waist. "Well…sweetheart, you could fulfill your promise and make love to me before you go skiing."

"That's an offer that's hard to turn down." Feeling guilty he said, "By the way, I'm sorry about last night. I was bushed. I'll make up for it later. If I made love to you now, I wouldn't have the energy to walk out the door. I'd better ski first. When I get back, I want to show you a place I discovered years ago. It's a spectacular view. Bird watchers love to go there and observe the eagles. I know you'll love it."

"That sounds interesting. I'll be ready."

Without another minute to waste, Jack rushed to the closet and jerked his ski suit off the hanger. He dressed quickly and crossed the room to kiss Lauren on the cheek. "I'll be back in a couple of hours. Thanks for understanding about last night."

"Goodbye, honey. Be careful and have a great time." She watched him trudge through the heavy drifts of snow until he was out of sight. Lauren sat on the couch to read a book. There was a chill in the air and when she looked at the fire it was nearly out. The log holder was empty, too. She couldn't wait for Jack or else the fire would be totally gone. There was nothing else to do but for her to get the logs. When she went to the closet to get her heavy coat, Jack's leather coat was lying on the floor. "Uh-oh!" she muttered. "He'd have a fit if he knew his precious jacket had fallen off the rack." Dust was on the collar, so she grabbed the bottom of the jacket and shook it to get the dust off. Five photographs fluttered to the floor. As she bent down to pick them up, she recognized Jack with a strange woman and a little boy. Sinking to her knees, she stared at the pictures. "My God!" she cried. "I wonder when these pictures were taken." She thrust her hand into the inside pocket of his jacket and pulled out a folded piece of paper. Her body shook uncontrollably with anger as she read the note out-loud that Lisa had written, "Your son and I love you very much." She cried out, "Damn you, Jack! The date on these pictures is the same time I went to Falmouth to see Ann Goodman."

Lauren began to feel queasy. Slowly she rose to her feet, staggered across the room, clutched the back of a chair for support, and made her way to the bathroom. When the retching stopped, she soaked a bath cloth in cold water and put it on her forehead. After several minutes, she managed to walk back into the main room and collapsed in a chair. Her mind began to clear, and she wondered how many other times he had lied. Maybe all those nights he claimed to be working on his research papers were lies, too.

Lauren went to the kitchen to get a coke. After a few sips, she muttered, "I've got to pull myself together. I can't let Jack see me like this." Lauren paced around the room wringing her hands distraughtly. She cried out, "I was so in love that it made me blind from seeing Jack as he really is. I should have realized something was wrong with his unpredictable mood swings. Why didn't I listen to the wisdom of Ann and Camille?"

It was too late now. Time had run out. Jack would be coming back soon. Everything she had ever wanted, except for her baby, had fallen apart. Slowly she took several deep breaths and regained her thoughts. He'll not get away with his game. She would get a divorce as soon as they get home. She'd play along with his scheme and pretend nothing was wrong. Lauren decided to put two of the pictures of Jack and Liza in her purse, the other three and the note would go into her jacket pocket. "Oh, my gosh! The fire!" she cried. "He'll throw a fit if the fire goes out."

She looked again in the log holder. No logs. The cold fresh air soothed her flushed face as she stepped outside to gather more wood. Tucking a few twigs under the smoldering coals, the flames flared up again.

Lauren jumped when she heard Jack call out cheerfully. "I'm back!" He hurried over to the fireplace. "Man, this fire feels good. You did a good job keeping it going. Doc, before I take my gloves and ski suit off, I want you to see a place called Eagle Nest Cliff."

In case the puffiness in her face hadn't gone completely away, she walked over to the kitchen counter to keep some distance between them. Her response was stoic, "Okay, let's go." She kept her back to him as she slipped on her warm jacket, hat, and sunglasses.

"Hey Doc. Are you feeling all right? You don't seem as excited about this trip as you were when I left this morning."

"I felt a little queasy earlier but I'm okay now."

As they walked out the door and down the snow-covered

steps, Jack held her arm. Just his touch made her want to jerk her arm away. It took all her stamina to remain the placid, stupid woman she had been since she met Jack. It was slow walking down the path to the cleared main road but once they got to it, Jack pulled her along at a brisker pace. He said in a husky voice, "It's only a short distance before we'll branch off on another path leading up to the cliff." Lauren noticed his voice was more tense than usual. Ten minutes later, she saw a small sign nailed to a tree, "Eagle Nest Cliff." She trudged slowly and silently behind Jack as they made their way along the rutted and over-grown path. Her mind was oblivious to the tangled vines and low hanging branches that struck her on her head and face as she tried to push them out of the way. The pictures had seared her brain like a branding iron. The path became harder to climb the higher they went. The crusty snow made it even hard to get a foothold.

She shouted to Jack, "How much farther?"

Impatience showing in his voice, he yelled, "Can't you go any faster?" Then he paused. "If you can see that tall gnarled tree with the straggly limbs growing out of the top of it, you'll see an eagle nest clustered in the branches. The cliff is just below it! It won't be long! We're almost there!" Jack forged on ahead not waiting for Lauren until he was within twenty feet of the edge of the cliff. There he spread his arms out like the wings of a bird and exclaimed, "Have you ever seen anything more beautiful than this sight. It's just amazing. It's a miracle anything can grow out of these rocks, but somehow that old tree and the nest have survived many hardships."

Breathing heavily, she stopped several feet from Jack and stoically said, "Yes, it is a spectacular sight."

Jack stepped closer and took her hand and pulled her closer to the edge. "Come on. You can get a better view if you stand near the edge. You can see the river winding through the valley. It looks like a silver thread from this height."

A cold blast of wind made Lauren jerk away, and she moved farther away from him. With her back to him, she thought, how can he be so charming? Once she would have been ecstatic sharing the beauty of those mountains, but now—nothing was pretty. All her dreams had been destroyed.

"Come back to me, Lauren. The wind has died down."

Lauren was near the edge of the cliff when she turned her head and with a look of rage, pointed her finger at him and yelled, "You are the spectacular sight, Jack Harper!"

He shouted, "What in the hell is wrong with you? You haven't been yourself since we left the cabin!"

With a clinched fist waving in the air, she moved even closer to the edge of the cliff as she screamed, "I didn't know you had a son! Who is Lisa? You son of a bitch! You were with her while I was in Falmouth! You've been lying to me for months! You bastard! Your Christmas present will be a divorce!"

Stunned by her outcry, Jack screamed back, "What in the hell are you talking about? Are you crazy?"

"No! I'm not crazy but I think you are!" Lauren pulled the pictures out of her pocket and held them out of his reach.

He tried to grab them but Lauren stepped further away from him. "Where did you get those pictures?" he yelled.

"They fell out of your precious jacket you've been guarding for the last month!" With his anger rising to a fever pitch, she realized she had better make her move. She quickly tossed each picture to the wind which caught them up like feathers and sent them flying in all directions. Jack stood dumb-founded and speechless as he watched the photographs spiral down into the valley. He recovered from what she was doing and sprang toward her like a tiger. Lauren heard the crunching snow from behind, and as she looked back, saw Jack with out-stretched arms running toward her. As he bore down, she screamed, "No! No!" Then in an instant, she stepped aside. Jack couldn't stop the momentum of his body. He grabbed at her arm to keep from falling but to no avail. His body tumbled over and over as his arms flailed in the air. A blood-curdling scream broke the tranquil silence as it echoed from mountain to mountain. His broken and bloody body ricocheted from one jagged surface to the next as he plummeted against the unforgiving rocks. No one heard the dull thud of his body as it lay shattered.

When Jack grabbed her arm, Lauren lost her balance and fell over the side of the cliff. Her life was spared by a handful of scrubby trees and bushes that had grown within the crevices of the mountain. As Lauren fell, she was knocked unconscious.

CHAPTER 30

An elderly couple, who were avid bird watchers, were hiking along the same trail and discovered Lauren. The man called the police in Newburg on his cell phone. He told the officer how they happened to see a woman lying on a ledge just below Eagle Nest Cliff. The police asked the couple to stay with the woman until the emergency vehicle arrived.

It wasn't long before the couple saw four paramedics. They scrambled up the bramble-covered path loaded down with equipment. They located the woman and two of the medics climbed down the treacherous cliff and found that she was still alive. They cautiously slipped a stretcher under her and lifted it up to the other two medics standing on top of the cliff. Before the medics took Lauren to the ambulance, one of them yelled to the medics who were still on the ledge, "I see another body further down the mountain. It looks like a man. While we're treating this victim, you'll have to go down and get him."

The elderly couple left the scene and continued their journey to find other places suitable for avid bird watching.

* * * * *

When the medics arrived at the emergency room, the doctor turned to a nurse and said, "Call the police department. There's no identification on either of the victims. I need to know their medical history."

The nurse placed the call. A clipped Yankee voice answered, "Newburg Police Department."

"Sir, this is Newburg General Hospital. We have two unidentified victims. One is dead and the other one is unconscious. It appears they fell from a cliff in the Forest Hills Resort area. Please send someone to establish their identities."

"Okay! I'll send someone immediately."

* * * * *

Detective Mark Preston leaned back in his wooden swivel chair. He propped his feet up on his well-worn desk that was littered with letters, clippings, and magazines. He was reading the daily newspaper when the phone rang. "Hello, Detective Mark Preston here."

Mark was an assistant to the State's Attorney and worked in the homicide department. He was in his mid fifties, of average height, and in good physical condition. His face was creased with lines that came from his job of making serious decisions.

The Chief of Police responded, "Mark, I want you to go to the hospital and see what you can find out about two accident victims. Neither has any identification. Better go right now!"

"I'm on my way!" Mark grabbed his trench coat and slapped on an old baseball cap he had worn for years. The letters across the bill had long faded away through numerous washings, but he wore it regardless of its appearance. He climbed into his white, 1994 Toyota station wagon and sped off down Main Street.

When he reached the hospital, he pushed his way through the crowd of people. A security guard took him to the morgue where they had Jack's body. Mark said to the guard, "I want to see all the victims' clothing and view the body before the coroner takes over."

The guard opened a pair of stainless steel doors. Mark was accustomed to the surroundings and was not intimidated by death. He scanned the corpse but couldn't make any judgment about his condition because it was so battered. It was up to the coroner to make the decision as to the cause of death. He whistled quietly as he zipped up the bag and turned his attention to the clothing. Meticulously, he went through every pocket. He found a ski lift ticket and a key with a cabin number. The clothes were shoved back into the bag and stored away. Mark got in touch with the doctor in charge of the victims. When he answered, Mark said, "I have to travel to the Forest Hills Resort to find out about these people. But first, I have to get a search warrant in order to finish my investigation."

Mark said to the officers that he took with him, "I'll go in and inquire about the ticket and key to the cabin." The receptionist was hesitant at first until Mark showed his credentials, then she obligingly gave him the information.

Detective Preston was like a bloodhound on the scent of his quarry. He rushed out of the lobby and drove the officers to the cabin that Jack and Lauren had rented. Mark assigned duties to the officers: one would dust for fingerprints and the other would go through the luggage and take pictures of everything pertinent to the crime. Mark opened a closet door and found a lady's purse. He emptied the contents on the bed. In it were two pictures: one was of a lady, a small boy, and a dog; the other was of a man standing next to the lady and the boy. He also found Jack Harper's driver's license as well as Lauren's. In their wallets, were personal calling cards of Mr. and Mrs. Vernon Harper and Mr. and Mrs. Ben Fulghum. Mark was anxious to see the place where they had fallen—now that he had some evidence.

The officers followed Mark to the path that led to Eagle Nest Cliff where they scoured the surroundings. Mark found a picture caught in a bush on the edge of the cliff. He called to one of the officers, "Come over here and take pictures from every angle. Be sure to get the ledge where the lady fell and those roughed up places in the snow near the edge of the cliff. The medics might have taken pictures, but I just want to make sure

I have a back up. When you're through, we'll go back to town."

* * * * *

Mark returned to his office to make the calls. When he walked into his office, it was dark to match the mood he was in. Telling people of a tragedy that had befallen one of their loved ones was the worst thing about his job. Slowly Mark picked up the telephone and dialed the Harper's number. After a few rings, someone answered.

"Hello. Is this the Harper's residence?"

"Yes, it is."

"Mr. Harper, this is Mark Preston of the Newburg, New York, Police Department. It is my sad duty to inform you that there has been an accident at the Forest Hill Ski Resort. Your son has died, and it seems in a fall from a mountain at the Resort."

The color drained from Vernon's face. His mouth dropped open in despair. His hand clutched his forehead as he nervously asked, "Are you sure it's Jack Harper?"

"Yes, sir. I found your son's driver's license. You and your wife should come as soon as possible to the Newburgh police station to make a positive identification."

"Yes! Yes! We'll leave right away."

"When you get here, ask for Detective Mark Preston."

Vernon's hand shook. His voice quivered as he turned to Sarah and said, "That call was from Detective Mark Preston. He wants us to come to Newburgh as soon as possible to identify a person named Jack Harper, who has been killed in an accident."

Sarah clutched her face with her hands and cried out, "Oh-h-h no, not my baby!" She pounded the kitchen table venting her anger and sorrow. Vernon stood motionless and watched her wring her hands in disbelief. She kept repeating, "No! No! No! It can't be true. My baby isn't dead! I won't believe it until I see his face!"

Vernon didn't know how to comfort Sarah. His voice

nearly a whisper said, "Sarah, it's getting late. We have to go. Since there isn't much daylight left, we may have to stay overnight. Pack a few extra clothes just in case we have to stay longer."

When they arrived at the Newburg Police station, Vernon climbed out of his snow splattered Cadillac and walked around to help Sarah. Vernon took her arm and led her to the front desk. A policeman in a tailored dark blue uniform decorated with badges greeted them and asked, "What can I do for you?"

Vernon replied, "I'm Vernon Harper and this is my wife, Sarah. We're looking for Detective Mark Preston."

The officer got up from his chair and said politely, "He's expecting you. Come with me." The officer paused in front of a door and knocked. A husky voice answered, "Come in."

"Detective Preston, this is Mr. and Mrs. Vernon Harper."

Mark's face held a sad expression as he extended his hand and said, "I'm sorry about your son."

"I'm sorry we're late. The roads were covered with ice." Vernon said coldly.

"I understand. I'm really sorry to put you folks through this ordeal, but it has to be done. Now, I'll take you to the hospital to identify the body."

Vernon held his body rigid, ready to face the unexpected, and prepared himself not to show any emotion. In his mind, he was certain that it couldn't be Jack. Sarah followed behind as they walked outside and got into Mark's car. When they arrived at the hospital, an officer escorted them to the morgue. Mark opened the door and crossed over to a wall that was lined with rows of large drawers. He pulled out one, and asked the Harpers to come and look at the corpse.

When the sheet was pulled back, Sarah cried out hysterically, "Jack! Jack!" It was such a shock; Sarah fainted in Vernon's arms. Mark rushed to her side and helped her to a chair. He found a bottle of smelling salts and passed it under her nose. Soon Sarah regained consciousness.

Detective Preston pushed the body back into the vault and said, "I'm sorry to put you through this. We have to investigate accidents. The first thing to be done is for the coroner to make his report."

Vernon spoke up, "We'll spend the night in a motel and then return home tomorrow."

"That's a good idea. There are several motels about two blocks from the police station. In the morning, I'll talk to you again."

Vernon asked, "Detective, how did Jack die?"

"He fell from a cliff called Eagle Nest Cliff."

Vernon remained silent, but as they got ready to leave, Sarah asked, "Where's Lauren?"

"She's been admitted to the hospital. Lauren was knocked unconscious, and she's in a coma. Otherwise, she doesn't appear to be injured, but the doctors are watching her carefully due to her pregnancy."

"Pregnant! cried Sarah, "Jack never told us they were expecting!" She looked at Vernon for an explanation. Vernon stood silent, clenching his jaw. Detective Preston apologized for the unexpected news.

* * * * *

Ben and Polly were dressing for church. Ben wanted to see the weather forecast, so he picked up the remote control and surfed through some of the channels. A "NEWS FLASH" came across the screen.

"A man and a woman fell from Eagle Nest Cliff at Forest Hill Ski Resort.

The man fell to his death. The woman was rescued by the Newburg Rescue Squad. The names of the victims to be released after the nearest of kin are notified." A mournful sound came from Polly as she said, "Oh, my Lord, those poor people.

What a shame." She leaned forward and said apprehensively, "Ben, honey, you know that's where Lauren and Jack are vacationing."

"Yeah, I know. That's the first thing I thought about." He hesitated and said, "Polly, for goodness sake, surely you're not thinking that's Lauren!" Ben started to change channels when the telephone rang. "I'll get it, Polly."

A man's voice asked, "Sir, is the residence of Mr. and Mrs. Ben Fulghum?"

"Yes it is. May I ask who's calling?"

"This is Detective Mark Preston. I'm calling from the Newburgh Police Department in New York. Do you have a daughter named Lauren and is she married to Jack Harper?"

Ben gripped the phone. "Why do you want to know?"

"Sir, there's been an accident. She's unconscious in the hospital in Newburgh."

Ben cried out, "No! It can't be Lauren!"

Polly jumped up from her seat, took the phone out of his hand and cried out, "Who is this?"

"Ma'am. I'm Detective Mark Preston. I'm sorry to have to tell you that your daughter fell from a cliff. The hospital spokesperson has released a report on your daughter's condition. She's in a coma but at this time, we don't have a complete report on her over-all condition."

Polly said hysterically, "We'll be there as soon as possible."

"Mrs. Fulghum, as soon as you and your husband arrive, get in touch with me at the Newburgh Police Department."

* * * * *

Early the next day, Mark Preston's phone rang. Vernon Harper said, "Detective Preston, we're getting ready to leave. What did you want to ask us?"

"I need to know the names of Jack's closest friends and where they live."

There was a moment of silence and then Vernon replied,

"I don't know any of his friends. He wasn't employed because he was studying to be a lawyer at Harvard University. Before that, he attended North Bridge Military Academy." Vernon hesitated and then he rudely said, "That's all I have to say." There was a click and the line went dead. Mark didn't like the brusqueness of Vernon Harper's voice. It was apparent he wasn't going to get any information about Jack Harper from his parents. He would have to dig it up by himself.

CHAPTER 31

The Fulghums landed at the airport early Sunday morning and immediately called Detective Preston. He told them the name of the hospital and room number where Lauren was hospitalized. Detective Preston said, "As soon as your visit is over, please call me again. There are some questions I need to ask you."

Ben replied, "Okay, we'll do that, but right now we're anxious to see our daughter." They hurried to the hospital, worried at what they might see. As soon as they entered the room, Polly began to sob when she saw Lauren's head bandaged. Slowly, she regained her composure and wanted desperately to hold her hand; but she couldn't because two nurses were huddled around her as they took her temperature and blood pressure.

Lauren stirred and through dimmed veiled eyes saw faces near her. Their voices sounded muffled. Suddenly the film lifted from her eyes, and she saw a woman smiling down at her. Confused, she asked, "Who are you?"

Polly looked shocked and gasped, "I'm your mother!"

Just as quickly as Lauren had opened her eyes, she closed them again. Ben sprang from his chair and rushed over to Polly to console her. He said quietly, "She doesn't know us yet.

When the doctor comes, we'll find out exactly what's wrong." Ben and Polly pulled their chairs close to the bed and kept a vigilant eye on their daughter.

An hour passed when Lauren was awakened by the shrieking sound of an ambulance siren. She flinched as if she remembered something. She tried to focus her eyes again as she looked around the room. She saw a man and woman staring at her.

She heard the woman say softly, "Lauren, baby, how are you feeling?"

"I'm sorry. I don't know you?"

"Honey, surely you know me?" Polly began to cry again.

"Please, can't you tell me where I am?"

Polly said to Ben, "I don't understand. She looks all right."

At that moment, a tall lean man walked into the room. He had a rather swarthy, athletic look in spite of his semi-bald head and brown beard sprinkled with gray. He walked over to Lauren, picked up her hand and patted it and said reassuringly, "I'm Dr. Charles Roberts. You're in a hospital. You fell and hit your head on a rock. The blow has caused you to have amnesia. As you heal, your memory will return." The Doctor noticed Lauren looking at Ben and Polly and said, "Mrs. Harper, these people are your parents, Ben and Polly Fulghum. They want to stay with you until you have recovered."

Lauren nervously moved her legs under the sheet. Her eyes darted back and forth at the strangers. Dr. Roberts patted her hand again to calm her down and to assure her that everything was going to be all right. The doctor needed to examine Lauren. So, he asked Ben and Polly to step out for a few minutes. The Doctor checked her eyes, ears, and nose, pressed her stomach, and asked, "Does this hurt?"

Lauren flinched. "Yes! That hurts."

"I think you're pregnant."

Lauren thrashed wildly and started screaming, "Pregnant! How can that be? I don't even know who I am! How did I get here! What has happened to me?"

"Mrs. Harper, please calm down and listen to me," the doctor said calmly. "You're going to be all right. You have a mild case of amnesia. In the meantime, trust your parents and me.

Eventually, something will trigger your memory and when you least expect it, you will remember everything. I'm going to give you a mild sedative to make you relax. I'll be back to check on you later." Dr. Roberts walked out of her room and motioned to Ben and Polly for them to go back in.

They returned and stood by Lauren's bed. Polly said, "Honey, we would like to be with you every day, if that's okay?"

Sleepily, Lauren muttered, "Thank you. That's very kind of you." In a few minutes, she fell asleep again.

* * * * *

As soon as the Fulghums left the hospital, they went to the motel and called Detective Preston. "We're here at the Hospitality Motel."

"Okay. I'll meet you in the lobby in twenty minutes. I appreciate your co-operation."

Ben had an uneasy feeling about the nature of this meeting. Why was the Detective so anxious to question them? Twenty minutes later, they saw a man in a trench coat amble through the front entrance. Ben got up and met him halfway and asked, "Are you Detective Mark Preston?"

"Yes, and you must be Mr. Fulghum." They shook hands and Ben introduced Mark to Polly. The three of them went to a table in a remote part of the lobby. Mark took out a notebook and asked, "I need a list of Lauren's friends."

Polly said, "Lauren didn't have many friends. She didn't have time to acquire them because of her work schedule. Her closest friend is Dr. Camille Bloomfield. She works at Mass General Hospital with Lauren."

Ben interrupted, "Don't forget Dr. Ann Goodman and Attorney Rita LaBaron. I don't know their addresses; maybe you can call the hospital and ask Dr. Bloomfield for them. By the way, we need to call the Mass General and tell them about Lauren. They'll be expecting her to come back to work Monday."

Mr. Fulghum stopped abruptly and asked, "Wait just a minute. Why do you have to know all about her friends?"

Detective Preston responded, "Mr. Fulghum, the police has to investigate accidents, especially since there weren't any witnesses. It's a procedure we have to go through. In case you don't already know, her husband died in the fall."

Polly was shocked and choked back her sobs as she cried, "We didn't know. I'm so sorry."

Ben put his arms around Polly to comfort her and asked, "Do the Harpers know about their son?"

"Yes. I called them before I called you. They've already arrived." Mark closed his notebook and said, "I'm through for the time being. I'll be back in touch with you later." On his way out, he waved and said, "I hope your daughter has a speedy recovery."

* * * * *

Monday morning, Detective Preston began an intensive investigation. In Lauren's purse, he found business cards for Dr. Ann Goodman and Rita LaBaron and a piece of paper with Dr. Bloomfield's work number. He called Dr. Bloomfield's office. He tapped his fingers on his desk impatiently.

A pleasant voice answered, "Hello, this is Dr. Camille Bloomfield."

"Dr. Bloomfield, I'm Detective Mark Preston. I don't want to alarm you, but I have to tell you that your friend, Dr. Lauren Harper, has been in an accident."

"Oh my God!" Camille exclaimed. "Is she all right?"

"She doesn't appear to be hurt seriously, although, she's suffering from a mild case of amnesia." Mark explained where the accident happened and then added, "Mr. Fulghum will call Mass General to let the proper authorities know when Lauren will be able to return to work." But before he hung up, he asked, "Did Lauren and Jack have a good relationship?"

There was a pause before Camille answered. "Well...Lauren loved Jack very much, but I don't think the feelings were mutual."

"By the way, how is Jack?"

"He was killed when he fell over the cliff."

"What!" Camille cried. "He's dead?"

"Yes. Thank you Dr. Bloomfield for your information."

Next, Mark called Dr. Ann Goodman. When she answered, he said, "I'm Detective Mark Preston with the Newburgh Police Department." He explained what had happened to Lauren and Jack. "I would like to ask you a few questions. How well did you know Lauren?"

"We've only known each other since her honeymoon last August. She visited me about a month ago. We were becoming very close." Ann stopped short and said, "Wait just a minute, Sir. You've sprung some very tragic news on me. I would like to ask you a question. How is Lauren? Just how serious is her injury, and did she lose the baby?"

"Lauren has a slight case of amnesia, and the doctor says the baby doesn't seem to be harmed," Mark politely responded.

There was a pause before Ann continued. "Well...Lauren loved Jack very much. It was my observation, when we all met on a cruise, he didn't act like he loved her.

"Did she confide in you?"

"Yes."

"Can you tell me about her relationship with Jack?"

"Sir, why are you interested in such details?"

"Ma'am, you know the law. All incidents have to be investigated to the fullest."

"Sir, I don't want to seem rude, but I can't discuss confidential information without her permission."

"You're right, Dr. Goodman. Thanks for listening. Goodbye." He hung up and muttered, "Damn, I thought I would catch her off guard. I'm not through with her." He spun his chair around and looked out the dirty window at the traffic swishing by. He thought, I've got to make a trip to Boston. The Harpers aren't going to give me any information about Jack. There has to be a story about their relationship, and I'm afraid it isn't pleasant. I've got to make one more call. He dialed Lauren's hospital room number.

Polly answered, "Hello, this is Mrs. Fulghum in Lauren Harper's room."

"Good morning, Mrs. Fulghum. This is Detective Preston. I will be getting a search warrant to enter Lauren's apartment, and I wanted you to know what I'm about to do."

"Well...I don't know. Let me ask Ben."

Ben took the receiver, "Detective, why do you want to go into her apartment?"

"Mr. Harper won't talk with me, and I need information about Jack. It's just routine.

I might be able to find a name that would give me information about him."

"Well, in that case, it's all right."

"By the way, how is Lauren?"

"Dr. Roberts was in last night, and he seemed to think that everything will be all right. Thanks for asking."

"I'll be in touch with you when I get back." Mark hung up and called the airport for a flight to Boston. The light hanging over the desk cast a shadow of Mark's head as he bent over his notes. He tapped his pen in a drum-like fashion and muttered, "H-m-m, I'm beginning to see that there could be a possible motive for murder."

* * * * *

Tuesday morning the plane was filled to capacity because people were returning home from the Christmas weekend. Mark Preston walked through the crowded terminal while Christmas carols still played. He grabbed his bag off the conveyor belt and rushed outside to hail a cab.

A light snow fell as the windshield wipers clicked rapidly knocking the icy flakes to one side. The taxi threaded its way through the tangled mass of buses, cabs, and cars. The driver jockeyed his way to the exit that would take him to the address given. Once there, Mark told the cab driver to wait or to come back in a half hour.

"Okay! I'll be back."

Mark yelled at the driver as he drove off, "Don't you forget!" He opened the door to the apartment and with a trained eye scanned the interior. It was obvious that this had been a neat and organized couple. He opened cabinet doors, closets, and drawers. He found that Lauren fell short of being as neat as Jack when it came to putting her clothes away. Everything that belonged to him was organized to perfection. Mark sifted through the desk drawers looking for information. Nothing. He checked the top shelf of a closet and found a small file box. Carefully, he thumbed through bank statements, bills, important papers, and insurance policies. He noticed immediately that Jack didn't have a bank account. It was all in Lauren's name. Uh-huh, he thought, she supported him. Mark found the insurance policy for $500,000 and read that the beneficiary would be Jack Harper in case of her death. An envelope addressed to Lieutenant Jack Harper was filed behind the policy. The official letter was his dismissal from North Bridge Military Academy. On the dismissal paper was the name Colonel Bruce Hoffner. Mark stuck the policy and letter in his brief case and left the apartment.

* * * * *

Next stop—Harvard University. The next day Mark took an early flight to Cambridge, Massachusetts. Mark told the cab driver to let him off in front of the administration building and to wait. A directory in the front hall listed the room number for the Office of Admissions.

Candy Rogers leaned back in her chair after typing a letter, pulled out a fingernail file, and worked on her nails. Mark observed Candy through the window of the office door and formed an opinion before he knocked. The way she wore her clothes sent a signal that she was on the 'loose'."

She looked up when she heard a knock. "Come in," she said in her southern drawl.

"Hello, I'm Detective Mark Preston. I would like information about Jack Harper."

Candy squealed, "Jack Harper! I've been wondering where he was. I haven't seen him lately. I miss him so-o-o much." She jabbered on about how good-looking he was, and it was a shame that he and his wife didn't get along.

Mark interrupted her and said, "Miss…

"Oh! Everyone calls me Candy. You can, too. I'm glad to have someone to talk to. It has been really lonesome around here since everyone's gone for Christmas break. What can I do for you?"

"Did you know Jack personally?"

"I sure did…but please don't tell his wife. She would just die if she knew that he was going to divorce her after he graduates."

"Candy, would you mind giving me a schedule of his classes and professors?"

"Lordy mercy, that's no problem. You just wait right here, and I'll get it for you in a minute."

While Mark waited, he smiled to himself and thought, she is the first person who revealed everything—not only her figure, but also some interesting facts. She acts like a dingbat, and he'd bet she has had an affair with Jack. When Candy came back with the schedule, Mark said, "Miss Rogers, thank you for talking to me. I'll be in touch with you again real soon."

"By the way, is Jack in trouble or something?"

"I'm sorry to tell you this, Miss Rogers, but Jack and his wife were in an accident and Jack was killed."

Candy's mouth dropped opened in shock as she cried out, "Oh no! I can't believe that my honey's dead!"

Mark explained what happened and said, "I'm just doing some investigating. I'll be calling on you later."

"Okay, I'll be right here," sobbed Candy.

* * * * *

Mark got a flight back to Newburgh that afternoon. When he arrived home, he made a call to North Bridge Military Academy. A man's voice clipped off a routine response, "North Bridge Military Academy, what can I do for you?"

"Please connect me with Colonel Bruce Hoffner."

"Who may I say is calling, Sir?"

"Detective Mark Preston."

"Thank you, Sir."

A gruff voice answered, "All right. This is Colonel Bruce Hoffner."

"Sir, I need to know something about Lieutenant Jack Harper."

"Detective Preston, I'll not answer any questions until I have proof of your identity."

"Sir, may I make an appointment with you?"

Colonel Hoffner responded explicitly, "Meet me this afternoon at the entrance of the Academy at fourteen hundred hours. I'll talk to you then. Good day."

Mark muttered, "Wow, he's strictly military. I'd hate to cross him."

* * * * *

Mark immediately got into his car and headed to North Bridge Military Academy. More than once, his car spun on icy patches but he was able to keep control. It was more than a three-hour drive. He checked his watch. One thirty—fifteen more miles. Mark didn't want to be late—not for this man.

At exactly two o'clock, he stopped in front of the black iron gates of the Academy. An official car was parked on the other side. Colonel Hoffner got out and met Mark at the gate. The Colonel said, "Sir, show me your identification." Mark pulled out his badge, driver's license, and a letter with the Newburgh Police emblem on it. Satisfied, they got into the Colonels' car.

"What kind of questions do you want to ask me?"

"How long did Lt. Harper serve in the Academy?"

"Four years as a cadet, five years in the regular Army, and two years as an instructor here."

"How did you get along with him?"

The Colonel's face reddened. He gave Mark a scowling look and demanded, "Why did you ask me that? Why are you interrogating me? You had better tell me your reason before you ask another question."

"Sir, Jack Harper was in an accident and was killed. I'm only doing my job to investigate probable cause."

There was a complete transformation in Colonel Hoffner's demeanor. Mark thought he heard him say, "good riddance." His voice was so low it was barely audible. The colonel pushed his seat back a little farther, folded his hands in his lap, took a deep breath as though relieved and said, "Jack was an outstanding cadet, but he was devious, cruel, manipulating, and brutal to other cadets. I tried for years to catch him breaking the rules, but he put fear into the hearts of anyone who reported him. As he rose in rank, he put some of the cadets through extreme torture. It was only after he came back that I finally caught him breaking a strict rule. Before he could be court-martialed, he resigned."

"Do you mind telling me what his offense was?"

"He had an affair with one of the female cadets."

"What was the girl's name?"

"Cadet Lisa Mitchell."

"Do you know where she is?"

"We have her parents' address. That's all. I'll send it to you."

"Sir, you have been very helpful."

Colonel Hoffner looked at Mark with his steely blue eyes and asked, "How did Jack die?"

Mark explained everything he knew about the accident and when he told him how Jack had fallen on the jagged rocks, the Colonel smiled. "Sir, I hope I can count on you to be a witness if this case goes to trial."

"Yes. Just let me know ahead of time."

It was time to go. Mark thanked him, returned to his car, and drove back to Newburg.

CHAPTER 32

Lauren began to look forward to seeing the couple that came to see her. She liked to hear them talk about their daughter. It made her feel closer to them.

One morning, Ben and Polly were late arriving. Every time the door opened, she hoped it would be them. Orderlies, nurses, and the doctor came and went, but still her friends hadn't come. Maybe something had happened. Surely they hadn't forgotten her! They were the only people she knew, and they seemed to care. She felt anxious. Lauren remembered that the doctor told her they were her parents. Could it be? From her window, she could see the snowdrifts that looked like icebergs all along the sides of the street. Maybe the roads were too bad, and they couldn't get out.

Just as she was about to give up hope, Ben's cheerful voice sang out, "Good morning, Lauren! How's my favorite girl today?"

"Good morning! I was afraid something had happened to you. You'll never know how much your visits mean to me."

Giving a hearty laugh Ben said, "It was hazardous driving, but it would take more than ice and snow to keep us away."

* * * * *

Detective Preston went to his office Thursday morning around nine o'clock. He typed most of the documentation he planned to give to the District Attorney. It was the duty of the court to prove beyond a reasonable doubt whether she was guilty or innocent. Mark stapled his information together and walked up a flight of stairs to the D.A.'s office.

He knocked on the door and heard a gruff voice, "Come in!"

Mark entered the office of District Attorney Wilburt Newton. The D. A. stood a little over six feet tall, slightly overweight, and nearly bald with just a fringe of blond hair circling his head. He was dressed in a heavy brown coat sweater and tan corduroy pants. The D.A. was looking out the window, concentrating on something outside. Mark greeted him, "Good morning, Wilburt."

"Good morning, Mark. I'm looking at people trying to walk on ice-covered streets. It's really fascinating to watch. They look like they're walking a tight rope, and unfortunately some of them land on their butts." His sky blue eyes crinkled at the corners when he laughed. "People are funny. I don't know why we laugh when we see someone fall. I suppose it's because they look rather spastic when their legs and arms go in all directions."

Mark said, "Have you heard about the accident at Forest Hill Ski Resort?"

"You bet. That's all I've heard on the television lately. Have you finished your investigation?"

"Here's my report. It isn't complete, but there's enough for probable cause." He handed the papers to the D.A.

Wilburt glanced quickly at the papers. "Probable cause, huh? The news reporters made it sound like it was just an accidental death." Wilburt studied the report briefly and said, "I'll look over your report and let you know my decision this afternoon."

"Sir, I'll be in my office the rest of the day." Mark closed the door and hurried back to his office. Time wasn't on his side. A lot had to be done quickly before Lauren's due date. The waiting made him anxious. He mumbled, "I think I'll call the hospital to see how she's doing."

After a few rings, a man's voice answered, "Ben Fulghum, Room 208."

"Hello, Mr. Fulghum. This is Detective Preston. I'm sorry I haven't called sooner, but I've been away on business. How's Lauren?"

"She's healing nicely, but she hasn't regained her memory. Dr. Roberts said her prognosis is fine, and the baby hasn't suffered any harm."

"I'm glad to hear the good news. I'll be getting back in touch with you later on. Goodbye." Mark was relieved to hear she was healing so quickly. He dug into his paper work again.

It was late in the afternoon when the D.A. came to his office and said, "Mark, I believe you're right. We'll start the proper proceedings as soon as Lauren Harper regains her memory, and she's well enough to be booked."

"Okay boss." Mark's attitude brightened immediately.

* * * * *

The Fughums arrived at the hospital Friday morning around ten o'clock. Ben had brought the newspaper to fill in the crossword puzzle and Polly had a book to read. Before Lauren flipped on the television, she punched and fussed with her pillows until they were just right. It was time for the soap operas. The local news station, RWH-CL, flashed a news-bulletin. The reporter announced that a television crew had gone to Forest Hills Ski Resort to tape the site where the murder took place.

When she saw the cameraman standing near the edge of the cliff, a blood curdling scream came from her—"**HELP! HELP! PLEASE!...DON'T...JACK...HELP!**" Lauren flung the pillows and beat her arms against the covers as though she were fighting off an attacker. Ben sprang to his feet and tried to calm her. Polly ran into the hall yelling for a doctor. The emergency code sounded down the hall. Dr. Roberts ran to Lauren's room. A nurse came in right behind him and gave her a shot.

It didn't take long for the shot to take effect, and Lauren grew quiet. She continued to stare at the television. She heard the reporter tell how, at first, the man's death was thought to be an accident but upon investigation, it was alleged to be a jealous wife getting revenge on her unfaithful husband.

Lauren cried out, "Jack's dead! No, he can't be dead! How could they accuse me of killing him? I loved him!" Ben and Polly held Lauren's hand and tried to comfort her. Tears filled their eyes. They had mixed emotions—happy their daughter's memory was back but distraught about the accusation of murder.

Mark Preston was furious when he found out the news had been leaked to the television station. He called the D.A.'s office and yelled, "Wilburt, who in the hell told the news reporters?"

"Damned if I know!" Wilburt yelled back. "Now I have to issue the warrant for her arrest."

"I don't envy the person who tells Lauren Harper she has been accused of murder."

* ** * *

Dr. Roberts came into Lauren's room the next day and said in his best bedside manner, "Lauren, your test and examinations indicate that you can go home. You have my permission, providing someone is there to take care of you. I suggest you and your parents fly by helicopter back to Boston."

Polly spoke up, "Don't worry Dr. Roberts, Ben and I plan to be with her."

"Good. I can't think of anyone that could do a better job. As soon as Lauren talks to her lawyer, she may leave."

Ben said, "After we get her settled, I'll fly home, close up the house, pack some more clothes, and return to Boston."

CHAPTER 33

Monday morning a law enforcement officer walked briskly through the busy hospital corridors to the elevator. He pressed the elevator button and rode up to the second floor. There he paused at a nurse's station and inquired, "Where can I find Dr. Charles Roberts?"

"Who are you and why do you wish to see him?"

The Officer flashed his badge and then told her he wanted Dr. Roberts to be with him when he went to Lauren's room. The nurse picked up the pager and called, "Dr. Roberts, please report to the nurse's station on second floor."

Five Minutes passed. Dr. Roberts stopped at the counter and asked, "Who wants to see me?"

The nurse pointed to the officer, "That man over by the elevator."

The doctor crossed over to him and asked, "Sir, what do you want?"

The officer saw his name pinned to his white jacket and said, "Dr. Roberts, I have to do a very unpleasant job of issuing a warrant for Lauren Harper's arrest. I would like for you to be with me in case she becomes upset."

The doctor remarked, "I've heard the news and indeed I want to be there."

When the two men walked into the room, Lauren looked up surprised to see a strange man with the doctor. The officer said, "Mrs. Harper, I'm Sergeant Kirk Davis." Lauren clutched the sheets and pulled them up under her chin. The officer said, "Detective Mark Preston, who did the investigation, believes there is probable cause that you murdered your husband. The news leaked out before we could tell you. I'm sorry. Before you say anything, I must inform you of your rights. 'Anything you say, can and will be held against you in a court of law.' I suggest you get a lawyer immediately." The officer handed her the warrant and said, "I have to take you down to the police station and book you for murder."

Lauren started crying. Ben and Polly rushed to her side to comfort her. "I didn't kill Jack. I didn't kill Jack," she cried. The doctor gave her a shot to calm her.

The officer turned to the doctor and asked, "Is she going to be all right to go to the police station?"

"Sir, you'll have to wait until this afternoon. I'm sure she'll be all right by then."

The officer said, "It will be my duty to stay outside her door."

Ben spoke up, "Honey, we know you're innocent. You don't have a thing to worry about. The truth will come out. Detective Preston has a job to do, and what he has found is circumstantial. When Rita gets here, she will straighten everything out."

"Dad," Lauren said as she wiped her eyes and stammered, "Get Ann Goodman's and Rita LaBaron's telephone numbers."

"All right, honey. I'll do it right now. I'll call Detective Preston."

As soon as Mark heard Ben's voice he said, "Hello Mr. Fulghum. What can I do for you?"

"Lauren has been served with a warrant for the murder of Jack and she needs her clothes that were in her suitcase. They want her to go to the police station as soon as possible. Also, give me the numbers of Attorney Rita LaBaron and Ann Goodman."

" Okay. I'll get them." In a few minutes, Mark gave him

the numbers and told Ben he would send her clothes right over.

Lauren was listening to the conversation. When Ben hung up the phone, she said,

"Thanks Dad, I'll get in touch with Rita."

The police officer spoke up, "Mrs. Harper, I'm going to tell you some of the things that you will have to do when a person is booked for a crime. First, we'll go down to the station. They'll fingerprint you and take your picture.

Lauren's eyes were filled with fear. Ben and Polly hovered around her uttering reassuring words that Rita would make everyone see that they were making a terrible mistake.

* * * * *

It was noon when Lauren was able to get in touch with Rita. "Thank goodness you're home Rita, this is Lauren. You told me to call if I ever needed any help. Well—I really need you now."

"Lauren, it's so good to hear from you but from the anxiety in your voice you seem troubled. "What's happened? Are you all right?"

"A lot has happened since we last met. Yes—I'm in deep trouble. I'll get right to the point. I've been accused of murder."

"What! Accused of murder! When did all of this happen?"

Lauren told her about the weekend that Jack planned for them at the Forest Hill Ski Resort. Then she told her about the pictures, the accident that caused Jack's death, and her amnesia. "Rita, I'm calling from the hospital in Newburgh, New York. Detective Mark Preston is investigating the accident. He believes because of all the evidence he has collected that I killed Jack. I've been served a warrant for the murder, and I was advised to hire a lawyer. Will you represent me?" Lauren tried to keep from crying.

"Jack's dead! Oh, my God. Okay…okay now Lauren try to be calm. I have a heavy work schedule, but somehow I'll shove things around and fly out there tomorrow. Then you can give me all the details."

"They are taking me to the police station this afternoon. How can I get out of staying in jail?"

"Call me again as soon as you get to the station. I'll talk to the prosecuting attorney and see what I can arrange. Since you're pregnant, they may let you go if your parents will be responsible. I'll work on that premise. Lauren, I'm so sorry this has happened to you. I'll stay in touch. Please take care of yourself. Bye"

* * * * *

The clothes arrived and Lauren dressed. She notified the officer outside her room that she was ready to go. After Lauren was released from the hospital, the three of them and the officer went to the police station. She went through the procedure of being booked.

CHAPTER 34

January 1, 1995. Boston, Massachusetts. In the meantime, Lauren and her parents were flown back to her hometown by helicopter. In the mean time, Rita worked on the trial proceedings. Ben flew to Williamsburg to get more clothes.

One day, Lauren said to her mother. "Mom, since I have time, would you teach me how to sew? I need something to keep my mind off the trial."

"Of course, honey. I'll call Ben before he flies back and tell him to bring my portable sewing machine. While we wait for him, we'll go shopping for some material for baby clothes and blankets."

The next day, Ben came in with suitcases packed with clothes and the sewing machine.

Lauren and Polly spent many hours cutting and sewing blankets, bibs, and nightshirts for the baby. It filled many anxious hours for Lauren. Nighttime was hard for her. The horror of hearing about Jack's falling to his death gave her nightmares, but the lies he had told hurt even more.

* * * * *

Rita went straight to the judge and prosecuting attorney when she arrived in Newburgh. After a long debated discussion with the court and lawyers, Rita called Lauren about 9:00 p.m. to tell her of their decision.

"Hello," answered Lauren. "Who's calling?"

"It's Rita. Don't tell me you've already forgotten the sound of my voice."

"I'm sorry. I had drifted off to sleep while looking at TV. How are things in Newburgh?"

"That's why I'm calling. I'm in Newburgh getting things lined up for the trial. A decision has been made that the trial will start May 1st, after you've had your baby. I have a lot of work to do to prepare for the trial, and it would give you time to have your baby without the extra stress. I wish I could wave a magic wand and it would all be over, but the law does things in its own time. Now that all the legal talk is over, how are you getting along?"

"The memories of Jack are beginning to haunt me. The flight here was okay, but coming back to the apartment hasn't been easy. Everywhere I turn I see things that remind me of him. All his clothes are neatly hung and put in their proper place. His books and papers are just like he left them. I must admit that he made me a much better housekeeper than I had ever been; although, sometimes it drove me crazy that he wanted everything to be so perfect."

"Lauren, we'll talk more later," Rita said. "I have to get back to work on your case. In the meantime, call me if you have any questions. Good-bye."

* * * * *

Polly and Lauren made part of Lauren's bedroom into a mini-nursery. Mr. and Mrs. Fulghum occupied the second bedroom. They planned to stay until Lauren's trial was over, and she was able to take care of herself and the baby.

Each day she marked off a day that brought her closer to her delivery. Lauren read everything she could on "How to Take Care of a Baby." During the last week in March, in the middle of the night, Lauren called out for her mother. Polly woke up from a deep sleep and rushed to Lauren's room. When she saw the pain on Lauren's face, she knew it was time to go.

"Ben! Ben!" yelled Polly. "Get Lauren's bag and get the car ready! We're going to the hospital! Call the hospital and tell them we're on our way!"

Lauren tried to get dressed. Minute by minute the contractions became more frequent. Polly threw a bathrobe around Lauren's shoulders. She wobbled through the living room holding her stomach, trying not to cry. Polly helped her safely into the car. Ben was so nervous that words stuck in his throat. All he could do, at this time, was to drive as fast as he could without having a wreck. He hoped a policeman would stop him so that he could clear the way to the hospital. Lauren cried out several times as the contractions grew closer and closer. Polly tried to keep her calm.

Ben yelled, "There's the emergency entrance! We're here! Hold on Baby!"

The medics were there to put Lauren in a wheelchair and to rush her to the maternity ward. Dr. Koss was paged. In a matter of minutes, the doctor was standing beside Lauren. In a jovial, soft-spoken manner, she said, "Lauren, here you are again, but this time you'll be able to take your baby home. Try to relax and follow the directions you learned in Lamaze classes.

Your Dad and Mom will be beside you to keep you on course."

Four hours later, Ben and Polly stood beside Lauren's bed. She had a smile that stretched from ear to ear. Happily Lauren said, "Grandma and Grandpa, meet your beautiful granddaughter. God has blessed me with this tiny angel, and that is what I'm going to name her—Angel." Lauren pulled back the blanket for them to get a good look at her.

Polly said, "Oh Lauren, she really is beautiful. I can't wait until I can rock her like I did you. You know we're going to spoil her."

Smiling, Ben said, "I can't be happier. It will be like seeing you grow up all over again, and what a joy that will be."

* * * * *

Ben and Polly returned to the apartment for the night, leaving Lauren in the hands of the hospital staff. A nurse brought Angel in and placed her in Lauren's arms. She picked up one of the babies hands and stroked her tiny fingers. Lauren thought, it is really a miracle that she survived the ordeals that Jack had put her through. Softly, she stroked the blonde fuzz on top of Angel's head and wished that Jack could see her. In her heart, she still believed that Jack would have loved this beautiful baby and in time would have been a good father.

After two days in the hospital, Ben and Polly took Lauren back to her apartment with Angel tucked safely in her arms. For the next five weeks, all of Lauren's thoughts were centered around her precious bundle of joy. Annoucements were sent to all her friends, especially to Camille, Ann Goodman, Rita, and even to the Harpers.

* * * * *

The trial was ready. Rita sent a special delivery letter dispatched to Lauren. She included an itinerary for Lauren to follow: "Fly to Newburgh April 28th. Rooms have been reserved for you, your parents, and my office staff. Motel reservations are stapled to the letter. Call me as soon as you arrive. Rita"

Lauren's hands trembled as she held the letter and thought; the wheels of justice are beginning to turn. She looked at her parents and with a worried expression on her face said, "We'll be going to Newburgh tomorrow. The trial begins in a few days." Then she handed the letter to them and went to her bedroom. Lauren sat on the edge of the bed opposite the dresser and looked in the mirror. She stared at herself and thought, where did it all go wrong? She had tried to be a good wife. She'd believed in him and loved him with all her heart. Why wasn't her love good enough for him? Why would anyone think that she could kill him? Now, she thought, will Jack still have control of her life even though he's dead? Lauren got up from the bed and started packing for the trip to Newburgh.

* * * * *

When they arrived at the motel, Lauren told her mother that she was going down to Rita's room because they needed to discuss the trial. She knocked softly. Rita called out, "Who is it?"

Pressing close to the door, Lauren spoke in a low voice trying to avoid anyone from hearing, "It's Lauren."

Rita got up from the table where she had papers for the trial and opened the door. "Come in, Lauren. I want you to meet my assistant, Jeanette Edwards."

Lauren stretched out her hand to an attractive lady of average height, short blonde hair, and vivacious blue eyes. Jeanette clasped her hand and said warmly, "I'm glad to finally meet you after all the nice things I've heard."

Rita chimed in, "Before we get started, Lauren has a new member of her family; a precious little girl named, Angel Harper. You'll get to see her sometime during the trial. Now let's get down to business. Lauren, we've been discussing some important details, such as what you'll wear at the trial and how you'll answer questions when you're called to be a witness. Do you have something that you think will be suitable to wear?"

"Well, at least I won't have to wear a maternity dress. I have a yellow striped silk blouse that looks nice with my navy blue pantsuit, or I could wear a purple linen sheath dress with a short jacket."

"The navy suit sounds perfect!" Rita exclaimed.

Rita stood up like an army commander ready to give orders. "Ladies, tomorrow is the big day. Lauren, there will be a lot of curious people, cameramen, and reporters badgering you with questions. Stay close to me and don't say anything. I'll do the talking. I've rented a van to take all of us to the courthouse in the morning. Lauren, you need to go back to your room and get a good night's sleep."

"It's easy for someone else to tell you not to worry," Lauren mumbled to herself as she went back to her room. "They can't begin to know how it feels unless they have walked in your shoes."

* * * * *

By eight-thirty the next morning, everyone had taken his seat in the van. Lauren, Polly, Ben, Rita, and Jeanette wore somber expressions on their faces. Silence prevailed over the group as the van approached the courthouse. Lauren stared out of the window and saw a throng of people gathered in front of the colonial style, red brick building. Some spectators waited on the Georgian style porch. They huddled around the four large columns that supported the roof up to the second floor of the three-story building.

As the van drew close to the courthouse, she noticed a copper dome that was covered in verdigrise; and on the dome sat a huge eagle, signifying justice. Lauren said a silent prayer that justice would be served. As soon as the van stopped, the crowd converged on them yelling questions as they stepped out. Rita grabbed Lauren's arm and hurriedly pulled her inside away from the press of people.

When they entered the large mahogany paneled courtroom, people turned and stared at Lauren as though she might be some circus curiosity. She looked straight ahead, oblivious to all the activities in preparation for the trial to take place. Guards checked for security. Reporters jostled for space, and spectators scrambled for the best seats. Whispering in the courtroom sounded like bees in a beehive. Rita escorted Lauren to her table. A railing separated the spectators from those involved in the trial. The Fulghums sat directly behind the defendant's table. Lauren sat down, turned, and raised her hand timidly to acknowledge her parents. Then she looked around the courtroom and saw Mr. Vernon Harper sitting behind the prosecutor's table. Hatred seemed to spill out of his eyes.

The lawyers took their places at the counsel tables, and the court recorder sat ready to transcribe the proceedings. The prosecutor and the defense attorney had already carefully selected the jurors a week before. The jury consisted of seven women and five men. They were in the Jury Room waiting for the trial to start.

Judge Clark was in her forties and had a reputation of being brilliant but quick-tempered. She was attractive, with brown hair cropped close to her head. Judge Clark came out of her office with a look of confidence and self-control. The bailiff called out: "All rise. The Honorable Elizabeth L. Clark is now on the bench. The circuit court, criminal division, is now in session." The crack of the gavel echoed in the courtroom. When the door opened, members of the jury filed out and sat in their appointed seats.

Judge Clark addressed Prosecutor Wilburt Newton and Defending Council Rita LaBaron and asked if they were ready to give their opening statements. They responded that they were ready.

District Attorney Newton, wore a blue and white seersucker suit, a white shirt with a button down collar, and a red and blue striped tie. He stood up before the court and dramatically unfolded his story:

"This trial is about a woman so filled with revenge, that she pushed her husband over a cliff. He plummeted to his death as he fell hundreds of feet down a rocky mountain side."

Newton walked up and down in front of the jury with his hands behind his back. Without warning, he nimbly twirled around and pointed a finger at Lauren and shouted, "That woman killed her husband, and I'm here to prove it!" Lauren bolted out of her seat, ready to shout back at him. Rita grabbed her arm and whispered in her ear, "Calm down Lauren. You have to control your feelings. You could damage your case if you make any outburst." Reluctantly, Lauren sat down.

After the State had presented its opening statement, the Judge called Counselor Rita LaBaron and asked if she was ready to present her statement. Rita replied, "Yes, Your Honor." As she walked toward the jurors, Rita looked more like a fashion model than a lawyer. Her jet-black hair was pulled back in a neat French twist. She wore an emerald green suit with a skirt that was short enough to reveal a pair of shapely legs. Triple strands of snow-white pearls and a pair of clustered earrings framed her beautiful face. Rita stood poised and spoke in a compassionate but compelling voice.

"Lauren Harper was reared by parents who loved her dearly. She was and still is the center of their lives. They taught her to believe that love could overcome many trials and tribulations that arise in a person's life. Lauren fell in love with Jack Harper. It was her belief that she could make him happy. The burden fell upon her to pay for all the financial responsibilities, regardless of whether he worked or not. She wanted him to accomplish a dream of his, and that was to become a lawyer. She never complained. Soon after they were married, she discovered that she was pregnant. Jack didn't want children, but Lauren wanted a baby more than anything in the world. She was sure that after the baby was born, Jack would love it, too. I am here to prove that Lauren Harper would never have killed the man she loved."

For the first time, Lauren relaxed. After hearing Rita's opening statement, she felt sure she would be exonerated from the accusations made against her.

* * * * *

Judge Clark asked in a clear sharp voice, "Is the State ready to call its first witness?"

"Yes, Your Honor," Wilburt Newton said loud and clear. "I would like to call Mrs. Lisa Mitchell Cannon." Lauren turned and saw a sedately dressed but elegant lady, with beautiful auburn hair. She walked confidently from the witness holding room to the witness stand. All witnesses are sworn in before testifying in the case. It made Lauren furious knowing that Jack had been with her. Her body grew tense as she leaned forward and placed her clasped hands on the table. Rita saw that Lauren was getting upset. Lauren's eyes blazed with anger as she stared at Lisa. Rita reminded Lauren not to cause a disturbance.

Prosecutor Newton fired his first question. "Mrs. Cannon, when did you first meet Jack Harper?"

"I met him when he was an instructor at the North Bridge Military Academy, and I was a cadet."

"How would you describe Jack Harper?"

Lisa entwined her fingers nervously as she kept them in her lap. With an air of melancholy, she answered, "There was a charisma about Jack that attracted me immediately. I admired him because he had the ambition to become one of the top leaders at North Bridge. I too, would like to have become an officer."

"Mrs. Cannon, I have a letter written by you and received by Jack Harper in the middle of November as part of the evidence in this case." Newton walked back to his table, picked up the letter, and handed it to Lisa. He waited for her to look at it. Satisfied, he asked, "Is this the letter that you wrote to Jack?"

"Yes, but I didn't know he was married at the time."

"Mrs. Cannon, would you mind telling the jury why you wrote this letter?"

"After my husband died, I thought it would be all right if I wrote Jack to see how he was doing, and maybe we could get together and reminisce about the days at North Bridge Military Academy. He knew that I was pregnant when we both resigned from the academy. Our son was three years old at the time I wrote the letter, and I thought he might like to see him."

Vernon Harper jumped to his feet and cried out, "That's a lie! My son would never fraternize with a female cadet!"

Judge Clark slammed her gavel on the desk and shouted, "Sir! Sit down. If you disrupt this court again, you will be arrested and taken out of this courtroom." Lauren turned in her seat to see Vernon's outburst.

Prosecutor Newton continued to question Mrs. Cannon, "How did you know where to send the letter?"

"I sent it to his parent's address in White Plains, New York."

"In your letter did you give him your address and telephone number?"

"Yes."

"Did Jack call you?"

"He called as soon as he received the letter."

Mr. Newton continued, "Did he tell you that he was married?"

"No, he didn't."

"What happened next?"

"I asked him when we could get together. I was surprised, but thrilled, when he could come the next weekend."

"Did Jack ask you anything about your deceased husband and what he did for a living?"

"Yes, he did. First, I told him how much my husband loved Travis and treated him like he was his very own. I also told Jack that my husband had invented a program for the computer that made him a multi-millionaire and that I would never have to worry about money again. After I filled Jack in on some of my personal life, I told him I would send my personal plane to pick him up at an airport near his home."

Newton stepped a few feet closer to Lisa and leaned toward her and asked, "How did Jack react to your remarks?"

Lisa said, "Jack sounded very excited about coming to see me."

"What time of year did this meeting take place?"

"It was the middle of November of last year." A disparaging groan came from Lauren as she remembered that was when she went to visit Dr. Ann Goodman.

"What was the purpose of his visit?" "At first, I thought it was just to reminisce about our days at North Bridge. When we saw each other, however, we realized that we were still in love. He told me he was unhappy in his marriage and that he was going to get a divorce. Then, he said, we would get married."

The courtroom began to buzz with excitement. The judge rapped her gavel to bring order in the court.

Newton quickly changed the subject. He said, "Ladies and gentlemen of the jury, I'm going to pass a picture and a letter around for you to see. In the letter, Mrs. Cannon told Jack he was the father of her son." A murmur rolled through the courtroom. Lauren hung her head and thought she might have felt like killing him had she known what he had been doing. Newton continued, by asking Lisa to identify the people in the photograph.

She responded, "They are, Travis, Jack Harper, and I."

Newton asked, "When was this picture taken?"

"This picture was taken while Jack Harper was visiting me about three weeks before Christmas."

Newton exploded, " That's when Lauren Harper decided to get revenge!"

Rita cried, "Objection! Prosecutor Newton is making an assumption."

The Judge said, "Objection sustained."

Wilburt Newton wasn't bothered by Rita's objection and smiled as he waited for the reaction of the jury. The jurors' expressions were exactly what he wanted to see. They seemed to believe her to be guilty. "Thank you, Mrs. Cannon, that's all the questions I have at this time."

Judge Clark asked the prosecutor if he had other witnesses.

"Yes, Your Honor, I would like to call Colonel Bruce Hoffner to the witness stand."

Colonel Hoffner marched briskly into the courtroom. His uniform was pressed to perfection, the creases in his pants were razor sharp, and his shoes shone like glass. The Colonel's eyes quickly surveyed the crowd until he caught sight of Lauren. She sat straight up in her chair when she saw Colonel Hoffner show a slight sign of compassion. The Colonel took the witness seat and folded his hands in his lap.

Prosecutor Newton looked at the Colonel and said, "Sir, all I want from you is to help me establish what kind of man Jack Harper was at the academy. Colonel Hoffner, how long did you know Jack Harper?"

"I knew him the four years while he was at North Bridge and two years after he returned following his completion of a mandatory five years service in the regular Army."

"Was he a good cadet?"

"He was until he became a leader in one of the barracks."

"What happened then?"

"He went beyond the normal hazing of plebes and cadets."

"Could you give me an example?"

The Colonel frowned as he spoke, "Jack Harper made his cadres line up with paddles and forced one cadet to run the line as they hit him. Then he made the same cadet stay outside all night in freezing weather. He nearly died." The Colonel continued to tell the court about many cadets who went to the infirmary with broken fingers, broken noses, and horrible bruises from paddling. Other injuries were inflicted when cadets failed to make perfect scores in drills under his command. The Colonel ended his speech, "I tried to get the cadets to report him, but they feared the repercussions if Jack found out who reported him. I could never catch him in the act." The Colonel clenched his fist, raised it before the court and declared, "I vowed, one day, I would see him punished for his malicious acts to the cadets."

"Colonel Hoffner, did you succeed in having him kicked out of North Bridge?"

"Yes, but it was after he came back from serving his Army obligation and became an instructor at the Academy. I became suspicious during the second year of his employment. I discovered that he was fraternizing with one of the female cadets, Lisa Mitchell. Jack was shrewd about covering his tracks, but she made a mistake in signing out to go home one weekend. I followed my hunch and caught them together at the ski lodge close to where Jack fell over the cliff. Jack and Lisa resigned before I had the pleasure of seeing them court-martialed. Jack Harper was the most devious, cruel, self-serving military man I have ever known."

Wilburt backed sway from the witness stand and said, "Colonel Hoffner, do you believe that Jack Harper would do anything to get Lauren Harper mad enough to leave him so that he could go to Lisa Mitchell Cannon."

Rita stood up and yelled, "Objection. It calls for speculation! Colonel Hoffner only knows what Jack Harper was capable of doing while in the Academy."

Judge Clark said, "Objection sustained. Colonel Hoffner can't predict what a person will do. In this case it's just one person's opinion."

Wilburt nodded at Colonel Hoffner and said, "Thank you, Colonel Hoffner. I have no further questions."

Colonel Hoffner stepped down from the witness stand. Lauren sat motionless. She was having a hard time absorbing his testimony.

The courtroom returned to the whispering as it often did after a dramatic scene. Judge Clark rapped her gavel several times. Then she raised her voice and called out, "Since the prosecutor has no further questions and since it's so near lunch time, we will adjourn and resume this trial at 2:00 p.m."

* * * * *

The spectators were eager to get back to court. It had been

a long time since they had seen very much action in their little town.

Judge Clark walked briskly into the courtroom and took her place behind the massive oak desk. She asked, "Does the prosecutor have another witness?"

"Yes, Your Honor. I would like to call Mrs. Vernon Harper to the stand."

Rita leaned over to Lauren and said, " Her testimony may really shake you up. Please try to stay in control of your emotions."

Lauren whispered back, "I'll try but keeping my feelings under control has really been hard."

Mrs. Sarah Harper was dressed in a black suit, hose, and shoes. She was wearing a black bow that held her faded blonde hair in a bun on the back of her head. The only color to break the bleakness of her attire was a small white collar and a pair of small pearl earrings. Her face was colorless except for her wide-open gray-green eyes. She sat rigidly in the witness chair.

The prosecutor asked, "How well did you know Lauren Fulghum before she became Mrs. Jack Harper?"

"I only knew what my son had told me. I never saw her until the day of the wedding. I can honestly say I never drew any conclusion as to the kind of woman my son was marrying. It was on such short notice."

"What do you mean, 'short notice'?"

"They had only been going together for a few months when Jack announced they were going to be married. The first thing I thought of was maybe they had to get married. My husband told Jack if he married her, we wouldn't support him any more in his education.

"Would you mind describing your son to the jury?"

Sarah's face relaxed. "Jack was disciplined about keeping his body in perfect condition. He was a natural born athlete and excelled in every sport he played. On one of his rare visits to us, he told me how he wanted to be a great lawyer. I believed he would have made it." Sarah smiled slightly as she continued, "I thought he was the most handsome young man in our town. When he was growing up, his father made sure that he did everything perfectly. He was extremely strict with Jack." Sarah's face began to tighten. "Jack knew the consequences if he failed to win in sports or fell below excellence in all his studies."

"Did you ever see Jack behave in a violent manner?"

"He...uh...well, sometimes he would hit a playmate."

Prosecutor Newton's head jerked, and he asked quickly, "How did Jack get along with you?"

Sarah smiled. "We got along fine. I knew he loved me. I tried to show him how much I loved him by cooking things he liked. I hugged and kissed him when I could." Lauren saw Sarah glance at Vernon as if worried about her husband's reaction.

Mr. Newton continued, "Mrs. Harper, when Jack was a little boy and failed to live up to his father's expectations, what did Mr. Harper do to him?"

Sarah Harper rubbed her hands and wavered back and forth in her seat. She clenched her teeth as though she were in pain. Lauren watched her look at Vernon. Her lips tightened and her voice rose higher as she answered, "His father beat him with a belt or a large wooden paddle until blood ran down his back."

Wilburt waited for the sounds of anguish from the spectators to subside. Then he continued, "What did you mean when you said earlier that you loved Jack when you could?"

"His father didn't allow any affection to be shown in our house. If it was, I received a harsh reprimand from Mr. Harper."

Lauren was riveted by what Mrs. Harper was saying. It seemed to her that she was expressing pent up emotions that she had held back for many years. Lauren was now beginning to understand Jack's mood swings. He always wanted to be in complete control, and everything had to be perfect.

Sarah stared at Vernon for a moment. Hot tears flooded her eyes. She straightened in her chair, set her jaw, and threw her shoulders back as if ready to fight. Then Sarah rose slowly from the witness chair, leaned forward, and pointed her finger at her husband and shouted, **"You killed my son. You succeeded in cloning him like yourself! You made a monster out of him! You tried to keep him from loving me!"** Sarah crumpled back into the witness chair in a torrent of tears.

Lauren wanted to put her head down on the table and cry. Instead she watched the Judge make no attempt to stop Sarah from releasing her feelings. Lauren glanced, in time, to see Vernon jump up from his seat and shake his fist at Sarah. He screamed at the top of his voice, **"She's a liar!"** The Judge banged her gavel repeatedly for order in the court and sent an officer to eject Vernon from the courtroom. The only sound in the courtroom was the icy rain that pelted the windowpanes. All eyes were on Vernon. Lauren thought, as she looked at him, his image had been destroyed like a sand castle on the edge of the ocean. All his strict regulations, selfishness, and self-centeredness wouldn't save him now. She wondered what Jack would have thought had he seen his father's head fall forward and his shoulders droop as he cowardly slipped out of the courtroom with the officer.

Wilburt Newton softened his voice as he asked Mrs. Harper, "How did Jack treat Lauren?"

Mrs. Sarah Harper's voice was so weak that her response was hardly audible. She managed to say, "If Jack treated Lauren the way Vernon treated me, I wouldn't blame her for whatever feelings she had toward him."

Assistant James Ferrell, a tall, robust man, rushed up to Sarah and helped her to return to the witness room.

The spectators were buzzing again after witnessing the dramatic out-pouring by Mrs. Vernon Harper. The judge brought silence to the courtroom with the threat that if there were anymore outburst; the courtroom would be cleared of all spectators. The judge continued by asking the prosecutor if he had any other witnesses.

Newton responded, "No, Your Honor. I have no other witness."

Judge Clark asked Defense Counselor LaBaron, "Are you ready to call your first witness?"

Rita responded, "Yes, Your Honor. I would like to call Dr. Camille Bloomfield to the stand."

Rita had advised Camille to wear something simple. She said sometimes jurors judge a person by the clothes he wears. Camille would have worn something in good taste anyway. Her coral linen two-piece dress with short sleeves was a perfect choice.

"Dr. Bloomfield, how long have you known Lauren Harper?"

Camille glanced at Lauren and smiled. "Mrs. Harper came to work at Mass General Hospital as a Pediatrician about two years ago. That was my lucky day. We became friends. Not only do I think highly of her, but the staff does, too. Children adore her. The ultimate gift a doctor can receive from children is their unconditional trust and love, and that's what she has from her patients. She has more compassion and forgiveness than anyone I've ever known."

"Doctor Bloomfield, did Lauren confide in you about Jack?"

"Yes. Lauren and I are very good friends. We talk to each other about our problems. We know that anything we say will be confidential."

"Dr. Bloomfield, will you give me an example of a problem she had with her husband?"

"If it will help her case, I think Mrs. Harper will understand why I'm telling the court about this event." Camille saw Lauren nod in agreement. "One day at lunch, she told me how Jack had gotten her drunk on wine and talked her into changing the beneficiary of her life insurance policy to him. The policy was for $500,000 with her parents as beneficiaries at that time. She told me she had planned to change it over to Jack when she was sure he would love the baby when it was born. But, Jack had insisted that she sign the new policy immediately."

"Were there other incidents she told you about?"

"Yes! One morning, she came to the hospital and she looked terrible. She told me Jack had beaten her. Lauren said he pulled her out of the shower, slapped her, knocked her down on the floor, and kicked her several times. She said he apparently tried to make her have a miscarriage. I sent her to a doctor for an examination. It was a miracle the baby wasn't hurt, and in time, Lauren was able to go back to work."

"Why didn't Lauren report or leave him?"

"I asked her the same thing. She told me she was afraid of what he might do to her. So she tried to live separately in the same apartment by locking her bedroom door. After several weeks, she forgave Jack and was the happiest I had ever seen her. She was especially happy when she said Jack had surprised her by making reservations for them to spend Christmas at the Forest Hill Ski Resort."

"Thank you, Dr. Bloomfield. I have no further questions."

The Judge asked, "Does the State wish to cross examine, Dr. Bloomfield?"

"Yes, Your Honor. Newton approached Dr. Bloomfield. "If you had a husband who treated you as Jack Harper allegedly treated Lauren, would you stay with him?"

"No, sir, I certainly wouldn't, but I don't have the same kind of faith and loyalty that Lauren possesses."

"Isn't it true that Lauren could have pretended to forgive Jack in order to carry out her plan to kill him."

"Absolutely not! She had never seen the place where he was taking her."

"Lauren saw a chance to get revenge when she saw this opportunity to push Jack over the cliff and be rid of an abusive husband!"

Camille sat stunned before she responded, "Sir, I have never met anyone so sincere and honest as Mrs. Lauren Harper."

"Dr. Bloomfield, I have been in crime work for many years, and I have seen the sweetest, kindest little old ladies become killers when they were pushed beyond their limits. From what I have heard today, Lauren had more abuse from Jack Harper than most women would have tolerated without striking back."

Camille's face flushed at the state's accusation. In a surprise outburst Camille shouted at Newton, "Sir, perhaps you've never loved anyone but yourself. Maybe you've never had a child that was your responsibility. Love is the greatest and strongest emotion anyone can have. I've seen miracles happen in my line of work where love has made people well. Lauren wanted Jack to love her more than anything in the world. She wanted to give him a home full of love because he never had had that experience. She was so confident that her love could change Jack that she was willing to do anything. I believe she was getting close to changing him until greed took away her dream." Camille dropped back in her seat and wept.

The courtroom fell silent. When noise returned, Judge Clark rapped her gavel and asked Counselor LaBaron if she had any more questions for the witness?

She said, "No other questions. Thank you, Dr. Bloomfield."

Lauren was crying so hard she couldn't control herself. The Fulghums reached over the rail to console her, but she was out of reach. Rita tried to comfort her, but nothing could soothe the pain of a broken heart.

Judge Clark rapped her gavel and said to the court, "Since there isn't much time left to continue the trial, I'm going to call it a day. We'll begin again in the morning promptly at nine o'clock. Court dismissed."

The courtroom emptied quietly. Lauren was mentally and physically exhausted. Rita and Jeanette assisted her out of the courtroom, but when they reached the outside, reporters, television cameras, and curiosity seekers swarmed around them.

Questions flew through the air, "How did you feel when you found out Jack was unfaithful to you? Were you surprised to find out Jack had fathered another child?" Hurtful questions rang in Lauren's ears and she desperately wanted to get away as fast as possible. Rita and Jeanette pushed their way through the crowd as best they could until two officers came and dispersed the people.

CHAPTER 35

The motel room was a haven of peace. Lauren didn't waste anytime taking a shower and crawling into bed. Exhaustion caused her to fall asleep, but it wasn't long before voices from the witness stand began to haunt her all over again. It was as though she were another person sitting in court listening to horror stories about someone she didn't know. She wondered why she couldn't have seen the signs. Camille was right: I let my love and dreams blind me from seeing beneath his charming façade.

A knock on the door awakened Lauren. So sure that it was going to be Rita, she didn't ask who it was. Instead, when she opened it, she was shocked to see Vernon Harper standing at the door. Lauren was speechless, but Mr. Harper wasn't as he blatantly screamed, "Why did you kill my son?" The look on his face was so frightening that she slammed the door in his face, and locked it. Immediately she called Rita.

Rita ran as fast as possible, knocked on the door, and called to Lauren. When the door opened, she could see that Lauren was about to collapse. Rita helped her to the bed and made her lie down. Calmly as possible, she asked, "Lauren, what happened?" She told her what Vernon Harper had done. Rita was furious. "I'm going to report this incident to Judge Clark as soon as I know that you are all right. I believe you might feel better if we ordered some food to your room." Twenty minutes later food was delivered, and Rita called Jeanette to join them.

Lauren was ravenous. She consumed a sandwich and a bowl of soup in record time. She immediately began to feel better. After Lauren had finished, she said, "Mom, Dad, and Angel are in another room so that I can get some rest. I didn't want to wake them. I'm glad you could get here so fast. Vernon really scared me."

Rita said, "I shouldn't have let you be by yourself tonight. Today was horrible for you to hear all the bad things that Jack has done in the past. Tomorrow is a new day, and I believe we'll be victorious."

Jeanette spoke up, "Lauren, Rita and I have decided that I will sleep on the extra bed here in your room. You don't need to be alone, in case someone else comes knocking on your door in the middle of the night."

Lauren said, "Yes, by all means. I know that would make me feel a lot safer. Thank you."

* * * * *

When Lauren woke up the next morning, she saw that Jeanette had slipped out and gone back to her room. It was time for her to get up, too. She pulled back the drapes and saw that it was raining. H-m-m, she thought, maybe the rain might keep away some of the curiosity seekers. Rita had given orders for the family members to be ready to go to the courthouse promptly at eight-thirty this morning. Lauren dressed in her dark purple linen dress with a short jacket. She brushed her hair to let it fall softly around her face. When she had finished dressing, she called her parents to see if they had eaten breakfast. They all met in the motel hospitality room where all kinds of breakfast foods and drinks were served. It was the first time she had been with her parents since the trial started. It felt good to be near them again. She knew it had been hard on them, too. Angel was kept in a nursery until the trial was over.

Rita joined them in the hospitality room. "Well folks, it's

time to go. I don't want to be late. I certainly don't want to make the Judge unhappy." Lauren noticed that Rita was wearing a tailored black suit trimmed with three gold buttons on the jacket. Her jet-black hair was down and hung loosely around her shoulders and her makeup subdued, but enough to enhance her beautiful eyes. She surely would get the jurors' attention.

They arrived at the courthouse and there weren't so many people around as yesterday. Although, reporters were like wolves ready to pounce on their prey as soon as they had a chance. Jeanette took Lauren to a private room to get her away from the crowd. Lauren said to Rita, "To me, it's beginning to look like the jury is thinking I should have killed Jack. They might wonder why I stayed with him since he was so mean. That day on the cliff, I told him I was going to divorce him. I certainly wasn't going kill him."

Rita said, "Don't worry Lauren, this trial is far from over. Jeanette and I have planned our strategy. All we want you to do is to remain calm."

After Rita, Jeanette, and Lauren took their places at the defense table, David Williams quietly took the same seat he had had yesterday in the back of the courtroom. Again, he had a clear view of Lauren and thought that she had never looked lovelier. He had succeeded in keeping his presence a secret, so far; he was here to offer whatever solace she needed. The bailiff called, "Court is in session."

The Judge asked, "Does the defense counselor have another witness?"

Rita answered, "Yes, Your Honor. I would like to call Mrs. Lauren Harper to the stand."

As Lauren rose to approach the stand, all eyes in the courtroom followed her every move. She held her head erect and walked gracefully toward the witness stand. Her once pregnant body had returned to the shapely figure Jack had admired when he first saw her. Lauren's flowing blonde hair and flawless complexion never looked more beautiful than it did today against the dark purple linen dress. With the grace of a lady, she took the witness stand.

Counselor LaBaron asked, "Mrs. Harper, how long did you know Jack Harper before you married him?"

"About four months. We met the first of May and were married August the 28th."

"Did you know anything of his past history?"

"No, I didn't, but I tried very hard to get him to tell me about his family. He always told me not to ask him about them. It didn't really matter to me because I loved him, and we would make our own history."

Rita stepped closer to the witness stand. "We've heard many bad things about Jack and especially when he hit you while you were pregnant. You're an intelligent woman. Why didn't you leave him after that episode?"

Lauren gestured with her hands. "In a way, I did. I isolated myself in part of the apartment for several weeks, hoping that maybe he would change or say that he was sorry. At the end of three weeks, he did change and I couldn't have been happier."

Rita took a few steps back and said, "What did he do to make you think he had changed since you were locked in your bedroom?"

Lauren shifted in the chair and said, "After the first two weeks, I was leery about coming out of my room when he was there. It was getting hard to avoid him. When I'd go to work or come home, I'd see that he had cleaned the house. During the third week, he insisted that I eat with him. My resistance began to wane. As always, his charming manner won me over."

"Mrs. Harper, from Jack's behavior while you lived together, did you ever discover any clues to his infidelity?"

"No, I didn't. In my demanding job and in trying to keep house, I was too tired to question why he was out late. I believed him when he said he was at the library or hanging out with friends."

Rita moved closer to the jurors so that they could see her

face as she asked, "When he made reservations at the Forest Hill Ski Resort, were you suspicious of his actions?"

Lauren's face relaxed as if to smile as she said, "Absolutely not. I was thrilled to death. It was going to be the first vacation we would have since our honeymoon."

"Mrs. Harper, when you saw the pictures of your husband with another woman, did you give him a chance to explain them?"

"When I saw the dates that the pictures were made, all I wanted to do was go back home and divorce him."

"What was so disturbing about the date on the pictures?"

"I had gone to visit a friend in Falmouth that very weekend. While I was there, he went to visit Mrs. Lisa Cannon."

Rita took a chance with the next question. She thought it would show the jurors how much Lauren wanted a divorce. She asked her, "You were so angry, didn't you want to kill him?"

Lauren cried out, "No! No! I decided right then I would ask for a divorce as soon as we got back home. I would never have tried to kill him. I still loved him, but I'm sure I would never be able to trust him again." Lauren tried to control her feelings by gripping the armrest of the chair. What she really wanted to do was stand up and scream at everyone that she was innocent.

Counselor Labaron retreated to questions less explosive and asked Lauren, "How did Jack treat you when you got home from your visit with Dr. Goodman?"

Lauren said, "It seemed that every time I'd get mad with him, he would do something so sweet and romantic that I couldn't stay angry with him."

"At this time in your relationship, what do you think upset Jack the most?"

"When he found my $500,000 life insurance policy and saw that I hadn't changed the beneficiary, he became upset. Also, he would get upset when the subject of having children came up. Since he didn't want children, I was afraid that if I got pregnant, he wouldn't love the child and might even abuse it. I told him if that should happen, I would divorce him."

"Mrs. Harper, what makes you think that he would be abusive to the child?"

"He had told me repeatedly he didn't like children. He had hit me hard enough to knock me to the floor in hopes of causing me to have a miscarriage."

"Did he ever convince you to change the policy before you became pregnant?"

"He thought he did, but I was already expecting. I decided not to tell him. I hoped by the time I was showing, he would be receptive to being a father. One night he cooked supper and made it a very romantic event. He kept my glass filled with wine until I was quite tipsy.

I was so happy for the way he was treating me that I would have signed anything. Jack had already gotten forms, earlier in the day, for me to sign. So, with his insistence, I signed a new insurance policy making him the beneficiary."

"Mrs. Harper, when did Jack Harper find out that you were pregnant?"

"Jack had stopped having sex with me when I was about three months. I couldn't understand why, but now I know. He was having sex somewhere else. At that time, I was glad not to have sex because he would have discovered my pregnancy. Overblouses and jackets concealed my stomach until I was five months along. One afternoon, as I was taking a shower, Jack came home unexpectedly and saw my silhouette through the glass shower door. He went ballistic and dragged me out of the shower and hit me repeatedly. He screamed at me and said that if I didn't have an abortion, he'd make me have a miscarriage."

"Why didn't you report him or leave him?"

"I've read and heard stories about women who loved their husband so much that they wouldn't leave or report the assault. I didn't think that would ever happen to me. A friend of mine told me that I was blinded by my love for him, and she was right. I tried living separately from him, as I stated earlier, but he made a gallant effort to win me over and it worked…that's when we went on our vacation in the mountains."

"Mrs. Harper, the court has pictures that were submitted as evidence." Rita walked over to the evidence table and picked them up. She handed them to Lauren and said, "Are these the photos you found in Jack Harper's jacket while at the Forest Hill Ski Resort?"

Lauren's head dropped forward as she recalled the day that she had discovered them. Her eyes filled with tears. In a choked-filled voice, she answered, "Yes…they are the pictures."

"Mrs. Harper, when you found the pictures of Jack, another woman, and a child, what went through your mind?"

"There wasn't any doubt in my mind after seeing the pictures—I would file for divorce as soon we returned home."

Rita took the pictures and handed them to the foreman to pass among the jurors. While they looked at them, she studied their faces for some reaction. The jurors did a good job of concealing their feelings. Rita retrieved the photos, turned to Lauren and said, "Thank you, Mrs. Harper. No more questions."

Counselor Newton spoke up and said, "I would like to cross examine the witness." Wilburt moved rapidly toward Lauren, staring steadily into her eyes. "Mrs. Harper, why didn't you show the pictures immediately to Jack when he came back from skiing?"

"I thought about it, but he was so excited to show me the beautiful view of the mountains from a cliff that I decided to wait until we got back to the cabin."

Newton narrowed his eyes and asked, "Mrs. Harper, why did you throw the pictures over the cliff?"

"When we reached the cliff, I noticed a change in Jack's attitude. He acted nervous and kept pushing me toward the edge of the cliff. He kept telling me to get close so I could see the view better. A strong gust of wind blew, and I jerked away from him. I ran about twenty feet away from him to the edge of the cliff and held up the pictures. That's when I told him that I was going to get a divorce when we got home. I turned my back to him and one by one I tossed them over the cliff. I was angry for all the lies he had told me, and I wanted to hurt him. I knew he wouldn't like it if I threw the pictures away. He had hidden those pictures in his jacket ever since he got back from Mrs. Cannon's home. When I heard footsteps crunching the snow, I turned around. He was charging at me with his arms outstretched. I moved but not fast enough to get out of the way as he grabbed my arm to stop his fall. I lost my balance and fell, too."

Wilburt Newton was sorry he had asked that question. It looked like her answer might defeat his case. He dug his hands deep into his pockets and walked a few steps away from Lauren and turned deftly around, pointed his finger at Lauren and said loudly, "My, my, what a fascinating story! No witnesses to prove what really happened! You knew he would try to get the pictures, and you lured him to the edge of the cliff. Your Honor, I have no further questions. I rest my case." Counselor Newton returned to his chair with a look of victory on his face.

Lauren valiantly held herself erect in order not to show disappointment. She prayed silently that the jurors would believe her.

Judge Clark asked Counselor LaBaron if she had any more witnesses. Rita answered, "No, Your Honor, I do not. I rest my case."

Judge Clark rapped the gavel down on the desk and said, "Court is dismissed for fifteen minutes. When we return the state and the defense will present their closing arguments. After that, the jury will be dismissed to the jury room to decide the verdict."

Rita whispered to Lauren, "Go with Jeanette. I want to be by myself while I go over my closing statement." She was well aware that Lauren's future would depend on her presentation to the jury. Her hand shook as she held the transcript. She prayed, "Please God, help me to say the right words. You know she's innocent."

* * * * *

When the fifteen minutes were up, Judge Clark took her seat and asked, "Counselor Newton are you ready to give your closing argument?"

"Yes I am, Your Honor." Lauren watched the prosecutor amble over to the jury and searched their faces. A few of the jurors fidgeted when he stared at them. Lauren jumped the same as the jurors did when he turned abruptly to face her. Prosecutor Newton shouted, "Do you see that woman over there? She probably believes she should be tried for justifiable homicide. Just in case you don't know what that means, she thinks she had the right to kill her husband. He was abusive to her mentally and physically. She had had enough of his cruelty, and it was time to strike back. The Defense said over and over again that Lauren Harper wanted a divorce. When she saw the pictures of her husband with another woman and a child, who looked a lot like Jack, she felt like murdering him. There's no doubt that any of you ladies sitting here today would want to kill your husband if he treated you the way Jack Harper had treated his wife. I've had a lot of experience in cases where wives kill their husbands. I understand human nature. I believe that Lauren Harper planned to murder Jack the day she saw those pictures. She lured him to the edge of the cliff and when he was close enough, she pushed him. He reached back to grab her, and that's when he pulled her over the edge." Counselor Newton stepped back from the jury box, turned and looked at Lauren, and said in an accusing voice, "Jack Harper never…never…had the opportunity to grant Lauren Harper a divorce. She had taken all the abuse and unfaithfulness she could stand." Newton yelled, "Jack Harper's fanaticism for perfection drove Lauren Harper to murder! Ladies and Gentlemen, you may call it justifiable homicide, but in my book, a man was deliberately killed." In a booming voice that could be heard outside the courtroom, he shouted again, "I call it premeditated murder!"

Lauren stood up and let out an ear-piercing cry, "I didn't kill him!"

Rita sprang out of her chair and put her arms around Lauren to comfort and to keep her from getting into more trouble with the Judge. One rap of the gavel brought the courtroom back to order.

The D.A. returned to his seat, never taking his eyes off the jurors.

The Judge asked, "Is the defense ready to give her closing argument?"

"Yes, Your Honor." Lauren watched Rita as she confidently glided over to the jurors, looked each one of them in the eye, and said, "Ladies and Gentlemen, you have been selected to decide whether Lauren Harper is guilty or innocent. You must realize that no defense witness made a single derogatory remark against Lauren Harper. I have letters from the hospital staff where she works, friends, and even her children patients telling of their love and respect. She was reared in a family that believed family was the most important part of life. Her parents made sure that she attended church, had a good education, took part in social life, and was exposed to cultural activities. All these things bore fruit as she went off to college and excelled in her studies. Lauren Harper wanted more than anything to become a pediatrician because of her love for children."

"Family was important to her. From what little Jack had revealed to her about his past, she was determined to give him the love he was deprived of as a young boy. Her parents had taught her that love could overcome many obstacles in life."

"After the first two weeks of their marriage, Jack returned to his controlling ways.

Perfection was a way of life with him and he expected his wife to keep a perfectly clean house, wash his clothes, iron every piece, put everything away in an orderly manner, have his meals on time, and let him spend her money like he wanted." Rita looked at the jurors and said, "Please remember she was the bread winner. She had to work long hours, and there wasn't enough time to do the things Jack expected of her. He not only abused her physically but verbally when things weren't done to perfection. He was obsessed with being a perfectionist."

"Lauren wanted to make sure that Jack got his law degree and, therefore, didn't press him to work. He thought he was above working as a common laborer and refused to take a part-time job to help with his education. Therefore, it was up to her to pay for his education and for living expenses. As time went on and she became pregnant, she was forced to make a terrible decision. Regardless of how much she loved him, her unborn baby's life was more important than taking a chance that he would harm the baby. Since he had shown that he didn't love her anyway, she would get a divorce and set him free."

Rita scanned the jurors' faces one more time and said, "Ladies and Gentlemen, Lauren Harper is innocent."

The courtroom was filled to capacity with spectators and each one hung on every word Rita LaBaron said. The silence was broken when Judge Clark banged her gavel. She looked at the jury and said, "Justice must be served, and it is in your hands to decide whether Lauren Harper is guilty of murder or is innocent. Consider all that you have heard in making your decision."

Just at that moment there was a lot of commotion just outside the courtroom doors. The Judge stopped the jurors from leaving until she could find out about the noise. She sent the bailiff to see what was going on. When he opened the doors, an elderly man and woman charged through the entrance and went directly to the judge's bench.

Judge Clark cracked her gavel down hard to bring order to the court. When she had everyone's attention, she asked the elderly couple to come forward.

"Would you please tell me why you have crashed into my courtroom?"

The man spoke up and said, "I'm Bill Gillette and this is my wife, Pat. We saw what happened at Eagle Nest Cliff."

Judge Clark interrupted Mr. Gillette's statement and said, "Bailiff, please escort the jurors to the jury room until I give them further instructions." Judge Clark said to the court, "This is a very unusual situation. If everyone will sit down, we'll get the Gillettes sworn in and allow them to give their statement."

After the jurors were back in the jury room, Judge Clark asked Mr. Gillette to continue his statement.

"We are avid bird watchers and are returning from an extended vacation traveling to various bird aviaries. It was during our drive here to Newburg that we heard, over the radio, about this trial and that a verdict was about to be reached. Pat said to me that we have to get to the courthouse. We can't let that lady be convicted of murder. We saw what happened. I stepped on the gas and drove as fast as I could.

"It was the third weekend in December when we visited Forest Hill Ski Resort. There is a wonderful view near a place called, 'Eagle Nest Cliff'. We were looking through our binoculars when we saw a man and woman who appeared to be arguing. She threw some small pieces of paper over the side of the mountain. The man was about fifteen feet or more from her when he started running toward her. She looked back and saw him coming and must have realized what he was about to do. The woman stepped back just as the man reached her. He lost his balance, tried to grab her arm, but it was too late. He fell to his death. When he grabbed her arm, she lost her balance and fell over the side of the cliff. We called 911 and reported the accident and waited until the emergency vehicle arrived."

Judge Clark asked, "Why didn't you report it to the police?"

"We were sure the medics would take care of that since it was an accident."

"Didn't you hear anything about the accident on the radio or television?"

"No, Your Honor. We left the resort the very next morning and traveled around the countryside looking for other aviaries."

Judge Clark said to Mr. and Mrs. Gillette, "Please have a seat. This is a matter that the court will have to discuss." She motioned for Counselor LaBaron and Prosecutor Newton to come to her chambers for a consultation.

The excitement in the courtroom rose to a fever pitch. Newspaper reporters, television cameras, and curiosity seekers crowded around the outside of the courthouse jostling for the prime spot to get the news.

* * * * *

Judge Clark sat down behind her simple mahogany desk. With concern in her voice she said, "Both of you have presented good arguments for your case."

Prosecutor Newton said as he smiled, "I don't have a problem believing Mr. and Mrs. Gillette. I don't think anyone knew about them and, therefore, had no chance to coerce them into this situation. I move that this case be dismissed."

Judge Clark rose from her chair and the three of them returned to the courtroom. She ordered the Bailiff to bring the jurors back into the courtroom. The noise level rose again, but the Judge banged her gavel, and the crowd immediately became quiet. The Judge looked at the jury and said, "Ladies and gentlemen, it has been decided that Lauren Harper is innocent of killing her husband based on the statement from Mr. and Mrs. Gillette who witnessed the accident."

Pandemonium broke out in the courtroom. All Lauren's family and friends gathered around her crying and laughing with joy. Mrs. Fulghum left the crowd and then came back with Angel. Lauren broke away from everyone and cradled her baby in her arms. Tears streamed down her face for more than having her baby but also for wishing Jack could have loved her like she loved him.

Lauren looked around the room for Mrs. Sarah Harper. She saw her standing where Vernon had been sitting. She noticed Mrs. Harper looked sad and lonely. Lauren walked over to her and said, "Mrs. Harper, meet your granddaughter, Angel. I would like for you to feel free to visit us whenever you can." Lauren held Angel out for Mrs. Harper to hold. A smile spread across her face as she held and kissed Angel on her rosy cheeks. After they talked for several minutes, Lauren said goodbye.

David Williams was waiting for Lauren in the hall outside the courtroom. When she opened the door, she was shocked beyond words. "David," she stammered, "How long have you been here?"

"I've been here since the trial began. I wanted to be near if you needed me. This isn't the time to talk about the past. I know you need time to get over this traumatic experience, but I hope you will see it in your heart, in the near future, to give me a chance to redeem myself." David handed Lauren a present as she went toward the van. "When you open this gift, remember where we were and what I asked you."

Lauren looked up into David's compassionate brown eyes and said, "It will take time for me to recover, and as I told you on the phone, we can still be friends. I have to go now. Please keep in touch." After Lauren walked some distance away, she turned, smiled, and waved goodbye. She opened the gift. It was a picture of a sailboat named, "GOTCHA."

THE END

Printed in the United States
52478LVS00001B/115-159